$25.00

5/16/2019

MW00834746

UNDER PAIN
of
MORTAL SIN

Other titles by Donald Cozzens

Nonfiction

Notes from the Underground:
The Spiritual Journal of a Secular Priest

Freeing Celibacy

Faith That Dares to Speak

Sacred Silence: Denial and the Crisis in the Church

The Changing Face of the Priesthood

The Spirituality of the Diocesan Priest (Editor)

Fiction

Master of Ceremonies

UNDER PAIN
of
MORTAL SIN

DONALD COZZENS

in extenso

UNDER PAIN OF MORTAL SIN
by Donald Cozzens

Edited by Michael Coyne
Cover design by Courter and Company
Text design by Patricia A. Lynch
Front-cover photo by Tom A. Wright
Photo of Donald Cozzens by Tony Dejak

Copyright © 2018 by Donald Cozzens

Published by In Extenso Press
Distributed exclusively by ACTA Publications, 4848 N. Clark Street,
Chicago, IL 60640, (800) 397-2282, actapublications.com

Library of Congress Catalog Number: 2018938762
ISBN: 978-0-87946-972-6 (hardcover)
ISBN: 978-0-87946-973-3 (paperback)
Printed in the United States of America by Total Printing Systems
Year 30 29 28 27 26 25 24 23 22 21 20 19 18
Printing 15 14 13 12 11 10 9 8 7 6 5 4 3 2 1

♻ Text printed on 30% post-consumer recycled paper

For my sister
Maryellen
whose goodness, warmth, and joy
bless everyone she meets

1

Laura Spivak took a deep breath, sucking in the clean air as a smoker would suck in the first deep pull of a freshly lighted cigarette. With her lungs full, she felt the cincture under her vestment tighten around her waist. Spivak wondered if it would ever end—the confounded internal wrestling with her new identity as one of the first female Roman Catholic priests in the Cleveland diocese. One moment she would find herself bathing in a blissful calm, a sense that she had arrived at a place she was meant to be. The next she would feel harried by dark doubts over her canonically irregular—some would say forbidden—ordination. At this moment, however, at a rustic lodge deep in the woods in the heart of Cleveland Metroparks North Chagrin Reservation, she was experiencing the pure delight of greeting her small flock after celebrating Mass. Connecting with people, she knew from a lifetime of experience, was the key to effective ministry. And Spivak was determined to be an effective priest. At five foot ten, she stood straight as a soldier, as if her shoulders had just been pressed against a wall. Yet she moved easily, without a hint of stiffness, her height accenting the folds of her green monastic-cut Mass vestment. Her prematurely white hair, stylishly cut just above her shoulders, completed the picture. Her easy smile and wide hazel eyes invited people to come close. The connecting was effortless for her, a private confirmation of her lifelong vocation to be a priest.

Early in her ministry the Reverend Laura Spivak had discovered the simple pleasure of mixing with the congregants, asking sincere, safe questions about their families, and on most occasions nodding a modest "Thank you" to their affirming comments on her homily. Yes, the light banter that marked the mixing after Mass came easily to her. "I'm glad your mother is adjusting to the nursing home" to one middle-aged woman. "When will you know if the transfer to Cincinnati is more than a rumor?" to the young father holding his ten-month-old daughter on his left hip while carefully sipping coffee. These good people would be out the door in a few moments. And so would her light-as-air glow be gone.

Alone after the service, Spivak stood still for a moment at the card table serving as her vestment case. Offering Mass, more than praying her breviary or saying the rosary, nudged awake the divine still point at the center of her soul. That's how the mystics spoke of it—a deep sense of communion with the divine. She was God's beloved. She was a priest of Jesus Christ. This sense of deep reality, this comforting sense of God's presence, kept its own time—it would wax and wane. Laura knew full well that moments of attunement with the divine mystery, moments of graced consolation, were transient by nature. They come, they go, and only a fool would think otherwise. But it wasn't just the occasional absence of priestly joy and bliss that she found disturbing. The deep sense of unease that often took their place was the more serious problem. Spivak pressed her eyes tight as the familiar knot of guilt once again sabotaged her calm communion with the mystery she called God. Here it was: this unbidden, suffocating conflation of anxiety and guilt. Under Canon Law she was, and had been since the moment of her ordination, *latae sententiae* excommunicated. *Latae sententiae*. Sentence passed. The very act of receiving the holy orders she had longed for since girlhood was considered by the hierarchy of the church to automatically cut her off from every sacrament save penance.

She should think of the feelings of guilt, she told herself again and again, as a temptation of sorts. A silly temptation. Her vocation was real. Her ordination was real. She could not give into this gray gloom. She knew in her heart that she was a priest by the grace of God. Her disobedience to an unjust law merited praise, not shame. The decision to seek ordination had taken more courage than any other decision she had ever made. She should feel only pride.

Trying to focus, Spivak deliberately, as if for the first time, lifted the simple monastic chasuble from her shoulders, brought it over her head and set it on the table. She unknotted the tasseled white cincture at her waist. She removed the green stole, folded it twice, kissed it, and then stepped out of her tailored alb, arranging it on a wooden hanger and then slipping it into a plastic garment bag. She glanced around the lodge serving as her chapel. In a few more weeks the autumn chill would be softened by a wood fire in the blackened stone fire-place dominating the west wall of the lodge. Her Mass was not a catacomb Mass but a Mass in the forest, surrounded by silent, ancient maples creating a gothic ceiling of deep green in the growing dusk.

No more regrets, no more guilt, no more doubts, she promised herself again. She would pack her Mass kit, gather her vestments, and join her husband and a few parishioners for a light supper at Austin's restaurant. Their company and conversation, like the crisp fall air, would wash away the bitterness rising in her throat.

Placing the cincture over the hanger's hook of her garment bag, Laura noted with curiosity the crunch of car tires on the gravel drive in front of the lodge. Maybe a park ranger coming to secure the lodge for the night. The door of the lodge opened slowly, and she turned to see instead, standing full in the doorway, a man of average height in a nylon workout suit. He stood still for a second, as if posing for a picture, his shadowed eyes dark and unblinking.

"May I help you?" she asked, her voice thin and tight.

"You have sinned, woman," his voice sharp and cold as a condemning judge. "You have sinned mortally. You have wounded God's Holy Church with your blasphemous ritual, with your sacrilegious pretense of celebrating Mass, with your contempt for God's law."

He steeled himself and moved towards her as she, by instinct, moved to the other side of the folding table. The fear in her eyes disturbed him. But the guilty must pay for their sins. And his mentor had assured him that those who attack the church must be destroyed. As an agent of God, he would exact God's vengeance. Without another word, he reached for the limp white cincture, soon to be an instrument of divine retribution.

2

Peter Bryn Martin, the newly-appointed twelfth Bishop of Cleveland, was still settling in to his sixth-floor corner office in Cathedral Square Plaza, an architecturally uninspired eight-story office building across the street from the Cathedral of St. John the Evangelist, close to the corner of East Ninth Street and Superior Avenue. A dozen boxes of books, photographs, and other personal memorabilia hugged the wall under the windows looking out on East Ninth, waiting to be shelved. Martin hoped to have already attended to the task, to have found himself more established in his new domain, but his full calendar of meetings continued to scuttle that idea.

A schedule of his afternoon appointments lay at the center of his mahogany desk. He had only twenty minutes before his first meeting, a reporter from the *Cleveland Plain Dealer* doing a profile piece on the new bishop. She was scheduled for thirty minutes but would take an hour at the minimum, the bishop guessed. The diocese's chief financial officer was next on the list, with a number of major maintenance contracts that had been held for Martin's signature. Then two priests from the personnel board with appointments of pastors and associates that needed his approval.

As soon as he could gain some control of his schedule, Martin was determined to begin the process of meeting the priests, deacons, and key lay ecclesial ministers of the diocese. Most of the women religious, he presumed, although anxious about their own future, would likely be supportive.

What Martin really needed to do right now was get to know the top lay and ordained chancery staff he had inherited. He was already comfortable with his Executive Assistant, Therese Reeves. A Yale-educated lawyer, Therese "Terry" Reeves had made it to the upper levels of Jones Day, a leading Cleveland law firm the diocese often turned to, but had grown tired of both the relentless pressure to clock billable hours and the frequent seventy-hour work weeks. She appeared to be savvy, professional, competent, and discreet, and had an air about her that somehow—perhaps it was the frank intelligence reflected in her soft brown eyes—signaled inner depth.

Martin's chancellor and moderator of the curia, something like his chief of staff, was Father Trace Dunmore, an Anglican convert born south of London who had studied medieval history at Oxford's Balliol College. Martin sat back, elbows on the arms of his leather high-backed chair, cocked his head slightly as he often did when he was puzzled, and wondered how in the world Dunmore ended up in Cleveland. Martin found his chancellor's formality off-putting. He remembered then why the name Dunmore had a familiar ring. Martin's father had been an American history buff and the colonies' struggle for independence was a common dinner-table topic. The Royal British governor of Virginia, and Thomas Jefferson's nemesis, had been the Tory John Murray, Fourth Earl of Dunmore. Might Dunmore's family have ties to nobility? Time would tell about this English-educated Trace Dunmore.

"God, let this work," Martin said, in honest supplication. What the new bishop of Cleveland was anxious to discover in the weeks ahead was whether he could trust Trace Dunmore and Terry Reeves.

Christina Tommaso from *The Plain Dealer* sat a bit stiffly in one of the four upholstered chairs that circled a coffee table in the conversation area of the bishop's office. Bryn Martin sat in the chair across from her, thinking she looked like a cub reporter fresh out of college. Terry Reeves had given him a snapshot profile of the reporter an hour before she arrived. Tommaso was in her third year with the paper, held a master's degree in journalism from Northwestern, and, if the rumor was to be believed, was being courted by the *Washington Post*. Reeves, Bryn realized, knew the importance of background.

"Thank you for seeing me, Bishop Martin. I can see you are still getting settled," Tommaso said, glancing at the sealed boxes piled beneath the window.

"Yes, I'm still very much in the 'getting to know you' stage, Christina. But let me thank you for doing this interview. I am hopeful that your piece will help the people of the diocese get to know me a bit."

"I know you're from Baltimore and that you have a sister, Nora. Can you tell me about the rest of your family?"

"My parents are deceased," Martin replied with a slight softening in his voice. "In addition to my sister Nora, I have two married brothers, wonderful nieces and nephews, and a slew of cousins. Nora teaches psychology at Johns Hopkins and is doing pioneering work on the impact of contemplative living on both individual health and on human relations. She's just a terrific person, a terrific sister."

"We know of course that you come to Cleveland from the Archdiocese of Baltimore where you served as an auxiliary bishop to Archbishop Charles Cullen." Tommaso paused. "We also know from reports in the *Baltimore Sun* that during your tenure there the retired archbishop, Wilfred Gunnison, died tragically during the celebration of his Golden Jubilee."

Martin nodded, remembering Gunnison's purported suicide,

just minutes before a celebratory dinner in his honor. There was no way, Bryn assured himself, that Christina Tommaso could know that Gunnison had very likely been murdered. But before he could say anything, the reporter looked directly into his eyes and said reassuringly, "That difficult event, Bishop, will not be a part of this story."

Christina Tomasso saw the new bishop of Cleveland nod again in a silent thank you. *Get a grip,* she told herself. *Stay focused.* While today's interview was intended largely to be a soft story, she had a few hardballs in her bag, including the limited role of women in the Catholic Church and the church's bungling of the sexual abuse of children by members of the clergy.

But before she could speak again, Terry Reeves, after two sharp knocks, entered the office. "Bishop, I need a word." Turning to Tommaso, Reeves said, "You should check your cell. Your city editor will be looking for you. I need a moment with the bishop." Tommaso frowned in puzzlement but stepped towards the doorway, took out her cell phone, and fanned through her new messages.

Reeves got straight to the point with Martin.

"I just heard a report that a woman named Laura Spivak was found murdered in a lodge in the North Chagrin Metropark." Martin's eyes narrowed. "She was strangled with a cincture."

"A cincture?" Martin said incredulously. "That's an odd choice of a murder weapon."

"Spivak considered herself a Roman Catholic woman priest, one of a number in our diocese."

"Let's get Trace in here," Martin said to Reeves. Tommaso, standing at a discreet distance, was already on her cell talking, he guessed, to her editor. "We can't continue now, Ms. Tomasso, but please call Therese later to reschedule," Martin said, breaking into the reporter's conversation and guiding her gently toward the door.

"I'll need a statement about—"

"We'll have a prepared statement in time," Reeves said. "Not now."

Dunmore and Reeves sat in two upholstered chairs across from Bishop Martin.

"What do we know?" he asked his aides.

"She was fifty-two years old," Dunmore began, "married," he said looking at his notes. "Husband's name Carl. Two grown children living out of state. About a year and a half ago she received a sham ordination from a retired bishop in Pittsburgh claiming apostolic succession. The whole affair really ought not be a concern of ours. She was excommunicated *latae sententiae*." Turning to Reeves, he added, "That means she excommunicated herself, *ipso facto*, by the very act of attempting ordination."

Reeves gave Dunmore a weak smile and inwardly bristled. She knew very well what the Latin phrase meant. Maybe the chancellor would offer next to translate *ipso facto* for her.

Dunmore continued, apparently oblivious to Reeves' reaction. "Spivak was strangled with her own cincture after saying one of those fake Masses at a Metroparks lodge. No witnesses. She was found by her husband after she failed to meet him and some friends at a nearby restaurant. There were no signs of robbery," his voice dropped to a whisper, "and it doesn't appear she was sexually assaulted."

"We may get the Feds on this," Reeves said. "It's too early to say with any confidence, but this could be considered a hate crime. She may have been murdered because she was a Roman Catholic woman priest."

"A purported priest," the chancellor corrected.

"Well, it wasn't a purported murder," Reeves said.

"That she was killed because of her ordination was the first thing to cross my mind," Martin said, looking squarely at each of them in turn. They sat in awkward silence for a moment.

"I guess we'll just have to wait for the police reports," Dunmore said, almost as if despairing of any useful news from official reports. There was no doubt in his mind that Martin and Reeves were correct that this was a hate crime. But Trace Dunmore had his own ideas about this particular hate crime. *Hate the sin and, when necessary, punish the sinner,* he thought.

"What was her parish? Before she was ordained, I mean?" Martin asked.

Dunmore glanced at his notes. "St. Therese in Garfield Heights."

"Terry, please draft a statement for the media. Focus on the diocese's deep sadness for this apparent hate-inspired act of violence. And emphasize our sympathy for Carl and his children."

It was Dunmore's turn to bristle. Writing that press release was clearly his responsibility.

"Trace, please arrange a call with the pastor of St. Therese."

"Cyril Tosko."

"We need to talk to him about how to discuss this with his parishioners. It's going to be a delicate subject. A lot of them had to know Laura Spivak. And when we find out about whatever kind of funeral service is arranged, let him know that I'd like him to attend with me."

"Are you sure that's wise, Bishop?" Dunmore asked.

Bryn Martin didn't answer. Here it was again. Two cultures batting heads. The canonical, "Who's in, who's out?" culture up against the pastoral culture, the core message of the gospel— compassion, mercy, inclusion. There was a place for both, he knew, and each could be present in the other. Excommunicated or not, Laura Spivak was a member of the Catholic Church of Cleveland. She may have been an estranged member, but she was one of theirs.

"Make the call, please," Martin said, holding the chancellor's gaze. Father Trace Dunmore, the bishop suspected, would not soon forget this moment.

"And, Terry, see if you can get the name of the Cleveland detective heading up the investigation."

"The murder occurred in Willoughby Hills, Bishop. The jurisdiction will probably rest with them. And the Metroparks have their own police, though surely not a homicide unit. I know a couple of detectives who are retired from the force. I'll call them and see what I can find out."

Bishop Martin stood. "Get back to me with anything more that surfaces. One more thing, Terry. Get me Carl Spivak's home number. That's it for now."

Terry Reeves and Trace Dunmore left the bishop's office in tandem. One feeling deeply good about the new bishop of Cleveland; the other feeling deeply troubled.

3

Fergus Mann stared into the black coffee in the glass mug before him and said a silent "Bless us, O Lord, and these thy gifts..." This was not a meal that required a blessing, but his boyhood habit of saying grace somehow comforted him. Mann thought of himself as old-school. Old-school Catholic, old-school cop, old-school veteran. And old-school meant all that was true and right. Old-fashioned virtues like God and country and especially church, the Catholic Church. Old-school for Fergus Mann meant that he was willing to die for his faith and, yes, kill for it, if necessary. And his church, his beloved church, like everything else in our permissive popular culture, was going down the toilet.

Fergus Mann would do what must be done to fix it. He had the time. Still, early retirement from the force had been a bad move. Too many empty hours, too much beer, too much TV. Living alone since his wife's death, no kids, no real friends, only some cousins whose liberal values made him sick. Hell, none of them even went to Mass. Worse, they were soft on abortion and their kids shacked up before they got married. So it was fine with him that he saw them only around the holidays. He had always been a loner, but his retirement loneliness, he now realized, had been driving him to an early death. But all that had just changed. Now he had a mission, a dangerous mission that mattered. It mattered more than anything he had ever done.

He was early today for his regular Saturday morning meeting with a man he had come to think of as his mentor. They met at The Coffee House on University Circle, once a stately old home on the campus of Case Western Reserve University, across from the Cleveland Institute of Music. His coffee partner's true identity remained a mystery to Fergus, but that was okay. Three months ago they had struck up a conversation over coffee right here, right at this table. At first he had been put off by his new acquaintance's precise, slow way of talking—and with an English accent, no less. But they had hit it off. The guy was okay. He told Fergus to call him Alistair, which surely wasn't his real name. That was okay, too. He looked important and dressed like a professor, sweater vest and sport coat, a neatly trimmed brown beard sprinkled with a fair amount of gray and, for sure, a fifty-dollar haircut. But real friendly, easy to talk to. Alistair, he came to see, was very much like himself. Old school. They were both old-school Catholic to the core, really, super-Catholics. So, kind of by accident, they started meeting for coffee on Saturday mornings. They talked about a lot of things at first, but especially about religion. And then, only about religion...and eventually only about the Catholic religion.

Mann sipped his lukewarm coffee, looking up to see if his mentor had arrived. Not yet.

About a month ago, Alistair had revealed to him that he belonged to a network of traditionalists, true believers, authentic Catholics who were working to save the Catholic Church from its long and certain descent into hell. Although he didn't put it quite like that. This network of Catholics worked quietly, like underground, to bring the church back to fidelity with God's laws.

"Would you like to know more?"

"Sure," Fergus had said, glancing around the shop.

"The church we both love is being sold out to secularism and liberalism and an anything-goes kind of morality, as long as you act sincere."

The two sat in respectful silence, like two grown children at the deathbed of a failing parent.

"Can I trust you with a secret?" Alistair muttered.

"Absolutely."

"Among ourselves," Alistair said, just loud enough for Fergus to hear, "we know one another as the Sentinels of the Supreme Center. We are laymen, priests, and bishops who do what is necessary to keep the church obedient to the authority of Rome, the church's supreme center. We are a private, international network. We have Sentinels and sympathizers in positions of influence all around the developed world. Some of our bishops work in the heart of the Vatican."

Fergus Mann, eyes narrowed with interest, leaned forward over the table.

"We would like you to work with us," Alistair said. "We have a very important, very delicate…and very risky assignment for you. If you accept this mission, you become a Sentinel, a part of our international network of true and loyal Catholics. A soldier of Christ. And if you complete the mission we have for you, you would join our elite corps of special operatives." Alistair took a sip of coffee, hoping Mann would sense his sincerity. "Fergus, the church needs you. We need you. We need men with your strong faith and military skills to save our church." Alistair paused again and lowered his eyes. Fergus thought he might be praying.

As if in answer to that prayer, Fergus asked, "What do you need me to do?"

When Alistair had detailed the full scope of the assignment, Mann thought at first that he might be kidding. Or testing him. But the steady gaze in Alistair's eyes and the gospel tone of his soft accent made it perfectly clear that he was dead serious. Fergus remembered the wave of confusion that settled over him, a sense of danger, but at the same time a gripping excitement—like he had felt in Nam before going out on a dangerous patrol. He should have asked for time to think about it. But he hadn't. He held Alistair's gaze for only seconds and without even blinking nodded his acceptance. He understood that his life had changed forever at that moment. His chest had swelled that day, and he had felt the adrenaline rush of a man not half his age. Accepting the mission had broken through the cloud of boredom that had taken all that could be savored out of his world. He had a new life now. A real life. A life with meaning. Fergus Mann was someone who mattered again.

Fergus came back to the moment and out of his reverie as he watched his mentor walk across the parking lot toward the back entrance of The Coffee House. Alistair had never mentioned what he did, but Fergus guessed he was a professor at the university or a lawyer or maybe a doctor at University Hospitals, which anchored the east end of the campus. It didn't really matter to him, and now that he had undertaken the mission he figured it was best he didn't know any more than necessary about Alistair. There were to be no outbound phone calls, no emails, no text messages. No audit trail confirming their connection. Alistair would call him at home, always from a different phone, when a Saturday meeting at The Coffee House was in order.

Coffee in hand, Alistair raised an eyebrow in greeting as he took the chair across from Mann.

"Well done, Fergus. You've completed the first stage of your mission without a hitch."

"The first time I killed anyone since Nam," Fergus whispered. He took a tentative sip of coffee and glanced quickly at the other patrons, and then raised his eyes to meet Alistair's, not knowing what else to say.

Alistair leaned forward. He knew *just* what to say.

"Your assignment is too morally complex for most people to embrace. It requires deep trust in the wisdom and judgment of the church's orthodox bishops." Then, to give his position the strength of theological backing, Alistair gambled that Mann would know, at least vaguely, who Augustine was. "We draw on the teachings of Saint Augustine, a truly great and orthodox fourth-century theologian, bishop, and doctor of the church. Augustine taught us that it is morally permissible in times of war and persecution of the church to kill in order to maintain peace and law and order...and to punish sin and wrong-doing."

Alistair paused to let his little lecture sink in. Mann appeared to reflect upon his words—a good sign he was buying a highly unorthodox parsing of Saint Augustine's teachings.

"Very few men are called to do the work you are called to do, Fergus. Your strength of will and deep faith are gifts from God. What is being asked of you is for the good of the church. You do understand that, don't you?"

Mann seemed to cradle the question in his Catholic conscience and finally nodded. "Yeah, I do believe that."

"And," Alistair added, "You will soon feel the hero's inner joy of triumph. You are doing something necessary...something noble." Alistair withdrew two envelopes from the breast pocket of his blazer and placed them, one on top of the other, at the side of the table.

"Are you ready for stage two, Fergus?"

"I am," Fergus said, speaking softly but without hesitation, like a candidate for ordination answering the bishop's ritual question before the laying on of hands.

"Good," Alistair said picking up the first envelope. You will find here the name of the next subject, her address, where she works, where she celebrates her sacrilegious Mass. Though we hope you will be able to complete stage two within the next two weeks, the time and place of completion will be up to you."

Fergus resisted the temptation to ask about the "we" to whom Alistair referred. Other members of the Sentinels of the Supreme Center, no doubt. But who were these others, and where were they? Here in Cleveland? New York? Rome?

Alistair slid the envelope across the table and Mann slipped it into the inside pocket of his nylon jacket.

"This is noble work you do, Fergus. Remember that."

Alistair seemed to wait for Mann to say something, but Fergus only moved his coffee cup to one side. Alistair slid the second, thicker, envelope across the table and let it rest in front of Fergus, who looked down at it but did not move to touch it.

"This is for your expenses. We know how much time goes into the planning and preparation for such a delicate assignment. You must consider this a stipend for your fidelity to the Roman Catholic Church and its supreme center."

Mann knew what he would find in the envelope—twenty crisp hundred dollar bills.

"Let's meet here the Saturday after you complete stage two." Mann nodded his agreement. "Good," Alistair said simply. "Good."

He stood and left without speaking another word.

Fergus watched Alistair leave by the front door, opposite the one he had entered, and walk across Juniper Street. He had a deliberate, confident walk, unhurried, yet sure of where he was going. Fergus knew nothing about his mentor beyond his phony first name and his sketchy description of the Sentinels of the Supreme Center. On the other hand, Fergus felt Alistair knew a good deal more about him than he let on. He drew the first envelope from his jacket and, after assuring himself that none of the other patrons were close enough to see its contents, opened it carefully, even respectfully. Her name was Frances Hellerman. The stapled picture showing her in an alb and stole was a photocopy from a newspaper story about her ordination. Attached to the photo was the personal information he would need to complete his assignment. Frances Hellerman, a high school teacher, was divorced. Her only daughter was a graduate student at the University of Illinois. A faculty colleague lived with her. Fergus would begin his surveillance the next day, Sunday, after going to Mass.

4

Bishop Bryn Martin scrolled his iPhone's contact list for Ian Landers and then tapped the professor's cell number. Bryn's sister Nora's significant other had accepted a year's appointment in Case Western Reserve's religion department as the Archbishop Paul J. Hallinan Professor of Catholic Studies. Bryn knew the year-long appointment had a number of pluses for Ian—a light teaching load, only two public lectures, a grad research assistant, and more time than he would have had at Johns Hopkins for his current project on the history of mortal sin in the Catholic Church. And—a thought that very much pleased Bryn—Nora would be visiting Ian as often as her schedule would permit. Spending time with both Ian and Nora would help ground Bryn and ease the tension of settling into this new chapter in his life as the Bishop of Cleveland. But more to the point, he needed to discuss the murder of Laura Spivak with both of them. Ian and Nora each had a genius for putting complicated problems into a clear perspective, and Bryn remembered their wise counsel when he was dealing with events that had beleaguered the Archdiocese of Baltimore while he was auxiliary bishop there. Ian's command of the shadow side of church history and Nora's keen insight into human behavior had served Bryn well in dealing with the tragic end of Archbishop Wilfred Gunnison. Martin listened to Ian's voice-mail greeting and after dutifully waiting for the beep, said that he hoped they could get together for dinner, the sooner the better.

"I really need to talk to you about the murder of that woman priest."

"Do you have a minute, Bishop?" Terry Reeves said, sticking her head inside Martin's open office door. He nodded and she took the chair across from him. "A couple of things. Word's gotten out among the priests of the diocese that you attended the funeral service for Laura Spivak. I've heard you earned a split decision. Some of the priests are saying you made them proud. Others think your presence sent the wrong message."

"We could have predicted that," Martin said.

Reeves could see in his eyes that the new Bishop of Cleveland bore no regrets.

"I had a call from an assistant D.A. this morning," she said. "Laura Spivak's murder will very likely be considered a hate crime. Remember the Amish who cut off the beard of an elder because of some internal dispute a number of years ago? That was treated as a hate crime, and they're saying that's a likely precedent for seeing Laura's murder the same way. That makes it a federal case, and will bring the FBI into it."

"And probably a lot of national media," Martin added. "When we finish here, see if you can get the nuncio on the phone."

Martin stood and walked to the bank of windows along East Ninth Street. In the distance Lake Erie looked like a giant tabletop, her smooth surface a metallic gray, as if lying in wait of wind and rain. As he stared out over the lake's dark expanse, a woeful thought struck him.

"My God, Terry. What if Laura Spivak's murder was just the start of some twisted plan to rid the church of women priests?"

His face drained of color, Martin moved back to his desk and slowly eased into his chair.

"That's actually what I wanted to talk to you about, Bishop.

I've been doing a little research." She lifted a file folder up for his inspection.

"How many of them are out there?"

Reeves opened the folder and placed it on the bishop's desk. "We can name two other woman priests in the Cleveland area, Frances Hellerman and Ann Marie Ellsmere. But we believe there are more. We of course have no records. If they are excommunicated it's strictly *latae sententiae*, so no diocesan action has ever been taken. Trace is trying to get more names. It won't be easy. Some of these women are quite private, you might even say secretive, about their ordination. They're sometimes referred to by supporters as 'catacomb priests.'"

Reeves stood to go.

"Terry, make sure whoever ends up leading the official investigation into Laura Spivak's murder gets this," Bryn said emphatically. "And make sure the Cleveland police understand Frances Hellerman and Ann Marie Ellsmere might need police protection. And, Terry, can you come back after I've spoken with the nuncio? And bring Trace with you."

An hour later, Martin, Dunmore, and Reeves sat at the table in the conference room adjacent to the bishop's office.

Dunmore seemed irritated about the unscheduled summons to the bishop's office.

"We need to leave by five for the confirmation at St. Luke's," he said a little testily. "We're expected for supper at five-thirty."

Martin looked at his watch. "Let's cover as much as we can in the...thirty minutes or so we have. What do we know about women who are attempting ordination to the priesthood?"

Dunmore waded in first. "I've got somewhat dated information. According to a *New York Times* article in 2012, more than one hundred women claimed to be Catholic priests, and eleven of them even claimed to be bishops. And that's just in the U.S."

"My figures are pretty close to Trace's," Reeves said. "Apparently there are two…I don't know what to call them, ecclesial bodies, or organizations, whatever…generating these ordinations. The principal one's called Roman Catholic Women Priests, and what looks like a splinter group is called the Association of Roman Catholic Women Priests. Here in the U.S. there were 106 women from the Roman Catholic Women Priests group awaiting ordination to the deaconate, priesthood, or bishopric in 2016. The Association of Roman Catholic Women Priests claims it already has fifty-six priests, four bishops, and eight transitional deacons. In 2016, Europe and Canada had about sixteen priests each. I don't know what the figure is today, but I wouldn't be surprised if the total number of women priests here in the States is already over 200."

Martin and Dunmore exchanged a glance. How had Reeves gathered this information so quickly—and from whom?

"Terry has the names of two other women priests here in the diocese," Martin said to Dunmore.

"Please, Bishop, women *claiming* to be priests, not women priests," Dunmore said with an air of frustration. "It's an oxymoron."

"Frances Hellerman and Ann Marie Ellsmere," Martin continued, ignoring the interruption. "If we're right about Laura Spivak's murder being a hate crime, we need to consider that the murderer might already have one or both of these women in his sights."

"I'll make sure the authorities have their names," Dunmore said.

"They've already been notified," Martin said, raising an eyebrow to Reeves, who nodded.

"The nuncio," the bishop said, "didn't offer much in the way of direction. He wants to be kept informed, of course. He hopes like hell that this was a random act of violence and asked that we play down the possibility of a hate crime."

"When did the church ever get into trouble playing down the possibility a crime has been committed?" Reeves offered with unrestrained irony, and pointedly ignored Dunmore's sharp frown.

"I wouldn't be surprised," Martin said, "if tomorrow's *Washington Post* and the *New York Times*, despite the nuncio's fervent prayers to the contrary, report it just that way."

5

Fergus Mann sat in his black Ford Focus waiting for Frances Hellerman to approach her car after classes at Shaker Heights High, where she taught advanced placement history to juniors and seniors. It was 4:25 on a Wednesday afternoon. Most days, he had noted, she got away earlier, usually around 3:30, so he was beginning to feel a bit unnerved.

Hellerman lived in a spacious home on Falmouth Road, not ten minutes from here, where she celebrated Mass for her small congregation in her living room, judging from the dozen or so cars parked on the street and in her drive both Saturday evenings on which he had surveilled the home. She did her regular shopping at the Heinen's on Green Road and at Beachwood Place.

It was too early for Mann to conclude much about Hellerman's social life. He figured his best opportunity, really the only one he'd spotted so far, would be on a Wednesday night after her weekly volunteer tutoring session at Ursuline College. Hellerman routinely parked in the unsecured staff lot next to the college's Wasmer Art Gallery. It was usually empty when she left around 9:30. She was a well-organized woman, predictable in her comings and goings. Which was good for him. And too bad for her.

At a quarter past nine that evening Mann chose a spot four spaces from Hellerman's car on the Ursuline lot. In the Ursuline Sisters' motherhouse that loomed like a massive, moored freighter in the night, the residents appeared to be turning in for the night. Lights winked out one after another. Mann liked the early fall chill and had the driver's window rolled down a few inches, as a smoker might. An empty red carton of McDonald's fries rested on the passenger seat and less than half of a Diet Coke sat in the cup holder. He tried to calm himself, praying the Our Father. Recently Fergus had begun to think of himself as the church's James Bond—a secret agent bearing a license to kill for the good of the Catholic faith. But that image came with its own problem. Ian Fleming's 007 was promiscuous—bedding down every woman he could. As a fornicator, he was committing mortal sin after mortal sin. And mortal sin demanded punishment. Mann leaned forward and took his wallet from his left-hip pocket. He removed a folded piece of paper and turned his head to face the parking-lot light that intruded like unwanted grace into the darkened Ford. Holding the smudged paper toward the dim light, he read aloud his favorite lines from Psalm 149.

Let the praise of God be in their mouths
and a two-edged sword in their hands,
to deal out vengeance to the nations
and punishment upon the peoples;
to carry out the judgment decreed.
This is an honor for all God's faithful.

"May God have mercy on her soul," Fergus prayed sincerely.

The instrument of punishment would be the same as with the Spivak woman—a cincture. Neatly coiled in his glove compartment, wrapped in cellophane, was a white cincture, a smooth and shining cord of braided silk, almost sacramental in its purity. Tonight Fergus Mann would once again act as God's avenging angel.

Father Trace Dunmore, red-faced and breathing heavily, stopped at the door of Terry Reeves' office.

"Have you heard?"

He could see from Reeves' expression that he was not the first to bring the disturbing news of a second murder. She followed him unbidden down the hall to the bishop's office.

"It's all over the local stations," Dunmore blurted. "Some national media outlets have already called for a statement."

The anchors' leads had all been pretty much the same: Serial Killer Strikes Second Woman Priest. The grisly reports followed. Frances Hellerman, a history teacher at Shaker Heights High School claiming to be a Roman Catholic woman priest, was found strangled in her car on the campus of Ursuline College. From the marks on her neck, it seemed the killer used a rope similar to the cincture used to strangle Laura Spivak two weeks earlier.

Bishop Martin was on the phone but waved them in. They moved to their chairs and waited as he finished the call.

"That was the nuncio's secretary. He'll call as soon as he can. What can you tell me about her family?"

"She was divorced," Dunmore said, raising an eyebrow, "with a daughter in Illinois, a sister in Michigan, and a brother in Pittsburgh. Another teacher from the high school, also a woman, lived with her."

Both Dunmore's and Reeves' cells vibrated.

"Hold those," Martin said, and they dismissed the calls. "We need to make sure that Ann Marie Ellsmere has security," Bryn said.

"We'll both be working on that, Bishop," Reeves said quickly.

Martin knew that he himself would be working on it, too.

As soon as they left, Martin called a longtime friend from Baltimore he thought could help. George Havel, a retired Secret Service Agent, had provided unofficial security for Archbishop Wilfred Gunnison when the archbishop's life had been threatened in the weeks leading up to his Golden Jubilee. As Martin was placing the call, the wrenching memories of Gunnison's tragic death and the unsolved mysteries surrounding it dampened his mood even further. Neither he nor Havel would be likely to broach the subject.

He caught Havel in and filled him in on the murders of Laura Spivak and Frances Hellerman.

"How many potential targets are out there?" Havel asked.

"We have—I should say had—three practicing women priests in the greater Cleveland area that we are sure of. Two are now dead. There are probably more, operating under the radar. I want to do all we can to protect the third we know about and any others who may be out there."

"It's going to be the local prosecutor's call, but I think you're right, Bishop. The murders are likely hate crimes and a third attempt is highly probable. A high profile case like these might lead to a scrap over jurisdiction, but it's probably safe to say that the FBI will be taking the lead. But protection will be local law enforcement, not federal."

"We have to do better than that, George. Ann Marie Ellsmere, the third woman priest, lives in Brecksville, a suburb south of Cleveland. The Brecksville police say they will do what they can, but they don't get half-a-dozen violent crimes a year out there. I'm afraid they may be over their heads if we have a serial killer on the prowl. That's the reason for my call. Do you know any retired Secret Service agents in the area that we can hire to watch out for her?"

"Who's 'we'?"

"I need to be careful here, George. The diocese has certain

discretionary funds available for emergency needs. I'll leave it at that."

"Hmm..." Havel hummed into the speaker of his phone. "You know as well as I do how risky that is. I'm thinking of a headline that reads, 'Catholic diocese offers protection for excommunicated woman priest.'"

Martin said nothing for a few seconds, as if reflecting about the risk. "So does anyone come to mind?"

"As a matter of fact, yes. Let me make a call. I'll get back to you as soon as I can."

"Do you have a minute, Bishop?" Terry Reeves said, standing in the doorway of Martin's office. At his nod she closed the office door and sat down.

"There's something you need to know. Ann Marie Ellsmere and I are high school classmates. We've stayed in touch. We're life-long friends. Her maiden name is Nosek. We grew up together in St. Mel's parish. Already in the third grade Ann Marie wanted to be a nun. Then, as a senior, she talked about wanting to be a priest. Her husband's name is Richard Ellsmere. They met in college. Miami University. Ohio, not Florida. Rich is a sales rep who travels a lot. He's home mostly on weekends. I'm worried about her being alone during the week."

Martin nodded his concern. "Children?"

"Not for lack of trying." Terry leaned forward in her chair, "I've decided to stay with Ann Marie when Rich is gone, at least for the next couple of weeks—or until they catch this...this maniac."

Martin again nodded his assent. "I'll be worried about you Terry, but I understand. Why can't her husband arrange to stay close?"

"He sells surgical supplies, operating room stuff, that a lot of people depend on, and he's the sole rep in his territory. He has a lot of responsibility."

"I'm arranging some additional security," the bishop said without explanation.

Two sharp knocks sounded on the bishop's office door.

"Come in," Martin said, more loudly than necessary.

Trace Dunmore took the chair next to Reeves without so much as a "Good morning."

"Both the Willoughby Hills police and the Pepper Pike police—where Ursuline College is located—are referring us to the Cleveland FBI office. And the special agent I spoke to said they have no information to release at this time."

Reeves, holding a tissue in her hand, said, "I spoke with a *Cleveland Plain Dealer* reporter, who confirms Pepper Pike detectives say they have no clues, no suspects."

"It's still early in these investigations," Martin observed. "Sooner or later, something will turn up." Looking at Terry, the bishop said softly, "Trace needs to know what you just told me."

George Havel called back a few hours later.

"There's a retired Secret Service agent in your area, Bishop. We did some of our training together. He's a good man and says he's fit for his age. His name is Hugh McKenna. He has your cell and will call you shortly. But you do need to consider that close protection is not a one-man job. You would need at least two men working separate shifts to do it right. Three even better. But one is better than nothing. The visible presence of local law enforcement should help. We're talking about a strangler, not a suicide bomber. This guy likes to get away. And Bishop, if you need me I can be there in six hours.

Alistair and Fergus Mann sat at their usual table at The Coffee House. None of the patrons was within earshot, but they spoke just above a whisper.

"Remember," Alistair said, "that you are doing God's work."

"Yes," Mann responded, "I tell myself that often."

"The papers and TV reporters say police have no clues, no suspects, not even a person of interest. You are very good and very careful, Fergus. Competence and prudence, two character-istics highly admired by the Sentinels of the Supreme Center."

Mann seemed deaf to the compliment. Alistair knew well that he had to handle this meeting carefully. Fergus had rational-ized his taking of the lives of Spivak and Hellerman. He pro-fessed to be okay with it, but Alistair feared his good-Catholic super-ego might try to break through in the deep corners of his soul, sowing seeds of anxiety, and doubt, and guilt. "Just one more stage to the assignment, Fergus."

"I know." And then to Alistair's relief, Fergus went on. "Let's get this over with."

Alistair placed two envelopes on the table. Mann put both of them in his pocket.

"Your subject works as an account manager for the Cleve-land Clinic at their Business Operations Center in Indepen-dence. Her home is in Brecksville, just a ten-minute drive from work. Her husband's job has him on the road most of the week, but a diocesan administrator, Therese Reeves, is staying with her at night. She is not to be harmed, if at all possible. Everything you need is in the envelope."

"This one is going to be a real challenge," Mann said with a heavy voice, almost as if looking for encouragement. "She's got to know she's in danger, so she'll have a bodyguard whenever she goes out."

"Yes, that's likely, Fergus. You need to be especially careful with this last one."

Alistair sensed immediately that he may have blundered. Fergus Mann thought of himself as a man who was always careful, and seemed to bristle at the remark. "The operational details remain completely up to you. But it's probably best you lay low for a while. Let things quiet down. Let her and whoever is watching out for her lower their guard, eh?"

Mann shifted in his chair, looking a little agitated. He seemed ready to stand up and bolt out. *Don't lecture,* Alistair thought, *keep him calm and focused.* He stood to leave, but before turning and walking away, said softly but firmly, "It's best that we discontinue our Saturday coffees, Fergus, until the final assignment is completed. God be with you."

6

Simon Ashley, assistant professor of art history at John Carroll University, put the paper down as he finished his breakfast. Dr. Ian Landers, he had just read in the Sunday edition of the *Plain Dealer*, was the new Hallinan Professor of Catholic Studies at Case Western Reserve University. How strange, he thought, that two of his classmates from Oxford's Balliol College were now in Cleveland—Father Trace Dunmore, a major player at the headquarters of the diocese of Cleveland, and now Landers. Dunmore, though a convert to the faith, was a committed and trustworthy Sentinel. Also one who was very well-placed. Landers, as he remembered, was unctuous about the dangerous reforms of Vatican II. Ashley found such naïveté insufferable. Nevertheless, he would host a reunion dinner with his classmates. Landers would certainly have news of how the church of Baltimore was coping with the tragic death of their retired archbishop.

It was a sunny but cool fall Monday as Ashley gathered his notes for his 11:00 class. He was distracted, however, by a letter he had just opened from his mentor, the archbishop of Perugia. He looked again at the rich, cream-colored stationery with its embossed coat of episcopal arms, resting atop a pile of student essays on his otherwise clear desk. On the surface, Pietro Montaldo's move from Rome to Perugia appeared to be a promotion. But Ashley knew enough of Vatican politics to wonder if this was an appointment designed to remove Montaldo from his power base. While hardly close friends, Ashley and Montaldo were linked by another kind of intimacy. They had met in Rome when Ashley was doing research for his Master of Fine Arts thesis. Montaldo was a renowned collector of antiquarian liturgical books. Ashley soon discovered that his new acquaintance was not known among the Vatican's middle-to-high-level prelates only for his refined tastes; Bishop Montaldo carried a reputation for wielding more power in and out of church circles than one might have expected from his relatively humble post in the office of Vatican Protocol. Ashley admitted to himself, not without embarrassment, that he had been flattered by the attention Pietro Montaldo had paid him. The bishop could be charming, and his reputation as a player in the art circles of Rome and inside the Vatican had quickly seduced Ashley. After a number of exploratory lunches together, at which Simon Ashley apparently comported himself well, he was invited into a clandestine network of church loyalists. The Sentinels of the Supreme Center, as they dubbed themselves, without a hint of irony, were a relatively small, secret cadre of men vowed to use their talents, resources, and connections to return the Church of Rome to its rightful past glory and power. In Cleveland now, on this crisp fall morning, Ashley rose from his desk, reached for his dark blue blazer, and walked to the window of his Dolan Center office. After his class, he would make the fifteen-minute drive to the Cleveland Museum of Art, where he could sit undisturbed and give Montaldo's curious request the consideration it deserved.

The museum was Simon Ashley's personal cathedral and most everywhere he looked his gaze fell upon angelic beauty and elegance inviting contemplation. As a Sentinel of the Supreme

Center, he considered himself the sentinel of the museum's soul—the history and glory of Christendom's golden age.

Ashley stood silently, as if in prayer in the museum's spacious atrium. Visitors moved across the atrium's floor, a few with purpose, most walking slowly, dwarfed by the atrium's majestic scale, soaring glass ceiling, and vast open space that all seemed to lift them to their toes. Simon's thoughts returned to Montaldo's letter. He would do what he could to honor its request. Ashley moved to a bench along the north side of the atrium and took quiet pleasure in the private relationship he enjoyed with the Archbishop of Perugia, his rather mysterious mentor and patron. Montaldo's interest in the fine arts and his social circle had given Ashley the distinct impression that he was wealthy, quite wealthy. That was not such an uncommon thing among Vatican bishops and cardinals—even some members of the lower clergy. It was wise, one learned in Rome, not to question the source of clerical wealth. Montaldo, it was whispered, was a very passionate man, but his true passion, Simon believed, was not for wealth or pleasure, but for power—the almost erotic power of behind-the-scenes influence. Ashley had been invited to enough cocktail parties and dinners to see that this sophisticated lover of art was also a warrior for orthodoxy who bore grave suspicions about the so-called "fresh air" of the Second Vatican Council. Indeed, he had heard that Montaldo often influenced the appointments of like-minded, arch-conservative men to the episcopacy, especially in Western Europe and North America. And it appeared that Pietro Montaldo had a genius for creating and nurturing networks of conservative clergy and laity who shared his passion for orthodoxy, preserving the hegemony of the Curia, and for protecting, at whatever the cost, the church's supreme center.

Ashley rose slowly, conscious of the few extra pounds he had put on in recent months, and walked to the Provenance Café at the west end of the atrium. There he ordered an espresso and sat down again, still pleased with himself as Pietro Montaldo's secret agent in the United States.

7

Fergus Mann had every confidence he could rise to the challenges he faced in completing his third and final assignment. His subject, Ann Marie Ellsmere, was seldom alone. That Reeves woman stayed with her during the week and her husband hovered at her side on weekends. Moreover, she had what looked like professional security following her when she went out. This was likely to be his biggest challenge. But he was determined that it would not be insurmountable. For the last two days Mann had watched as Ellsmere almost ran to her car after work. Less than ten minutes later, she would pull into the attached garage of her home on Whitewood Road in Brecksville. Seconds after the door on the two-car garage went down, lights in the house came on. Ellsmere had the look of a very frightened woman. Mann didn't like frightened prey. He took no pleasure in the terror he saw in their eyes. As unfaithful and guilty as she was, he preferred to dispatch her, like the other pseudo-priests, as quickly as possible. Yes, he would do his best to kill Ann Marie Ellsmere as quickly and painlessly as possible.

Patience, patience, Fergus repeated. No reason to rush this assignment. After a few weeks, she and her protectors would begin to let their guard down a bit. That's all it would take. One slip. Perhaps they would think, hope, and pray that the media's coverage and the FBI's investigations of the Spivak and Hellerman deaths had frightened their assassin enough to make him cut and run. Mann smiled. They would be gravely mistaken. In the meantime, he needed only to be careful not to be spotted by Ellsmere's security people.

Simon Ashley moved pensively, like a monk walking his cloister, through the galleries housing the museum's medieval collection. The spot lighting and the dark maroon walls in gallery 10-B created a transcendent, time-out-of-time ambience that never failed to calm his soul and at the same time excite his imagination. Ashley nodded to the museum guard, then moved slowly to the case holding the *Caporali Missal*. It was a remarkable piece and the illuminations in this hefty altar missal were beyond exquisite. Standing inches now from the missal, Ashley suddenly stiffened, as if Archbishop Pietro Montaldo himself were standing a few steps away watching him. He shivered like a lover discovering a rival for his beloved. The Archbishop of Perugia was interested in more than the loan of a priceless book.

Back on the John Carroll campus, Simon Ashley left his Dolan Center office and with the strap of his weathered briefcase pressing into his left shoulder walked toward the Grasselli Library, mulling over the information he had recently uncovered in his post-thesis research on the provenance of the *Caporali Missal*. Every few steps his thoughts were interrupted as he exchanged nods and half smiles with familiar students who could not have suspected he was God's avenger.

Once settled into his faculty carrel in the library, Ashley studied his handwritten notes. Other scholars were familiar with the work of the Caporali brothers, Bartolomeo and Giapeco, who were the likely artists commissioned to execute the illuminations that made the missal so extraordinary. And other scholars discerned that the miniaturists had painted the little masterpieces adorning the missal in the latter part of the fifteenth century for the Franciscan monastery in Montone, a picturesque Umbrian city just north of Perugia. Ashley let a hint of a smile soften his face—this was the joy of scholarship. The Cleveland Museum of Art had purchased the *Caporali Missal* in 2006 from Dr. Jörn Günther, a highly regarded German art dealer, for a rumored 1.3 million American dollars. Gunther claimed to have purchased the missal from an unnamed Swiss collector. The identity of this anonymous collector had been the object of Ashley's research for more than a year now. No other scholar to his knowledge had been able to identify him. But Simon Ashley was confident that he was closing in on the discovery of his career. The collector, he had learned, was not Swiss at all. He was more than likely, according to Ashley's recent digging, an Italian. He was not yet able to prove it, but the evidence he had unearthed suggested that the anonymous collector who sold the missal to Jörn Günther was none other than Pietro Montaldo. Could the leader of the Sentinels of the Supreme Center be experiencing seller's remorse? Was this regret behind Montaldo's current request for the loan of the missal to his cathedral in Perugia? For the time being, this likely piece of the provenance of the missal would remain secret, held *in pectore*, in the bosom of Simon Ashley.

Ashley feared Montaldo overestimated his connections at the museum in seeking his help in arranging the loan. He would write to the curators he knew and would make a few calls, but an assistant professor at a neighboring university just didn't have the clout to influence such a decision. Ashley hoped the loan would be made. The missal was the major focus of his own academic work, and his mentor, Pietro Montaldo, was equally obsessed with it. And Ashley thought he knew why. It was universally believed that the missal was created in the Caporali brothers' studio in Perugia. It was, therefore, a Perugian masterpiece, and Montaldo wanted to bring it home.

44

It was late in the afternoon by the time Ashley got back to his office. It had been a good day overall and now it was time to meet Trace Dunmore for a drink at Pizzazz, a faculty watering hole at the edge of the John Carroll campus.

8

B ryn Martin heard a ping from his cell. The text was from
Ian Landers. "Reminder: dinner tonight at my apartment,
23201 North Park Blvd., #104. 6ish. White wine if conve-
nient."

Martin drove slowly east on Chester Avenue, caught in the
tail end of the rush hour traffic creeping out of the city. Dinner
with Ian was just the break he needed from the dark events of
the past weeks. At the same time, he looked forward to learning
what Ian thought about the murders of the two women priests.
Landers would know of the historical precedents of violence in
the intramural world of Catholicism. Still in exploration mode
in his new city, Bryn drove onto Fairmount Boulevard and found
himself driving past long rows of stately mansions. Strangely,
they seemed uninhabited, ghostlike in their isolation among vast
gulfs of perfectly trimmed lawns, empty of any sign of life.

Martin found Ian's building without difficulty, pressed in
Landers' apartment code, and waited to be buzzed in. A Puligny-
Montrachet that never failed to please in hand, he found number
104 down the corridor to the right of the entrance. The door
opened before he could knock.

"Bryn…welcome." The two exchanged a brief hug, with a
couple quick pats on the back. Before Bryn could say a word, Ian
added, "Someone's joining us for dinner. Hope you don't mind."

To Bryn's great surprise, Nora appeared from the dining
room. Bryn's eyes teared as he hugged his sister.

"You look good, Bryn, considering what you've run up against. Two women priests murdered and God knows what else you've been dealing with."

"Yeah. It's been rough, really rough."

"What I figured. I don't have a Friday class this semester at Johns Hopkins, and I can always stay at the Carmelite monastery, so I thought a weekend in Cleveland with two of my favorite men would be a good idea."

"A very good idea," Bryn said almost in a whisper. "Ian, thank you."

"My pleasure, Bryn. I'm hoping we can make it a regular thing."

"Amen to that," Nora added cheerfully.

Bryn handed the wine he'd brought to Ian, who whistled appreciatively.

"That'll need a little chill."

"Would you like a cocktail, Bryn?"

"Scotch on the rocks with a splash of water if you have it."

Landers said over his shoulder on his way to the kitchen, "Dewar's, right?""

"Perfect," Bryn replied.

Ian returned with Bryn's drink. He and Nora seemed to be having the same.

Bryn eased into the chair closest to the front window. Outside the window two giant fir trees seemed to be standing guard over the gathering inside.

"How are you coping with all this?" Nora asked.

"It's been pretty cloak and dagger. Maybe you two can play Sherlock Holmes and Dr. Watson. We have—or had—three women priests in the diocese that we know of. Two are now dead, strangled with cinctures. It's probable they were killed because of their ordination. Someone or some group really doesn't like women priests. No, let me correct myself. They don't dislike

47

them, they hate them."

Nora asked, "How's the third woman doing?"

"Ann Marie Ellsmere. She's kind of a mess. Her husband's worse than she is. They've both lost weight. They're not sleeping. Pretty much what you'd expect."

"Any progress on the investigations?" Ian asked as he placed a tray of Stilton blue cheese, crackers, and red and white grapes on the coffee table. "The *Plain Dealer* said the FBI's involved."

"So far nothing—no witnesses, no clues, no suspects. The Brecksville police say they're giving Ellsmere as much attention as they can. You two might remember George Havel," Bryn said, unconsciously lowering his tone, "the retired Secret Service agent who helped protect Wilfred Gunnison after the threats on his life."

Nora and Ian each responded with a simultaneous, "Yes."

"I called George and asked if he could recommend any retired agents in Cleveland. He made a call and found one willing to help. His name is Hugh McKenna. He did some of his Secret Service training with Havel. He's with Ellsmere a good part of each week day, when she is between secure locations. But we can't give her even this minimal security indefinitely. And we have to consider that while it might be possible to protect her from assault and strangulation, the killer may change his *modus operandi*. Car bomb, rifle."

"Whoa," Nora said, "The brand new bishop of Cleveland is providing private security for an excommunicated woman priest?" She exchanged a troubled glance with Ian.

"They'll savage you if this ever gets out," Ian said.

Bryn furrowed his brow. "It's the right thing to do."

"And if the killer ever figures out you're providing security for his next victim?" Nora said. "You know where that puts you."

9

Ann Marie Ellsmere turned left off of Brecksville Road onto Whitewood, catching sight in her side-view mirror of Hugh McKenna's car making the turn behind her a moment later. As she pulled into the garage, McKenna eased to the curb two houses down from hers. He would keep watch until Terry Reeves arrived. Her drive from Ninth and Superior in rush hour traffic could take an hour on a bad day.

Ellsmere entered the side door, put her keys in the dish on the kitchen counter and started for her bedroom. Something wasn't right. She froze, listening. The house was quiet. Then she noticed it. The door to the laundry was closed. She always left the door open. "Terry?" she called out. But Terry's car hadn't been in the drive. The laundry room door swung silently open and a man in a black nylon athletic suit walked toward her. He was wearing a black ski mask and twined a white cord in his gloved hands.

"You have sinned mortally, woman. You have harmed God's holy church."

Ellsmere stabbed the button on a wrist alarm coded to Hugh McKenna's cell, but her killer was already on her, grabbing her by the shoulders and turning her so her back was to him. The white cord squeezed her throat, locking the air in her lungs. With all her might, she kicked her heels against her killer's shins. Her face felt as if it might burst, and the room began to blur. She felt, for a moment, dreamlike and weightless, until the room around her went dark at last.

"I called Richard," Terry Reeves said. She was perched on the edge of the couch in the Ellsmeres' family room, holding the cold hand of her friend Ann Marie. "He's flying in from Chicago and should be here before midnight."

McKenna was standing in front of the fireplace talking to two Brecksville policemen and two paramedics who wanted to take Ann Marie to the hospital.

"I'm shaken, but I'll be okay," Ann Marie said. "I want to stay right here." She was lying under a blanket on the couch in the family room with throw pillows under her feet.

"Your attacker must have seen Hugh coming up your driveway and taken off through your back yard. The police are waiting for your statement."

One of the Brecksville Fire and Rescue squad paramedics said, "At least keep her feet elevated. No food, no drink for at least an hour."

They collected their gear and went out the front door and back to their ambulance.

McKenna said, "Give us a minute?" to the two plain clothes police officers hovering inside the doorway and pulled an ottoman up to the couch as the policemen moved into the kitchen.

"Your doctor has prescribed some sedatives that should be here soon."

Ann Marie squeezed McKenna's hand.

"If you hadn't been here, I'd be dead." She shuddered, trying to break the spell of the unthinkable. "I'm cold." Reeves went looking for another blanket and McKenna turned up the gas in the fireplace and adjusted the speed of the fan. Terry placed a crimson Ohio State blanket on top of the one already tucked tightly around Ann Marie. "I'll make some tea when the hour is up. Is there anything else you want?"

"No," she said. "I just want Rich here."

Terry called Bryn Martin and updated him while a pot of

coffee brewed for Hugh and the officers. There was really nothing for him to do here, so they arranged to meet first thing the next morning. McKenna walked into the kitchen and asked the officers, "Any signs of the attacker?"

The older of the two answered, "We don't really know what to look for until we get a statement. We have the two other cars on this shift patrolling the streets around here for anything suspicious. As soon as we finish here, we'll be knocking on the neighbors' doors to see if they saw anything at all. Whoever did this knew what he was doing. The house alarm was disabled at a little after 4:50. Mrs. Ellsmere got home at about 5:10. This was no burglary gone bad."

Fergus Mann walked at a steady but unhurried pace to St. Basil the Great Catholic Church, a little over a mile away. As he had rehearsed three days earlier, he made the walk to the church in under eighteen minutes. Mann slipped through the right back entrance just in time to catch the final blessing of the weekday 5:00 Mass. After a short prayer of thanksgiving for his deliverance, he joined the fifty or so parishioners moving to their cars. Just another Catholic stopping for Mass at the end of another work day.

10

W ho is this Hugh McKenna?" Trace Dunmore asked after Terry Reeves reported her firsthand account of the near-tragedy averted by McKenna the night before. It was eight o'clock on Saturday morning and the bishop and his two aides found themselves alone at the Catholic Center.

Bishop Martin overrode Dunmore's question by asking Reeves, "How is Mrs. Ellsmere?"

"She seems okay, Bishop. No serious injury. Just mild shock, which had to be expected, and has passed. Her doctor and husband are watching for symptoms of post-traumatic stress. Richard made it home a little after midnight. Ann Marie really lost it when he walked in."

"But who is this Hugh McKenna?" Dunmore insisted.

Reeves signaled the bishop with a raised finger that she wanted to take Dunmore's question. "A friend of the family hired Hugh McKenna, a retired Secret Service agent, to provide security for Mrs. Ellsmere in light of the murders of Mrs. Spivak and Mrs. Hellerman. As it turned out, he saved her life."

In that moment, Bryn Martin knew he could trust Terry Reeves. Terry had to have her suspicions about who brought McKenna into the picture. She held his gaze, only for a split second, but it was enough.

"Should the media want a statement," Bryn said to Dunmore, "keep it short. Something like, 'We are deeply grateful that Mrs. Ellsmere survived this attempt on her life. Beyond that we have no comment.' If you get pressure for anything more, Trace, run your statement by me before you release it."

Dunmore nodded peremptorily and remained silent.

"Maybe, please God, whoever's behind these attacks will back off. Thanks for coming in on a Saturday morning."

Dunmore knew Martin's thanks were meant for Reeves. He lived with Martin, after all. He didn't "come in," he simply walked across East Ninth Street from the cathedral rectory.

Back in his own office Dunmore drafted the media statement. It took him no more than ten minutes. On the surface, the early morning meeting with Martin and Reeves may have appeared to be a waste of time. For Father Trace Dunmore, though, it had been anything but that. Reeves had dissembled. He loved the word. She knew more than she had let on. He would find out all he could about Hugh McKenna, and who had hired him. The new Bishop of Cleveland, Dunmore noted with growing pleasure, had made three mistakes in less than three weeks on the job—he had gone to the funeral of excommunicated Laura Spivak, he had permitted his own Executive Assistant to stay in the home of an excommunicated woman priest, and, if Dunmore's hunch was correct, Martin had something to do with the hiring of Hugh McKenna.

As he always did, Fergus Mann arrived well before the appointed hour of nine at The Coffee House nestled in the heart of the Case Western Reserve campus. He recognized some of the Saturday morning regulars, including the gaggle of left-wing know-it-alls who hotly debated issues of religion and politics, as if anybody gave a damn what they thought. He ordered a zucchini muffin and ate quickly, wanting to finish it and clear the crumbs before Alistair arrived. He had no idea what to expect from his mentor.

At 9:03, Alistair walked across Juniper Street and entered

The Coffee House through the front entrance and took a seat across from Fergus without ordering. The two men sat in silence for a few seconds.

"Are you all right?" Alistair asked.

"Yeah, I'm all right," Mann responded flatly. "It was a close, close call."

To Mann's relief, his mentor said, "You did well. Avoiding apprehension was far more important than completing stage three."

Fergus studied Alistair's face. His expression was controlled, strangely cold, but seemed sincere at the same time.

"We are very pleased, Fergus. We consider your assignment completed. We have punished the enemies of our church and put the fear of God in the hearts of any women considering ordination."

We? Fergus thought. *I punished the sinners. I am the man who put the fear of God in women thinking of being ordained.*

Alistair pulled an envelope out of the breast pocket of his tweed coat. "This is for you, Fergus. We hope you will make a retreat or take a vacation. You need to just take it easy. You have met all our expectations. And we are very grateful."

Mann remained silent, looking casually around the room so he wouldn't have to look at Alistair.

"So, now what?" he said, bringing his gaze back to Alistair.

"You are now a Sentinel of the Supreme Center. Our 'special-ops' man, if you will. It would be entirely natural for you to have questions, Fergus, but this is all you need to know. As I told you earlier, we are a network of loyal, orthodox Catholics intent on saving the church from succumbing to the ravages of secularism and liberalism. We are only a handful of faithful souls, but any true, orthodox Catholic is our ally. That means we have thousands, even millions, of allies who know nothing of our mission but who sustain us and encourage us by their fidelity. Some of our strongest allies are in the media and some write far-reaching blogs that expose the sickness in our church and her false leaders in the clergy."

So, Fergus thought, I know a little bit more about the Sentinels. But he wondered, where does the money Alistair is so generous with come from? Who are the leaders of this network? Do they have the blessing of the pope? He balked at Alistair's admonition to ask no questions, but said nothing.

Alistair, back at his podium, interrupted his thoughts as if reading his mind.

"Let me repeat what I've said before—there are no meetings, no dues, no membership lists. You are now a part of a silent network of faithful disciples of Jesus. You need only to stand ready to defend the Holy Roman Catholic Church from the assaults of her enemies from within and without. And as you know, the worst enemies we must deal with are often within the church."

Fergus wasn't sure exactly what to feel or what to think. What he did know as an absolute certainty was that he was a part of something bigger than himself. It made him feel good. Powerful. Exalted. He said lamely, "I guess this is a big deal."

Alistair suppressed a chuckle at the naïveté of the statement. *You have no idea,* he thought. "Absolutely," he said. "The SSC is asking you to stand ready, to be on alert, so to speak, for the next time we have an operation, an assignment, for you. It could come at any moment, so you need to be ready."

Fergus nodded.

"When the assignment comes, and it could be next month or next year, we expect you to make it your top priority. Is that clear?"

Fergus nodded again.

"I will contact you when you are needed. I'm not permitted to give you any of my contact information. You must never attempt to contact me in any way whatsoever, or to try to discover my true identity. Is that acceptable?"

"I guess it has to be," Mann said.

"Now I must ask for your cell number, good man."

Alistair scribbled the number Fergus gave him on a napkin.

"I won't use this number unless I absolutely must. The usual way I'll contact you is to have a member of our network approach you and say 'Alistair sends his greetings.' That means I'd like to meet you here at The Coffee House on the following Saturday."

Fergus nodded his assent. Alistair could see that he embraced the little bit of cloak and dagger with pleasure.

"In the meantime, Fergus Mann, know that you have done the Catholic Church a noble service, a brave service, for which you can never be publicly acknowledged or thanked. Let the reality of your courageous service to God and Holy Mother Church sustain you in the months ahead."

Both men stood as Alistair shook Fergus's hand. Without another word, Alistair nodded farewell and walked away.

Fergus Mann sat back down, put the envelope into his pocket, and stared into the ring of black coffee at the bottom of his cup.

11

Christina Tomasso arrived ten minutes early for her 9:00 appointment with Bishop Martin. Wearing designer jeans, an off-white blouse, and a tailored dark sport coat, she sat next to a *Plain Dealer* photographer in the waiting area looking over her notes while surreptitiously peering through the open door to the office of Therese Reeves. She would try to get some comment from her on her new boss when she finished with the bishop.

"Good morning, Bishop," Tomasso said as Reeves ushered her and the photographer into Martin's office.

"Welcome back," Martin said shaking her outstretched hand. "Sorry for the interruption last time."

"This is, Wendy, one of our photographers," Tomasso said gesturing to the other woman, who was reading the office's lighting with a hand-held meter.

Martin and the photographer exchanged a nod.

"I thought we'd get the photos first," Tomasso said.

Wendy shot the bishop sitting at his desk, standing in front of his finally shelved book cases, and a few mood shots silhouetting Martin looking down at the city below.

"Maybe a photo of Christina asking me a question," Martin suggested.

Tomasso colored slightly as Wendy smiled her agreement and clicked away as the reporter and profile subject feigned conversation. *Like we'll use these,* she thought. Terry Reeves brought in coffee and mini-scones as Wendy slipped away. Tomasso and Martin settled into chairs in the conversation area of the office. She thought Martin looked a bit on guard compared to her first meeting with him. It had to be the attacks on the women priests.

"These three assaults were horrific, mindless acts of violence," Martin said, anticipating Tomasso's first line of inquiry. Tomasso smiled inwardly at this brilliant move on the bishop's part. He was taking control over the most dangerous, problematic topic they would be discussing. "My heart goes out especially to Laura's and Frances's families and friends," he said. "I'm praying for them every day." Martin paused, but Tomasso knew better than to jump in with a question. "Chief among the factors associated with these brutal attacks is the twisted motivation that must have led to the assaults on these women. That's about all I can say right now in light of the on-going investigations and the search for their killer."

Well-played, Tomasso thought, with a reluctant smile, taking a sip of coffee. But she'd let this go. Anyway, Martin may have said more than he realized. "Okay, let's move on. Tell me about your goals as you begin your ministry as bishop here in Cleveland."

"They're pretty modest, I think, and rather predictable. I want to get to know the people of Cleveland, especially the Catholics, and I want to catch the flavor and culture of a city that has been through a lot in recent decades. I'm eager to get to know the people who share ministry with me, the priests and deacons, the sisters and lay ministers, the teachers in our schools. I really want to get to know our priests. We've been through and are going through some very difficult times: the abuse scandals, the relatively small number of men in training to be priests, the median age of priests. More than half are approaching retirement. I could go on. But priesthood remains a very humbling, joyous way of following Christ. A mentor of mine used to say that priests have a front row seat at the unfolding of grace in the lives of God's people. If being a priest doesn't make a man humble, grateful, and joyful, then something's wrong."

"When did you discover that you had a calling to the priesthood? How old were you?"

"I was in high school, and the priests I met were the happiest men I knew. There was something special, something mysterious about them. But I want to go back to something I was saying just a minute ago, speaking about priests. We bishops need to heal the division we see in the ranks of priests today between what I'll call the traditionalists and the progressives. And I want to lead them, join them, in what the Second Vatican Council calls the reading of the 'signs of the times.'"

"What do you mean by that?"

"Well, what are we to make of the fact that in many parts of the Catholic world, especially in developed nations, only one in five Catholics goes to Mass on Sundays? In many places, weekly Mass attendance among baptized Catholics is in single digits. Just a half-century ago, seventy percent of Catholics went to Mass every Sunday. I'm afraid a number of Catholics, especially our young adults, have come to see the Eucharist and their parish as no longer meaningful in their lives. We church leaders need to find ways of listening to their reasons for not practicing their faith, and then taking seriously this particular sign of the times. What's it saying to us? And we also need to listen to practicing Catholics, the current faithful we see every week. What is it, exactly, that brings them to Mass every Sunday? I don't think it's fear of mortal sin anymore."

Christina tried to remember the last time she attended Mass. *Weddings and funerals don't count,* she thought. She could not name the day.

"Can't creeping secularism explain that drop in Mass attendance?" she asked.

"Sure, that's a big part of it. But something tells me it's more than just the hostile secular culture we find ourselves living in. Christians should always be in a certain tension with the prevailing culture. But I think many Catholics are suffering from a crisis in confidence when it comes to their church. To be more precise, many Catholics seem to have lost confidence in the credibility and integrity of their bishops and pastors. And I'm afraid that, too, is a big part of it."

"How do you plan to address that challenge?" Tomasso asked, surprised at Martin's frankness.

"Certainly not alone. If we Catholics truly believe the Holy Spirit is with us, then we must begin by looking fearlessly and honestly at the elephants in our room. I mean we need to look at issues that seemingly conflict with our long-held values and tradition. Mandatory celibacy for Latin rite priests is a prime example of what I'm referring to. So, we might begin with some really honest, respectful conversations. But history has proven to us that's never easy."

"Do any other goals sit high on the list, Bishop?"

"Maybe one or two. I'm eager to meet the Hispanic and Asian communities of our diocese. I believe we will be drawing on their faith and example in the years and decades ahead. And I'd like to meet the Protestant, Jewish, and Muslim leaders of Cleveland. I'm anxious to work with them…and learn from them. They know where our city needs healing far better than this new kid on the block. And I've heard so much about Cleveland's wonderful ethnic diversity. I hope to visit the neighborhoods. That might take time, but I'll get to it."

"I have to admit, Bishop Martin, that I'm surprised by your candor. So, in that vein, what weaknesses or short-comings do you bring to your new job?

"Did you pack a lunch? We could be here for quite a while."

Tomasso said to herself, *How can you not like this man?*

"I'm afraid I have all the frailties we associate with being human," the bishop said. "Criticism still stings a bit more than it should, so I hope to be less thin-skinned in the future. And my Spanish isn't very good, by a long-shot." Martin paused. He was at heart rather happy with Tomasso's edgy question. With a hint of a smile, he added, "And it won't take the priests and people long to discover the rest of my weaknesses."

Tomasso returned the smile and reached for her recorder, signaling that the interview was over. As Martin stood, he said with conviction, "I promise I'll give the people and priests of the diocese my best."

"Bishop Martin, thank you very, very much. And I promise to do my best with this piece. It should be out soon in a Sunday edition of the *PD*, maybe even this Sunday. I'll send you a tear sheet as soon as I see it."

"How do you think it went?" Terry Reeves asked a few minutes later, sitting across from Martin in the bishop's office.

"It's always hard to say, but we'll see soon enough. I was candid…maybe too candid. But I got a real sense Christina Tomasso will be fair. What her editor will do to her piece is another matter." He leaned back in his chair. "So how are the Ellsmeres?"

"Rich is taking family leave, so Ann Marie will never be alone until they catch the guy."

"That's a relief."

"She's still pretty shaky, up one day and down the next. Some days she says she feels strangely liberated by the whole experience. The next day she and Rich want to move to Alaska. But then she feels that her assailant won't dare try again and is determined to stay. I never quite know where she will be when I call. She wants her life back and is determined not to live in fear. I hope she can pull it off."

"I hope she's right about the assailant," Martin said wearily.

"She asked me to get contact info for McKenna, who I guess is off the case while Rich is around. She feels that she never thanked him properly. Can you give me a number where he can be reached?"

"Now Ms. Reeves, what makes you think I would know about that?"

12

Professor Ian Landers stared at his computer screen in his Tomlinson Hall office in the religious studies department of Case Western Reserve University. His one undergraduate course, "The Fear of Hell Fire in Medieval Christendom" listed in the catalog simply as "Sin in the Medieval Church" was going well, with both good participation and good energy. Most religion courses at Case, his department chair had informed him, had about a dozen students. Landers' class had twenty-two students and their buzz on the course had brought in a few student auditors. "That's unheard of," the chair told Ian one day, betraying a hint of envy.

But it wasn't the course on sin that had Landers' attention. It was his first public lecture, one of two scheduled during the academic year, and it was only three weeks away. This first talk was co-sponsored by the religion department and Newman Catholic Campus Ministry, and it was open to the public. He knew Bryn Martin had it on his schedule, Nora was flying in, and the theology departments of John Carroll University, Ursuline, and Notre Dame Colleges were advertising the lecture. Ian expected their theology faculty and students majoring in theology to make up a good part of the audience. The task before him was to tighten up the talk. An hour's worth of content had to be slimmed down to a seamless forty-five minute presentation. A lecture geared for a general audience, Ian believed firmly, should never go beyond forty-five minutes. Never. So, he would cut away. Overall, he was happy with it and felt he would engage both students and his fellow academics. He was especially pleased with the title of the talk, "Under Pain of Mortal Sin: Moral Motivation in the Medieval Church."

Landers took off his reading glasses and looked out the window. The trees on campus were in their full burst of autumn orange, yellow, and burnt red, and while he didn't believe Case's campus quite matched up to Johns Hopkins, he was overall quite happy he'd accepted the visiting appointment to the Hallinan Chair of Catholic Studies. It meant being away from Nora Martin much of the time, but only for a year. He loved Nora and had told her so. "I love you, too," she had responded. But they didn't speak much of "being in love," as if doing so would invite the question of marriage. Both of them, he knew with certainty, treasured their relationship. Nora even spoke of it as a grace. It certainly wasn't platonic in the usual sense of the word. There was chemistry, and from time to time, especially when they shared meals or talked for hours about religion, spirituality, and psychology, a transporting electric delight. So it came to pass peacefully between them that it was wise to move slowly or perhaps not at all. Their relationship achieved a kind of stasis—as if it were just what it was meant to be.

Turning off his computer, Landers sat for a moment at his desk thinking about the dinner reunion with two of his college mates planned for later that evening. The mild squirm of anxiety he felt going to school reunions turned in his chest. Strange, he thought, that two of his classmates from Oxford were now living in Cleveland. And with interesting jobs. Trace Dunmore, now *Father* Trace Dunmore, chancellor and moderator of the curia of the Diocese of Cleveland! *God help us,* Ian thought as he recalled his tavern debates with Dunmore. During their years at Balliol College, Trace had decided to convert from the Anglican Communion to the Roman Catholic faith and he hammered away almost daily about the liturgical beauty and doctrinal rigor and unchanging splendor of the Roman Church. To Ian, their beer-hall dialectics over fish and chips had become tedious and, quite frankly, boring. Still Ian was surprised—and the Dunmore clan scandalized—when Trace announced his decision to begin studies for the priesthood with the staunchly conservative Legionaries of Christ.

Simon Ashley, who would be their dinner companion, was an assistant professor of art history at John Carroll, the Jesuit university in Cleveland. Landers found him a tough nut to crack. His musty imagination had drawn him regularly to the stately libraries of Oxford, where he would probe, like a fifteenth-century Sherlock Holmes, the mysteries and scandals of medieval Christianity, with its glorious sacred art and surreptitious venery. Ashley—the thought made Ian smile—had seemed destined for epic intrigues and dark conspiracies. And of the three of them, Ashley, behind his English tweeds and British reserve, was without question the most passionate.

Ian decided to leave his car in the faculty lot behind Tomlinson Hall and walk to the Primo Vino restaurant in nearby Little Italy for this reunion dinner with his Oxford "friends," praying that the twenty-minute walk would give him ample time to brace his soul for the ordeal ahead.

Father Trace Dunmore stuck his head through the open door of Bishop Martin's office, "I'm leaving for dinner with two former classmates from Oxford, Bishop, both professors now. I believe you know one of them quite well. Ian Landers, on loan to Case Western from Johns Hopkins."

"Yes, I do know Ian. Tell him I said hello."

Dunmore nodded. "Do you have anything for me before I leave?"

Martin thought for a moment. "Yes, I think I do." Dunmore moved into Martin's office but remained standing. "I've been thinking that one good way I could get to know this city better would be to have someone drive me around for a few nights so I can get a feel for the neighborhoods. Do you think you could find someone suitable who might be willing to give me some of his time?"

Trace hesitated long enough to give Martin the impression that he needed to think about his answer. "Yes, I think I have the man for you. He's a member of St. Patrick's parish, the one on Bridge Avenue, but he comes to the cathedral for Sunday Mass. St. Patrick's is a bit too progressive for him. He's been retired from the Cleveland Police Force for a year or so. We've talked after Mass on a number of occasions. A nice enough chap. He lost his wife a few years ago and lives by himself. A bit on the quiet side, but he loves the church and knows Cleveland's neighborhoods as well as anyone. I'll give him a call tomorrow. His name is Fergus Mann."

13

The three Oxford University alums sat at a worn wooden table directly under an almost life-size print of an icon portrait of Emperor Justinian. The original mosaic, Ashley and Landers certainly knew, was hanging in Ravenna's Basilica of San Vitale. Smiling at Justinian's robes of Tyrian purple, Landers was reminded of the underground gang of self-proclaimed church saviors who once operated under the secret mantle of the Brotherhood of the Sacred Purple. Instinctively, Landers looked toward Ashley. The Simon he knew at Oxford would have been fascinated with a secret brotherhood committed to restoring the church to her undisputed place of power and prestige. Come to think of it, so would Trace Dunmore.

Back in the moment, Landers thought this must be Ashley's favorite table, a guess that was confirmed when Roberto, the owner, approached and greeted them, addressing Ashley and Dunmore like old friends. "I've prepared a nice antipasto for you, Professor, some of your favorites—cheese, pepperoncini, mushrooms, olives, artichoke hearts, but no anchovies. See, I remember," he said with a self-congratulating smile. "And we're decanting a bottle of the Ruffino Ducale D'Oro."

"Thank you, Roberto," Ashley said with an approving smile. Gesturing to Landers, Ashley said, "This is Professor Ian Landers. He'll be teaching at Case Western this year in the Hallinan Chair of Catholic Studies."

"*Benvenuti*, Professor, welcome to Little Italy," Roberto

smiled at Ashley and Dunmore as if approving of the good company Landers was keeping.

Ian returned the smile and sipped his sparkling water, anticipating the pricey Chianti. What he really wanted was a stiff scotch on the rocks.

"Roberto," Simon added, "was born in Ravenna and knows we like to dine beneath the great Justinian."

All three settled in at the table, looking pleasant enough but alert to issues that had provoked heated exchanges during their Balliol years—personal and political issues they hoped to avoid. Landers was glad he hadn't worn a tie. Like himself, Ashley and Dunmore wore open-necked shirts and sport coats. Dunmore wasn't in his Roman collar—a propitious sign. But Ian had been right. Their early conversation was strangely formal for classmates simply re-connecting, catching up, and ready to entertain themselves with selected memories of college high jinks and modestly abridged stories of their brilliant careers.

And so it went for the next few minutes. Restrained reflections in their now-mature years about the famed Balliol rivalry with Oxford's Trinity College, drinking sessions in their favorite pubs, a few flagrant flirtations recalled with wry grins, and an unnecessary reference to their college's 1263 founding as one of Oxford's oldest and most prestigious colleges.

To Landers relief, the Ducale D'Oro, having been given a proper chance to breathe, arrived in a crystal duck, just as Trace quoted a favorite line of H.H. Asquith's about Balliol men possessing "the tranquil consciousness of an effortless superiority." Roberto poured the ruby wine in the awkward silence that followed the priest's remark. Dunmore, apparently unaware that he was showing bad form, blundered on. "Tell us Ian, whatever became of that woman you were living with during your senior year?"

"Her name, Trace, was Emma," Ian said, somewhat sharply.

Still, there was a softening in his blue-gray eyes. "And though we may have been living in sin," he looked briefly at both his companions, "she was a kind of soul mate." Simon and Trace remained pointedly silent. Ian felt an unexpected wave of emotion fill his chest and heard himself say, "I'll never regret the months we shared under the same roof…in the same bed. It was during my time with Emma that I came to have, pardon the hubris, a kind of a revelation. As you both know, our relationship didn't last. But it was real, authentic…even holy." Ian didn't add that Emma loved him in a way that made him want to weep. He tried to sound matter of fact. "It was during my time with Emma that I came to desire some kind of intimacy with God."

Ian spun the Chianti in his glass, inspected its legs, and took a careful sip, embarrassed at his thoroughly un-English expression of romantic and religious feelings. Balliol men didn't go there—it inevitably smacked of the maudlin and sentimental. He feared he sounded like some would-be medieval mystic.

Dunmore bridged the strained quiet, "Now bring us up to date, Ian. Aren't you, shall we say, close to my new boss's sister, Nora, if I'm not mistaken?"

It hit Landers that in posing the probing question that way, Trace had said more than he intended. "Yes," Ian said, a little too casually, "Nora Martin and I are very good friends. She's on the faculty at Johns Hopkins, the psychology department. It amuses us both that our colleagues speak of us as an 'item.' But isn't that enough about me?"

A server cleared the antipasto plates and the oval platter with the leftovers of Roberto's special choices.

Wanting to force a change in conversation, Ian asked Dunmore, "How did you find yourself in Cleveland of all places?"

"The Legionaries, to be frank, seduced me. Our founder's close relationship with Pope John Paul II was a factor, as was the appearance of a deep and rich spirituality. But it wasn't until I was ordained that I saw how shallow it all was. Our hearts were supposed to be overflowing with the love of Jesus, but the whole approach was heavy with devotions and light on theology. I still don't understand why I didn't see it sooner. And then there were the rumors about our holy founder. I got out before Maciel was exposed for his heinous sexual seductions and financial abuses."

Ian asked. "Did you ever meet him?"

"He embraced me on the day of my ordination and kissed me on both cheeks, but thank God I was not one of his favorites, one of his drivers. Those were the men in real danger."

Ashley appeared to be watching the candlelight dancing off his wine glass, but he was really watching Landers' reaction as he listened to Dunmore's tale of his little odyssey. Simon, having heard it all before, smiled inwardly. Dunmore was smart and a bit smug about his family's aristocratic status, but he, Simon Ashley, had his own gifts. With all modesty, he was a master seducer, and not merely in the sexual arena. He was expert at finding the right people to do God's work and coaxing them ever so gently, almost effortlessly, with perfect pitch, exquisite timing, and inspired language, into meaningful action for the good of the church. Dunmore had come under his spell more than a year ago. Poor Landers had no idea how closely bonded he and Dunmore had become, bonded together in a sacred cause of ultimate importance. Nor did Landers have any idea of the power that rested in their hands, especially in Simon Ashley's hands.

"When I was in Rome working through the canonical red tape of leaving the Legionaries," Trace continued, "I met a priest from Cleveland working in the Secretariat of State who suggested I consider becoming a priest of the Cleveland diocese. I immediately took to the idea. And I knew a bit about Cleveland. My parents lived here while my father headed the U.S. offices of British Petroleum, located here for a few years. They loved the orchestra and the museum, of course, and they were stars of the social life that embraced them in the Hunting Valley, Gates Mills area."

"So you had a Cleveland connection," Ian said. "Was the adjustment difficult?"

"A little bumpy," Trace acknowledged. "I was only here a few years when Bishop Martin's predecessor appointed me chancellor and moderator of the curia. It didn't go down well with a number of local priests. But most of the chaps have accepted me, at least as far as I can tell. Anyway, the bishop will be appointing his own team, and fairly soon, I expect."

Ashley signaled Roberto for a second bottle of Ducale Gold. "I've pre-ordered for us, gentlemen. I hope you don't mind, but since I'm picking up the tab…Roberto will be serving us veal Marsala, steamed asparagus, and his renowned lobster risotto. I don't think you'll be disappointed."

Ian and Trace said, almost in unison, "Wonderful, Simon, sounds wonderful."

Over the meal, Simon brought Ian up to speed on his appointment to the art history department at John Carroll. "After Oxford, I earned a master of fine arts degree from the University of London." Ashley paused and took a sip of his Chianti. Dunmore, he knew, would understand the abridged version of events he was about to relate. "To my surprise, two months later I received an offer from the Gardner Museum in Boston to be an assistant curator. So I made the decision to move to the States. I'll spare you the dreadful details," Simon remarked coyly. "But that appointment didn't quite go as I had hoped. When I saw there was an opening in the art history department at John Carroll, I applied. And as they say, 'You know the rest of the story.'"

Dunmore dabbed at a spot of Marsala sauce on his shirtfront. He knew the details that Ashley chose to spare Landers.

While at the Gardner, he had been accused of sexual harassment by a colleague. But Simon had buried it so deeply that neither the search committee nor the dean knew anything about the allegation when he interviewed at John Carroll.

Ian Landers, trying to sift his jumbled feelings, walked slowly down Mayfield Road after leaving Ashley and Dunmore in the parking lot behind Primo Vino. He passed Guarino's restaurant, then Mamma Santa's, a favorite of cash-strapped grad students. Ian paused at the corner of Coltman Street, under the bright neon sign of Presti's Bakery, studying the facade of Holy Rosary Church rudely abutting the sidewalk, asserting its place of honor in Little Italy's nominally Catholic community. In the months ahead he knew he would get to know this area framing the southeastern edges of the university rather well. But as Landers walked under the railroad bridge over Mayfield and toward the lights of Euclid Avenue, he continued to sort the various bits of table talk, like pieces to a puzzle. So, Dunmore knew, and wanted to let him know he knew, that he and Nora were close. Where did he get that information? And he astutely avoided any personal comments on Cleveland's new bishop. Of course Bryn's pastoral instincts would clash with Trace's canonical, "official-church-teaching" approach to administration and ministry. And it was also clear that Ashley and Dunmore had grown closer over the years. His two classmates, he remembered, seemed to communicate during their meal with knowing glances and raised brows, like comrades of a sort, as if in possession of some shared secret.

He wished he could sip espresso with Nora and get her read on the little drama that had just unfolded at Primo Vino. Back on campus, Ian crossed Adelbert, slowed his pace to drink in the silent splendor of the lighted facades of Severance Hall to his right and Amasa Stone Chapel on his left, then continued to his car in the surface lot behind Tomlinson Hall. Yes, as soon as he was back in his North Park apartment, he would call Nora.

14

It wasn't hard to get Hugh McKenna's contact information, Terry," Ann Marie said to her good friend. Ellsmere, her husband, Rich, and Terry Reeves were sitting around the table in the breakfast nook of the Ellsmeres' comfortable two-story home on Whitewood Road a few weeks after the attack. "In fact, I've asked him to join us. Rich and I want to talk to both of you."

"Do you mean he's coming over now?" Terry asked, trying to hide her interest in talking to McKenna…her interest in seeing him again.

"Yes, he called just before you arrived. He should be here in a few minutes."

Reeves had suspected there was something specific Ann Marie wanted to talk about when she had invited her to stop over for coffee and bagels on this late Saturday morning. All things considered, Ann Marie looked reasonably good, though a little drawn around her eyes. Rich, on the other hand, seemed a bit defensive, even sad. He hadn't touched the bagels or sipped his coffee.

"Rich and I are so grateful for all you've done, and for what Hugh did when I was attacked," Ann Marie said.

Rich added, "There's no way I can ever repay either one of you. That flight home from Chicago the night of the attack was pure agony. When I came in the door and saw you and Hugh taking such good care of Ann Marie…" Rich looked out the kitchen window in an effort to hide his damp eyes. Ann Marie, sitting next to him, nudged closer and took her husband's hand.

Ann Marie rose to answer a knock at the front door and let Hugh McKenna in. The former agent glanced around the room, as if on duty, checking his perimeter. He hugged both Ann Marie and Rich and shook Terry's hand. Reeves wondered if she had held on just a bit too long.

"Thanks to both of you for coming over," Ann Marie said. "Rich and I want to ask your advice on a decision we've made. I guess I should say, are in the process of making. And maybe your blessing. But first a little update. The psychologist I've been seeing thinks I'm doing rather well. I'm still not comfortable being home alone, but there've been no terrifying dreams of late, no significant depression, no radical mood changes." Rich furrowed his brow at the "no radical mood changes."

"My appetite is okay and I'm back to exercising twice a week at the Brecksville Community Center," Ann Marie continued.

"You always were a rather tough cookie," Terry offered.

Rich said softly, "You have no idea." He leaned forward in his chair. "Ann Marie and I have thought seriously of moving, maybe to New England. I could easily arrange a transfer to my company's Hartford office, and Ann Marie would have no trouble finding a job she liked."

"But we've decided to stay," Ann Marie said. "We'll be doing things a little differently, but we really want to stay."

"We've had only one real scare," Rich said.

"I have a ridiculously short commute to work, just ten minutes to and from the clinic. Last week," Ann Marie said to Terry, "driving down Brecksville Road, just a few blocks from Whitewood, I thought I was being followed."

"And she was," Rich said with a wry smile. "It was Hugh."

"There have been a few days when I've been able to give Ann Marie a bit of protection," McKenna said modestly.

"We appreciate that so much, Hugh," Rich said. "But we

think it's time to just move on, carefully of course, but to live the way we did before the attack. To refuse to let this monster control our lives."

Reeves smiled her silent approval. McKenna looked like a man playing poker.

"I spoke to the police again this morning," he said. "There's been no progress in the investigation. Whoever attacked you is still out there. They've profiled a sick, fanatic Catholic, active and fit, maybe ex-military or law enforcement, probably acting alone. He thinks women priests are the work of the devil and that he is doing the work of the Lord. But he is so careful, his attacks were so well-planned that they don't believe he is completely insane. I think the odds that he has given up are in your favor. They've got his physical stats, now, thanks to Ann Marie's description. If anyone should be moving out of state, it should be him. While I'd feel better if we could get this guy, I think you two are making a prudent decision. This man wasn't after you, personally, Ann Marie, only what you represent. That's a huge factor in your favor."

Terry found herself agreeing with all Hugh said. Her attention drifted from Ann Marie's safety to the strong chin, clear eyes, and slightly freckled cheeks of Hugh McKenna. What did she know about her friend's unassuming protector? A retired Secret Service Agent—he had to be at least in his early fifties. Married? Divorced? A widower? She had noticed that he wore no ring the night she met him. Was he in a relationship? She found herself surprised at her own romantic, even physical, interest in Hugh. He caught her studying him, and she blurted, "Like Hugh, I think you're making a good decision."

"I will be taking a leave from ministry. I mean I'm not celebrating Mass or doing weddings or baptisms for a while."

"I think that's a really good idea," Terry said.

"There's one more thing Ann Marie and I need to know

before you two leave." Rich glanced at Ann Marie but his eyes moved immediately to Hugh. "Can't you tell us who hired you, Hugh? You must understand why we want to know."

McKenna hesitated a moment, catching Reeves' eye. "A certain new guy in town made a few phone calls to an old friend. Let's leave it there."

The Ellsmeres seemed satisfied with Hugh's careful response. They all stood, and Terry and Hugh hugged each of the Ellsmeres, who walked them to the door. Hugh walked Terry to her car, their elbows brushing as they moved down the narrow walk. Terry found herself blushing when Hugh asked for her number.

"Bishop," Trace Dunmore asked on the inter-office line early Monday morning, "do you have a moment? I have a retired policeman here in my office who might be just the man you're looking for. I'd like you to meet him."

"Great," Martin replied, "bring him over."

He rose from his desk as Dunmore ushered into his office an athletic-looking middle-aged man Martin thought he recognized from the cathedral's 8:00 Sunday Mass. He and Mann were the same height and about the same weight. He was black Irish, like Bryn, with the same sharp, west-of-Ireland chin.

"Bishop Martin, this is Fergus Mann."

The two men shook hands as Bryn said, "Good to meet you, Fergus. If I had an older brother, I think he would look just like you." Mann smiled at the remark. They sat around the coffee table in the conversation corner of the bishop's office.

"When Father Dunmore suggested you to show me the city I thought a retired policeman would be ideal."

"I'll be happy to do what I can, Bishop. I've been retired for more than a year now so I have the time, and I know the city pretty good. Born and raised here. Over the years I was assigned to three different districts. I can show you where to get the best ethnic food. And I know some neighborhoods not in the travel brochures where some pretty colorful people hang out."

Dunmore blanched slightly when Fergus said "colorful" people. "I told Fergus that you were thinking of taking an evening ride with him once or twice a week for a month or so."

"The city you describe is just what I want to see, Fergus. Do you think that might work for you?" Martin asked.

"Yeah, it should, even tonight or tomorrow." Mann said nodding to both Dunmore and Martin. "Shouldn't be a problem. Anything I can do for the church, I do."

Fergus Mann took in the spacious, well-appointed office. This poor kid from the Irish enclave known as the Angle was sitting in the Bishop of Cleveland's office with the bishop himself and his chancellor, his right-hand man. And they were asking him for a favor! The irony did not escape him.

15

Bishop Martin and Terry Reeves rode the same elevator up to the sixth floor of the Cathedral Square Plaza later that morning. "I had an interesting visit with the Ellsmeres over the weekend," Reeves said. "And Hugh McKenna was there."

"How are they?"

"It looks like they're doing all right, all things considered."

Martin consulted his wrist watch. "Stop by in about half an hour if you can, Terry. I'd like to hear whatever you're able to share."

Reeves liked that her boss wasn't going to pry, that he understood there were aspects of her friendship with Ann Marie that should remain strictly between the two of them.

Thirty minutes later, with coffee in hand, Reeves sat down across from Bishop Martin. "Well, they've finally decided against moving out of state. Ann Marie is still seeing a psychologist, which I think is really important."

"What a difference it would make if they could catch the murderer," Martin said.

"McKenna said there's been no progress in the investigation, and he didn't think there would be. The first forty-eight hours after a murder are critical. If they don't have strong leads in that time period, they're often left with a cold case."

"That's a sobering thought." Martin looked frustrated and tired. "When you talk to Ann Marie, tell her I'm thinking about her, and praying for her."

"I will, Bishop. By the way, both Ann Marie and Rich are very grateful that Hugh is still on the job."

Martin simply nodded with a knowing smile. Reeves hesitated, "I know you've had a few phone conversations with Carl Spivak, Bishop. How's he doing?"

"Not nearly as well as Ann Marie. He calls the FBI's Cleveland office almost daily. He's overwhelmed with rage and grief. Not a good mixture. If he had the money, he said he would hire a private investigator. He keeps asking, 'What kind of a Catholic would do such a thing?' He's convinced the man who killed his wife is some kind of reactionary nut, especially since Frances Hellerman was killed and the attempt was made on Ann Marie's life. I think Carl's surviving by drawing on the energy of an avenger. His kids are doing the best they can to support him, but they have their own sorrow."

Reeves stood to leave. "I thought Christina Tomasso's profile piece in the *PD* was quite good. Any reactions from the priests?"

"No, but I've only had contact with a few of them." Bryn hesitated, feeling a pinprick of guilt for saying something he perhaps shouldn't say. "Not one of the cathedral priests—the men I live with—has said a word about it."

16

Bishop Bryn Martin opened the passenger door and slid into the front seat of a black Ford Focus parked under the yellow stone arch connecting the cathedral rectory to the former chancery offices across East Ninth Street. He was wearing black cotton slacks and a black clergy shirt—without the white plastic Roman collar—and a dark windbreaker.

Fergus Mann, a bit uneasy about spending time alone with the new Bishop of Cleveland, said stiffly, "Good evening, Bishop."

Martin offered his hand, "Thanks, Fergus. I'm looking forward to these little runs to different parts of our city. I appreciate your doing this."

"Happy to do so, Bishop. Not a bad way to spend a weekday evening." As if the two men had coordinated their attire, Mann was dressed in black pants, a dark shirt, and a black nylon Under Armor workout jacket.

"Where to?" Martin asked.

Mann pulled out on to Superior and headed west to Public Square. "I thought we might begin with Ohio City. It's just across the Cuyahoga. It's a part of Cleveland now. Not sure when it was incorporated, sometime in the 1840s I think. During the Civil War there was a pretty large Union camp there, Camp Cleveland. Now there's shady streets and cozy restaurants and a lot of old, pretty well-kept homes. A lot of our movers and shakers live here, politicians and the like…even a congresswoman. Some of our upper crust call it the 'Paris of Cleveland.' Paris, my—"

Mann caught himself in time. "Believe me, this neighborhood has its share of trouble, but in the summer, it could be a nice long evening walk for you, Bishop."

Dark clouds attempted to smother an orange-red sky as the car moved onto the Detroit Superior Bridge. Across the river Fergus slowed down as they approached a busy intersection surrounded by century-old industrial buildings of brick and stucco, with no more charm than a prison yard.

"That's St. Malachi's on the right there, Bishop. It's one of our old Irish parishes."

"I'll be there next week for confirmation," Martin commented casually. "I'm looking forward to it. I've been told they do a good job of serving the poor and homeless of the area."

About a half dozen men in dark clothes, worn and looking lived in, sat smoking and talking on the steps in front of the church or on the low stone wall guarding the tidy but tiny lawn in front of the rectory.

Mann glanced quickly at the bishop, holding his thoughts for a moment. "Most of the parishioners are pretty liberal, Bishop. If you ask me, they're barely in the fold." Mann wanted to say that the church would be better off without the lot of 'em, but held his tongue.

They drew close to the Ohio City Farm, one of the largest urban farms in the country, that seemed to be a life-saver for a lot of Cleveland's refugees, but Mann thought better of showing it to the bishop. He turned left onto West 25th and headed south to Lorain Avenue. "Not long ago West 25th was a terrible area. Adult book stores, drug dealers, male prostitutes. Much better though now. That's the West Side Market on your left. A real Cleveland landmark. You'll see a good cross section of Clevelanders there on a Saturday morning. It's worth a visit." Mann turned west onto Lorain Avenue, "Coming up on your right, Bishop, is St. Ignatius. One of the premier Catholic high schools.

Great reputation for academics and athletics. Too expensive for my folks. I went to a public school, West High. Probably for the best. I'm not sure I would have fit in."

Bryn smiled to himself. Fergus Mann had a well-settled opinion on everything.

"The Catholic Worker house is down the street on your left," Mann said as they passed Fulton Road. "They run a few satellite houses in the neighborhood. And they have a storefront up ahead where they have a kind of open house a few days a week. The local riffraff show up and drink coffee and eat their free chili. Half of them, heck, most of them, show up drunk or high. Does little good. The police who work this area think the Catholic Workers are a little strange, but for the most part, the cops respect 'em. A lot of the Catholic Workers have a good education. Heck, they could live in the suburbs if they wanted. I think the neighborhood would be pretty much the same depressing place with or without 'em."

Bryn began to wonder whether his choice of tour guide had been such a good one.

Mann turned onto Bridge Avenue and drove past St. Patrick's Church, taking his foot off the pedal but not braking. "St. Pat's is the oldest Irish parish in the diocese—established in 1853—and the current church building opened its doors in 1873," he said, showing the bishop he knew his history. "Some dispute that, but they're wrong. But for sure it's one of the oldest parishes in the diocese. I guess you'd call it my official parish, Bishop. It's not the same as it was in the old days. It's gone pretty liberal, if you ask me. The Catholic Workers moved into the convent after the nuns moved out. But that didn't last. The pastor, or maybe downtown, wanted them out." Mann seemed unaware that the man sitting next to him was the personification of "downtown." "The parishioners have different stories of why the Catholic Workers got the boot. I don't go to Mass there much anymore, even though it's my parish and was my parents' parish and grandparents' parish. Too much guitar music. Too much jabbering about peace and justice. Can't remember when I heard a sermon about saving your soul, about sin, about hell. Just way too liberal for me. So, like I said, you won't see me at Mass at St. Pat's even though it's Cleveland's oldest Irish parish. I go to the early Mass at the cathedral.

"I've seen you there."

"We're close to the Tremont area now. Really trendy with hoity-toity restaurants, they tell me. But I'm not sure it's worth our time. Maybe some other evening."

Mann worked his way back to Lorain and headed west to 65th Street. "I want you to see St. Colman's, Bishop. Really beautiful inside. There's a big St. Patrick's Day Mass every year, but I don't really like it. Bagpipes, drums, flutes marching up and down the aisle. Not right for a church if you ask me."

"I've heard about St. Colman." Martin decided not to say anything about the parish's social outreach or its stabilizing effect on the working class neighborhood. Signaling Mann that it was time to head back to the cathedral rectory, Bryn said, "Thanks for this little tour, Fergus. You do know the city well, and you're giving me a real insider's feel for it."

Fergus looked straight ahead, unable to acknowledge the compliment.

"On the way back, Bishop, I'll take you down to the Flats for a drive-by. Lots of action. A really popular spot for anyone looking for nightlife. I know nightlife doesn't interest you, but it's worth having a meal there sometime." Out of the corner of his eye, Fergus thought he saw the bishop smile. He was pretty sure the new Bishop of Cleveland wasn't old-school, probably not his kind of bishop. Still, this guy was easy company. *I'll bet we're going to get along pretty good*, he thought.

Back under the arch, Bryn opened the car door, turned in his seat and instinctively shook Mann's hand, "Thank you, Fergus. This has been really helpful."

"No problem, Bishop. Unless I hear from you or Father Dunmore, I'll be here Thursday at seven. We'll visit Slavic Village. And I have a few questions for you about the church. Hope you don't mind."

"No, not at all." Martin smiled and gave Mann a short wave as he walked up the steps to the side entrance of the cathedral rectory.

Trace Dunmore glanced at the clock on the mantel of his suite of rooms. Eight thirty-five. Fergus should be bringing Martin back to the rectory after their first sortie into the city. Too risky to call him. He would wait until after Sunday morning Mass to ask Fergus what he and the bishop had talked about. Trace was not alone in his curiosity; Simon Ashley would be expecting a full report.

It was already dark as Trace walked to the window of his third floor sitting room and looked out at the light traffic spilling down Superior Avenue. A few office workers or store clerks, still as statues, wrapped in dark shrouds, waited at the bus stop while a couple—difficult to tell their age—stood at the curb waiting for the light to change. Not much movement on a Thursday evening in Cleveland, at least not at the corner of Ninth and Superior. But soon enough there had to be significant movement in Dunmore's life. How much time did he have left as chancellor and moderator of the curia? Months? A year or two? Martin had to be thinking about naming his own team of chancery staff, at least the clergy on his staff. Some of the priests would keep their posts, some surely would not. And from day one it had been clear that Trace and Bryn Martin weren't exactly on the same page. Dunmore smiled at his own understatement, turned from the window and went back to his oxblood leather chair and ottoman. No sooner had he sat down than he got up to pour himself a half inch of single malt whisky.

Back in his chair, his thoughts drifted between his present post and his uncertain future. One thing was clear, Martin trusted Terry Reeves more than he trusted him. Dunmore caved to the rising resentment filling his chest. She was competent, he had to admit, and would likely survive the inevitable reorganization of the diocesan staff. He, on the other hand, would likely not. So what could he angle for—a slot on the seminary faculty? That's not where the action is. A pastorate at a wealthy parish? At least he would have access to like-minded traditionalists with money to foster the mission that he and Simon were so committed to. If the right place opened up, he would seize the opportunity. Not much else to consider. A hospital chaplaincy? Too restricting, and too depressing! Dunmore sipped his drink and reached for the Gore Vidal novel *Burr* at his elbow, but didn't open it; he really wasn't in the mood for reading. He admired Aaron Burr. The man was smart, ambitious, cunning. And like himself, poorly appreciated by his titular superiors, especially by His Excellency, the overrated, inept General George Washington.

With Burr as his muse, Dunmore continued the inventory of his own considerable talents. His Italian was passable—maybe an appointment to a minor post in the Vatican. He had some contacts there and Simon's intimate friend, Pietro Montaldo, now reigning in episcopal splendor in Perugia, still had influence in those highly polished halls of the church's supreme center. All Trace needed was an entry position. For the present, he reminded himself, he would make the most of his place at the center of action right here in Cleveland. Simon Ashley would expect no less. *And,* Trace reminded himself, *you just never know.* With the right information, the right leverage, he might make it difficult for Bryn Martin to replace him. *Don't let me down, Fergus.*

17

"Do you have a minute, Dr. Landers?"

Ian Landers looked up to see an attractive, dark-haired, caramel-skinned undergrad standing at the open door of his Tomlinson Hall office. He pointed to the chair next to his desk. "Yes, I have a few minutes, come in."

"I have a friend in your 'sin class'...that's what he calls it."

Landers smiled, "You mean the 'Sin in the Medieval Church' class."

The young woman nodded as a spot of color came to her cheeks and to the sides of her neck. "Oh, I'm sorry, Professor, I'm Rachelle Pageotte."

Landers nodded in a welcoming gesture, "Nice to meet you, Rachelle."

"I know your office hours are for your students, but—"

Landers cut in, "Not really, they're for students of the university. I'm happy to talk to you."

"First of all, I'd like to ask if you would mind if I sat in on your class once in a while. My friend...my boyfriend really...we talk about your class all the time. I wish I'd signed up for it, but I'm in pre-med and the science courses are so demanding I have to be careful with electives."

"Come whenever you like. There are three or four empty chairs."

Rachelle smiled a "thank you" and relaxed a bit. "I'm here on a scholarship, which is a really big deal for my family. I'm from

88

Haiti." Rachelle looked down at her hands before continuing. "My father's Haitian but seldom goes to Mass. My mother's another story. She's from the States and very, very Catholic. She's even met our first cardinal, Cardinal Langlois. After graduating from a conservative Catholic college in Ohio, she did a year of volunteer service in Haiti…that's when she met my father. If my father is a bit lax, my mother is just the opposite. For her, being Catholic is all about avoiding sin, especially mortal sin…she lives in fear of committing a mortal sin. She'd rather face another earthquake or hurricane than commit a mortal sin. She loves God, but I think she fears God even more. She keeps reminding me that if a person dies in mortal sin, it's an eternity in hell." Rachelle took a breath and found the expression on Ian's face encouraging her to continue. "My mother's a good person, Dr. Landers, but she's not very happy." Rachelle's dark eyes watered. "Nick, that's my boyfriend, says she did a job on me, and I think he's right. I'm a lot like my mother, but I don't think everything the church says is a mortal sin is really a mortal sin."

Landers looked pleased. "I think I understand why you and your boyfriend are talking about my class."

For the first time, Rachelle's lips hinted at a smile and her eyes sparkled. "We talk about it all the time. I call home almost every Sunday and my mother is more worried about me committing a mortal sin than she is about my classes. She's heard that college students are partying like crazy and doing all kinds of immoral things when they're not in class or studying for exams. Really, Dr. Landers, I don't have time to party much. And that's okay. Nick and I don't really like the party scene. It can get pretty wild, especially if there's a lot drinking, and it seems there's always a lot of drinking. So we mostly hang out together and with friends who feel the same way. But my mom is really making me feel terrible about simply having fun, the normal fun college students have. I hardly party at all, I don't drink a lot…"

Rachelle thought better than to mention the recent, decidedly sexual, dimension of her relationship with Nick.

"Avoiding the party scene as much as possible sounds like a good plan, Rachelle. Sit in on my classes when you can. And I have a public lecture coming up that speaks to just this topic. It's hard to miss the posters advertising it. Campus ministry is pushing it pretty well. I'm calling it 'Under Pain of Mortal Sin.' If what you hear when you sit in on the 'sin class' and the lecture seem to help, you're welcome to come back and I'll try to be more specific, more concrete. The Catholic Church has a lot of wisdom when it comes to navigating the moral choices facing all of us today. But it also has an overly legalistic, rigid approach to morality that has focused too much on specific behaviors, especially sexual behaviors, and not enough on the fundamental goodness of life and the fundamental goodness of human sexuality. But that approach is changing. So, let's continue the conversation."

Rachelle reached for the backpack resting on the floor next to her chair, "Thanks, Dr. Landers. I'd really like that."

Hugh McKenna and Terry Reeves sat at a table across from the fireplace at The Harp, a popular Irish pub with a good view of Lake Erie. Dozens of boaters, both sail and motor, were taking advantage of one of the final days of the season, but the autumn chill had kept Terry and Hugh from choosing The Harp's outdoor deck. Terry was especially happy to be inside and close to the fire that sparkled in Hugh's light blue-gray eyes. She shivered as if a draft had taken her by surprise, but she felt strangely cozy...warm even, yes, cozy, and safe in this good man's company. A good sign, Terry thought, for their first casual date. Maybe it wasn't even a casual date. "Let's meet at The Harp around seven," Hugh had said without indicating whether this was simply to have a drink or if he had dinner in mind. She put him in his mid-to-late fifties.

Over Great Lakes Oktoberfest beers, the couple entered into the slightly self-conscious rite of trading the social fundamentals for Cleveland Catholics…East Side or West Side, parish and elementary school, high school, and college.

"After law school I spent a few years at Jones Day," Terry said, without mentioning she had a Yale Law degree or asserting that she had more than held her own at the prestigious firm. "The pace, pressure, and values, however, began to wear me down. They weren't good for my soul. So, I started looking. I'd done some work for the diocese, so I spoke to a few people I knew there and wound up working for them."

"It looks like the move was a good one," Hugh said before taking another sip of his beer.

"Overall, yes. Hands down, yes." Terry hesitated, blinking quickly after a brief knowing glance directly into Hugh's eyes. "But of course, there's always a down side. And it's not so much the deep cut in salary. It's the chancery culture. It's a little bit like medieval court life. We staffers to the bishop are like courtiers, all trying to make his job easier by doing our own jobs well. But a bishop isn't an ordinary boss. He's the lord of the manor. There's a part of most of us that wants so much to please him, and wanting to please too much really isn't healthy. Throw in human weaknesses—masked ambition, turf protection, petty jealousies, whispered gossip, and the ever-present class distinction between the priests and us lay folk—and it's not as idyllic as you might think."

"Never thought of it quite that way," Hugh said. "And I'm a life-long Catholic."

"Still, I'll take it over what I've seen in the corporate culture," Terry added, worrying she may have gone on a bit too long. "How did you like the Secret Service?"

Before answering, Hugh picked up his menu. "Let's order…

91

and this is on me. I recommend the walleye, it's always good here."
She's enjoying herself, Hugh thought, watching Terry settle comfortably into her chair and take another delicate sip of her beer. Easy company, easy on the eyes, intelligent, professional without being the least bit stuffy. *Be careful, man,* he said to himself, instinctively moving his eyes from hers to the flickering fire and then back to hers. All the while she held his gaze. Hugh ordered for them both, the walleye with The Harp's signature lemon pepper spinach cream sauce, a side each of buttery colcannon, and another round of beers. As the server left their table, Hugh played with his silverware, thinking how to tell his own story.

"The Secret Service...I liked it. After high school at St. Ed's, I went to Canisius College and double majored—criminal justice and sociology." He told her a few of his old stories, the kind of stories people tell when they want others to get to know them. How he played point guard for the Golden Griffins on what remains their worst team since their insuperably bad 1939 season when they went 0-13. He talked about enduring the great Buffalo blizzard.

"The funny thing is, there was no new snowfall during the blizzard."

"How is that possible?"

"It was all snowpack being blown in off the frozen lake. Residue of the past winter. When the wind stopped blowing we dug ourselves out and looked around and it seemed as if God had recreated the world overnight. The way it was supposed to be. People climbed out into the sunlight and started helping one another. Digging out neighbors with snow to their roof tops, sharing food, running extension cords to homes that had lost power, giving freely whatever they had to give, with no more sense of self than a bee in a hive. It is amazing the way adversity can bring out what is best in the human spirit. It is a lesson I've always remembered."

He told her about his unexpected recruitment by the Secret Service. "I was thinking FBI, but almost on a whim signed up for an interview with the Secret Service, and I guess nailed it. They made me an offer and I signed up. It was a good decision, overall. But the excitement of White House duty wore off soon enough. I seldom flew on Air Force One. Most of the time I flew ahead with the president's car and advance team. I never saw any greater threat to the president than some nasty looking egg salad. But the long hours, a lot of it pretty boring, made it easy enough to retire when I reached the twenty-five-year mark."

"How have you found retirement?"

"I like it. I like it a lot." My wife and I divorced right after our tenth anniversary. The Service is hard on wives. The long hours, the constant travel, always being on call."

Divorced. Terry shouldn't have been surprised, but the disclosure unsettled her. It complicated things. "Do you have children?"

"A grown daughter, Sarah. She's married and lives in Erie, so she's halfway between me and her mother, who is back in Buffalo. I visit her as often as I can." Their dinners arrived at just the right moment. The break in the conversation seemed to invite the delicate move to the topic of Hugh's role as Ann Marie's bodyguard. But Hugh found himself not quite ready.

"I keep myself pretty busy. I golf when I can, and I do some on-going training for the local TSA employees. I'm in D.C. once a month or so as a consultant for the Department of Homeland Security."

Both ate in silence for a moment. "How did Bishop Martin come to know of your..." Terry hesitated..."special talents?"

Hugh held her eye just long enough to make her feel the question was out of line. "I'm not sure we should be talking about that," he said.

"Really, I think it is okay. Bishop Martin has never admitted hiring you. But it was clear to me that he did. And he knows very well that I know he did. So, I think it's all right for us to discuss it."

Hugh paused again, but only for a moment. "Bishop Martin got my number from a friend and former colleague, George Havel. Havel lives in Baltimore and did some work—very delicate work—for Bishop Martin when he was an auxiliary bishop there. Havel joined the Secret Service a year before I did. We were often assigned together and became good friends. He knew I could, and would, help."

Terry nodded.

"Your bishop," Hugh said lightly, "is one shrewd man." Terry leaned in as if to make sure she would hear every word over the noise from the surrounding tables and bar area. "He asked me to meet him not in his office or the cathedral rectory. That was smart. He asked me to meet him in front of the Federal Reserve building. Said I would know him by the Baltimore Orioles cap he'd be wearing. I had read of the murders of the two women priests, of course, so I guessed what he was worried about. We took a walk, and he asked me to help with Ann Marie's security. He offered to pay me in cash, whatever I thought was fair. By our second pass around the block I was on board, not just because of George Havel's esteem for the bishop or because it was clear to me that Ann Marie Ellsmere was in real danger. I saw right away the kind of man Bryn Martin is. Smart, practical, caring, and not afraid to do what he thinks is right, no matter what."

"Do you understand that what the bishop did was extremely risky to him personally? It will be a huge problem for him if this ever gets out." Terry glanced nervously at the next table, as if concerned that they might be able to overhear what she was about to say. "There are people on his staff who would very much like to see him fail."

"Believe me," Hugh whispered, thinking of what Havel had

told him of Martin's role in preventing a sniper's assassination of a retired Baltimore archbishop, "I understand."

Over Irish Coffees, Terry asked what Hugh thought of the meeting in the Ellsmeres' kitchen the week before. He thought for a second or two. "I would stay in Cleveland if I were them."

"I think I would, too," Reeves said. "But there's still a murderer out there who might try again."

"This is a tough one for the Feds and the local investigators. There's no apparent personal motive and the killer was so careful. Too careful, if you ask me. I doubt that he's just some extremist, reactionary Catholic taking God's justice into his own hands. I don't think he's some lone crackpot acting on his own. I'd bet he has some kind of support, some friend or some people he knows who are reinforcing his conviction that women priests in the church are the work of the devil and deserve to be done away with."

"Do you think he'll try again?"

"If he's been acting alone, maybe not." Then Hugh added, "If he's part of something bigger, I really don't know."

18

It's me," Ashley's voice said when Dunmore answered his cell phone. The priest looked up from his desk in his Cathedral Plaza office to make sure his door was closed, then rose and walked to the windows overlooking Ninth Street as if moving away from his desk would somehow enhance the privacy of the call. "I'm calling for an update. Has our friend's little tour with the bishop born fruit?"

"Not much, I'm afraid. But we should be patient. Our friend and the bishop are just getting to know each other, and he's a bit nervous. He's never spent this kind of time alone with a bishop. They're going out again this evening. To the Slavic Village. You must understand, Simon, that nothing at all may come of it."

"We must make sure that something does. I'm counting on you, Father Dunmore. Bishop Bryn Martin is not our kind of bishop."

Trace remained silent, irritated at Simon's tone—the snarky formality a sure indicator of his edginess. They had been close friends in college, for God's sake. When Simon Ashley chose to use titles, *Father, Excellency,* it was more than a turn to British formality. It was notice of disapproval.

"By the way," Simon's voice softened, "does Fergus have any suspicion that my coffee house conversations with him were not coincidental?"

"Fergus, you must understand, is a rather uncomplicated, rather dull individual. No, Simon, he has no idea that it was I who suggested him as a potential operative. Or that you and I even know each other."

"Good," was all that Simon Ashley said, hanging up the phone, perhaps a little more curtly than he intended.

His call to Dunmore left Simon Ashley uneasy. He understood the priest's drive to safeguard the Roman Catholic Church from its dangerous turn to modernity and the world—and not inconsequently his equally strong personal ambition to rise in the church's ranks. Ashley's own ambition, his own "treasure," was quite clear. As much as he was committed to the Sentinels of the Supreme Center, to the absolute necessity of a papacy-dominated Catholic Church, Simon Ashley was, at his core, first committed to the transcendent glories of medieval art, to the almost erotic waves of private joy that little-known works like the *Caporali Missal* sparked in his soul. Archbishop Montaldo's motivation remained a bit of a mystery to him. Though he knew Montaldo wouldn't rest until the *Caporali Missal* was in his cathedral, his desire to possess it, unlike Simon's own obsessive passion for the missal, was but a dilettante's unholy mix of lust and greed. Ashley raised his eyebrows, his thin lips softening into a cynical smile. Now that Montaldo was the Archbishop of Perugia, a cardinal's red hat was more than a possibility. And once he was a member of the College of Cardinals there was only one greater prize. And, God willing—Simon found himself breathing heavily—if Pietro Montaldo were to be elected pope he would certainly reward his most faithful Sentinel in America.

So, yes, he would do his humble best to support the archbishop's request for a loan of the *Caporali Missal*. Ashley understood that if the loan were ever agreed to, it would be in "church time." Months would pass, even a year or two. But Montaldo, impatient man that he was, would know Ashley had tried to move the loan along. He had proven his commitment to the Sentinels, and at considerable risk to his own career—even his own life. It was he, after all, Simon Ashley, who had masterminded their operation against the heretic women priests. And should he be able to build a case against the orthodoxy of Bishop Bryn Martin, just so much the more would he be in the Archbishop of Perugia's favor.

A cold, steady autumn rain hit the windshield of Fergus Mann's car as Bishop Martin dashed from the door and ducked in. They pulled out from the cathedral archway onto Superior Avenue, then turned south onto East Ninth Street, and passed Progressive Field, home of the Cleveland Indians.

"Let me make a confession, Fergus," Martin said. "I'm struggling with my conversion from a Baltimore Orioles fan to an Indians fan." Then with a smile, he added, "I'm sure you will pray for me."

"Oh, yeah, for sure, Bishop. Father Dunmore says that with God all things are possible. But you might want to say a couple Hail Marys yourself."

"My conversion from being a Ravens fan, of course, is another matter."

Heading south on rain-slick Broadway, they drove in silence past dark, squat, aging buildings Fergus deemed unworthy of comment. Minutes later, he turned right onto East 55th toward Fleet Avenue.

"You're in Slavic Village now, Bishop. I thought I'd do a drive-by of St. John Nepomucene, once a Bohemian stronghold, and then show you St. Stanislaus. Too bad I can't show you inside. It's really something. All old-school European craftsmanship, unbelievable wood carvings, statues all over the place. Lot of people think it's too busy, too over-the-top. Not me, I like it. It's my kind of church. Traditional, you know." Mann hesitated,

"After that, if you don't mind, Bishop, I'd like to suggest we stop at the Red Chimney. It's right on Fleet Avenue. They have really good pierogis, decent coffee. And it's a hangout for Fourth District police."

"I'd like that," Martin said, sensing that Fergus remained slightly uneasy in his presence.

Over coffee and pierogis, Fergus explained how work in the steel plants and woolen mills had drawn large numbers of Poles and Czechs to the area a hundred fifty years ago. Fergus impaled a fat pierogi on a fork, spun it in the pool of melted butter on his plate, and took a bite. "The people here are solid, working-class folks. Real old-school types. I like them 'cause they're not uppity. The long-timers are struggling to hold on to their neighborhood. But if you ask me, I think they're doing okay. A few of the hangers-on I know think the village is never going to be what it once was." It was a nice feeling to have the bishop listening to him, taking him seriously.

"These are great," Martin said as he picked up his second pierogi. "And you're right, the coffee isn't bad."

Mann said, "When I was on the job I usually came in for the Weiner Schnitzel."

"Maybe next time," Martin offered.

"I have a question for you, Bishop," Fergus said, and paused as if waiting for permission to speak. Martin smiled and gave him a slight nod. "When I was a boy at St. Pat's, everyone went to Mass on Sunday. The place was packed. Nowadays, hardly anyone goes. Father Dunmore says that only about twenty percent of baptized Catholics go to Mass. And my relatives in Cork say it's the same over there, maybe even worse. Isn't it a mortal sin to miss Mass on Sunday anymore?"

"Let me put it this way, Fergus. For a long time now the

church has taught that going to weekly Mass is a grave obligation. In other words, we shouldn't miss Mass deliberately, without any excuse or circumstances that would make it unreasonable, or we risk separating ourselves from the love of God—one good way of understanding the consequences of a mortal sin."

A crack of thunder and a blink of the lights quieted the restaurant for a second as the evening's steady rain turned into a heavy downpour.

"So why aren't Catholics who don't go to Mass afraid of going to hell? Geez, Bishop, being in hell forever scares the daylights out of me."

"Your question makes a lot of sense, Fergus. And for an old-school Catholic like yourself, it can really mess with your thinking, with what you were taught in catechism class."

"It sure does," Mann said spitting the words out. "I was raised believing the church has the truth, that it never changes because what it teaches is God's will. And the supreme center of the church is the pope. What he says goes." Fergus glanced around at the other patrons. "These people, Bishop, are almost all Catholics. Believe me, most of them don't give a damn what the pope says, what the church says anymore." He paused again, now with a hint of disdain. "Most of them don't seem to care that they're going to face the judgment of God one day, and God isn't smilin' these days, that's for sure."

"Sometimes, I believe God does smile. I think God smiles often, Fergus. Maybe a sad smile, but still a smile, because we just don't get it." Mann frowned, finding the idea puzzling. "This might help you see what I'm trying to get at, Fergus. Pope Benedict, 'B-16' as some called him, once said that Christianity is not so much a law to be obeyed as a presence to be embraced. For many Catholics, maybe even most old-school Catholics, the faith is really about obeying the church, obeying the pope. When that's the case, then the Catholic religion is mainly about obeying the commandments. You know, about morality. And right along with morality, religion becomes mainly about dogma and doctrines."

"What's wrong with that?" Fergus felt his lower lip quiver and struggled to hide his irritation. "If Catholics obeyed the commandments and believed what the pope and bishops are teaching, we'd all be a lot better off."

Martin waited while the waitress refilled their coffee cups. "Yes, morality and the creed are foundational. They really are important. But at the heart of the Catholic religion, and I think at the heart of all healthy religion, is seeing that faith is really about trust. Trusting that God is good and life is good. Trusting that God is healing love, that God loves us even in our sins. Maybe especially in our sins."

"Well how in God's name, then, do you earn heaven?" Fergus asked with an air of smug confidence.

"You know, Fergus, we don't really earn heaven. That's one thing Martin Luther was right about. Heaven is pure grace, pure gift. Maybe that's the hardest thing of all to believe."

"But don't sinners deserve to be punished? There are enemies of the church out there. Something has to be done about them. They have to be punished." Mann wrapped his hands around his coffee cup and pursed his lips. "You believe in hell, don't you, Bishop?"

Bryn sat silent for a moment and then signaled for the check. "I think it's possible, Fergus, even probable, that God doesn't punish. I think that really self-centered, greedy people, people who don't care about God or others are the loneliest, and perhaps the unhappiest, people on earth. Their isolation is a kind of self-imposed hell."

Mann squinted as he tried to square what he had just heard with his childhood catechism image of hell. Of course God punishes. Why else would anyone try to obey the commandments?

Obey or face the punishment of hell. Accept the truth of the church or face eternity in a lake of fire.

"But hasn't the church always punished sinners, especially heretics?"

Martin took a deep breath. "For a long time the church imposed some really harsh punishments on men, women, and even children who were judged enemies of the faith. But not so much today, thank God." Bryn was silent for a bit, trying to read Fergus's thoughts. "The foundation of authentic faith, Fergus, is a humble heart. I'm still learning that. The church itself is still learning that." Martin reached into his jacket pocket and took out a pen, clicked the point from its barrel, and reached for a paper napkin. "Here's a quote I really like from a French philosopher. He lived in the seventeenth century. His name is Blaise Pascal."

"Never heard of him."

"Most people haven't, Fergus. But take this with you and give it some thought." Bryn wrote clearly enough on the thin, fragile paper: *Men never do evil so completely and cheerfully as when they do it from religious conviction.*

Fergus sat dumbfounded and seemed glad to see the waitress bringing their check. As the bishop reached for it she paused. "You look familiar," she said to Martin. "I've seen your picture somewhere. In the *Plain Dealer*, I think."

Mann looked at Martin for direction. The only help he got was a faint smile. "Well," Fergus ventured on, pleased with the surprise he was about to spring, "young lady, you've just served pierogis to the new Bishop of Cleveland. This is Bishop Martin."

"Nice to meet you, Bishop." "Nina" was stitched onto the front of her oxford-blue shirt. "I belong to St. Stan's." She rubbed her hands on her apron. "Welcome to Cleveland."

"Thanks, Nina," Bryn said, taking her outstretched hand. My friend here," he gestured to Fergus, "is showing me around the city."

After a quick glance at the check, Martin left an appropriate tip on the table and walked toward the cashier, a middle-aged man who needed a shave but reigned over the restaurant with a proprietary air. "The pierogis were delicious," Martin told him.

With their collars up and heads down, the bishop and his somewhat bewildered guide walked quickly through the evening's steady rain to the parking lot behind the Red Chimney. Mann's mind was racing. He had never heard anything like this before. The new bishop didn't believe in punishment. He didn't believe in hell. Fergus couldn't wait to tell Father Dunmore about his little chat with the bishop.

19

With the text of his lecture "Under Pain of Mortal Sin" on his lap, Ian Landers sat on a bench close to the Michelson-Morley Fountain in the Case Quad. The warm, late-October sun highlighted the gold-yellow and rose-red leaves still clinging to their trees, symbols of nature's patient acceptance of the rhythms of life. Classes were changing and Ian looked up to see a gaggle of students moving in and out of Yost Hall, math majors seemingly unburdened by the weight of sin—mortal or otherwise. Instead of editing his text as he had intended, Landers found himself thinking of his recent dinner with his Oxford classmates. On the surface it had been pleasant enough. But on a deeper level, he felt vaguely uneasy. Something he couldn't name seemed to forge a bond between the two, something beyond their years at Balliol College. Simon Ashley came to Cleveland because of an opening in the art history department at John Carroll. Landers suspected that he really coveted a faculty position in the acclaimed art history department at Case Western. But Dunmore's explanation of how he wound up in Cleveland seemed rather thin. So his father once headed the BP headquarters here, and his parents were charmed by the Anglophile friends they made in the quaint yet exclusive New England-like suburbs of Hunting Valley and Gates Mills. It strained credulity to think that those were sufficient reasons to choose the diocese of Cleveland for his ministry as a priest. During his studies in Rome, Trace would have met any number of American priests from more glamorous cities like New York, Boston, Chicago. And what could explain the rapid rise of an outsider to moderator of the curia and chancellor? Ashley and Dunmore had always been close, one might even say best friends, at Balliol. Ian was certain that his classmates were both very traditional, if not reactionary, Catholics. Their golden age of the church was the late Middle Ages: the pure visual glory of passionate religious art, ageless Gothic cathedrals rising to the heavens, the haunting drone of Gregorian chant, and the unchallenged sovereignty of the papal will. Still, there was something else at play here. Perhaps the months ahead would reveal it.

"Dr. Landers!" Hearing his name brought Ian back to the moment.

Standing in front of him was Rachelle Pageotte with two of her friends. "Just want you to know we're coming to your lecture. My friends," she said, looking at the two young students with her, "and maybe Nick."

"That would be wonderful."

"Sorry to interrupt your work," Rachelle said over her shoulder as she and her friends moved on.

Ian placed the manila folder holding his text on the bench. So, at least some students would be at the lecture. And he could count on a few theology profs from John Carroll, Ursuline, and Notre Dame showing up. Bryn Martin had said he would be there, and Simon had called to say he and Trace would attend after an early dinner at Primo Vino. And best of all, Nora would be flying in and staying for the weekend. The only downside to his year as the Hallinan Professor of Catholic Studies was the distance it put between him and Nora. Their separation was proving more difficult than he had imagined. In spite of their frequent phone conversations, he missed her in ways he could not have predicted.

Most of the students drifted off to class and the Case Quad

grew quiet, like a monastic cloister when the monks were in chapel. And like a monk in prayer, Ian sat still, his lungs expanding with the damp autumn air, savoring the smell of bone-dry leaves dancing like misshapen feathers through a surprisingly warm breeze. He leaned back against the bench and crossed his legs. Gratitude welled up in his chest, unsummoned. He had come a long way from his boyhood in Leeds and his years at Oxford. He wondered where Emma was. Was she happy? Married, no doubt. And his good fortune to gain a tenured post at Johns Hopkins. And Nora…she was such a grace in his life. The ease of her company, her reflective spirit, her joy for life, all this and the quiet pleasure of seeing her almost daily once she joined the faculty at Johns Hopkins. On top of everything else, she had led him to the treasure of the archives of the Carmelite Monastery in Baltimore, largely unknown to most church historians. What he discovered there reinforced his belief that reactionary secret societies of medieval-minded churchmen were still active today. Nora had explained that the Carmelite nuns were the first women religious in the thirteen colonies, arriving in 1790. They were led by intelligent, literate superiors, fluent in French, Italian, and English, who directed the sisters in their meticulous preservation of correspondence and other documents chronicling the thoughts and actions of church authorities and civic leaders.

He had learned of the archives during his first dinner with Nora, when their friendship was just taking hold. Ian smiled, remembering the frank yet trusting manner in which Nora told him that she had been a nun of the Baltimore Carmel—right up to final vows—before pursuing her doctorate in psychology. From their first meeting at a Johns Hopkins faculty convocation he had been taken by the contemplative depth of her personality. And yes, by her clear blue eyes and lean, athletic figure. The thought of spending a weekend with her made him smile again. Ian Landers picked up the text of his talk, stood and stretched, then headed slowly to his office in Tomlinson Hall, his footfalls crunching legions of fallen leaves, meeting without complaint their inescapable destiny.

20

Trace Dunmore left his sixth-floor chancery office without a hint of an explanation to his secretary and headed for the elevator. His mood was sour. He crossed East Ninth Street and marched to his silver Volkswagen Passat in the cathedral garage connected by a spooky underground tunnel to the cathedral rectory. He had remained out of sorts since his phone conversation with Ashley the day before. Trace detested resentment of any kind. But there it was. The scion of the Dunmore line resented Ashley's closeness to Montaldo, took umbrage with the protocol that Simon alone had access to the Archbishop of Perugia. Dunmore was acting now on impulse, determined to visit the professor in his office and clear the air. Dunmore turned east onto the Shoreway, immediately passing the Burke Lakefront Airport, an homage to Cleveland's elite. He glanced with smug irritation at the Navy and Air Force jet fighter planes balanced on their elevated moorings like vulgar athletic trophies. The World War II submarine, the USS Cod, locked in anchor nearby, didn't seem to bother him. Driving south on the park-like Martin Luther King Boulevard soothed his spirit a bit. So Ashley had behaved uppity to him. He knew very well that he probably should, as Americans like to say, "let it go." But he couldn't.

Simon Ashley's office door was open, but he wasn't alone; two coeds, artsy types, were standing on either side of him at his tall draft table, studying an illuminated manuscript page through a large, lighted magnifying glass on a stand mounted to the floor. One of the students was lean, with dark hair trimmed very short. She wore an apron over a gray, full-sleeved blouse and ankle-length black skirt. The other, conventionally pretty and wearing a blonde pixie cut, in a light denim shirt and jeans, looked more like a typical underclass coed. Both had that air of refinement Trace found in many artists and patrons of the arts. Ashley must have felt Trace's presence, but didn't look up. Trace stepped a few paces down the hall, miffed that Simon wasn't willing to wave him in and embrace him with an apology for his recent rudeness on the phone. After a five-minute wait that further aggravated Dunmore's ruffled ego, the students left and Ashley stood at his open door.

"Dunmore, this is an unexpected...pleasure. Is anything wrong?"

"Not really, Simon," Trace said, squeezing past him into the office. "I needed to get out of the chancery for a bit and thought I should fill you in personally on Fergus Mann's neighborhood visits with Martin."

Ashley closed his office door and waved Dunmore to a chair in front of his desk. Instead of moving to his high-tech desk chair, Simon sat in the open chair next to Dunmore—apparently as much of a gesture of equality as he would offer.

"Fergus, I'm afraid, is quite conflicted. He tells me that though he is appalled at the bishop's liberal views, he rather likes him." Dunmore paused for effect. "Bishop Martin, according to Fergus, doesn't believe in hell." Another short pause. "Furthermore, he doesn't think God punishes the sinner, even the heretic."

Ashley frowned. "So Mann is shocked by Martin's liberal theology, but likes him on a personal level. That could make it difficult for us to manage Fergus. As you know, Trace, the personal ever trumps the theoretical. Martin could turn Mann. You know where that would leave us."

"Fergus has planned two or three more evening drives with Martin. We'll see if anything useful surfaces, but it's probably best that his days as the bishop's driver come to an end."

"Yes, Fergus Mann needs careful monitoring." Ashley went still, tapping his desk with a pencil. "What else do you have on Martin?"

"Beyond what we have from Fergus, it is public knowledge that Martin went to the funeral of an excommunicated woman priest. And he invited—I might say 'ordered'—Spivak's former pastor to attend the funeral with him. Simply indefensible behavior, even scandalous behavior, for a bishop."

"Go on," Simon said dryly.

"Martin's administrative assistant, a former lawyer at Jones Day by the name of Therese Reeves, turns out to be a friend of Ann Marie Ellsmere. At least for the week or two following the death of Frances Hellerman, Reeves stayed overnight with Ellsmere when her husband was away. As a staffer to the bishop, you would think she would keep her distance from an excommunicated Catholic."

Ashley nodded his agreement.

"And Bryn Martin knew full well about this arrangement," Dunmore added with emphasis.

"Well," Ashley said, as if he were speaking to a student, "it appears we might be gathering an interesting dossier on our new bishop, after all."

"Ah, but I'm not quite finished, Simon. This Ann Marie Ellsmere, as we know, has been the beneficiary of a personal bodyguard. And I'm not talking about some local off-duty cop. That very bodyguard interrupted her moment of reckoning. I suspect Bryn Martin is using diocesan funds to pay for this protection." Dunmore paused as if to rest his case. *Yes, it had been a good idea, a very good idea, to make this unannounced visit to Simon Ashley.*

The chancellor felt certain that Ashley was impressed with his briefing, although he would not give him the pleasure of saying so. Trace added the icing on the cake. "I've done some digging. Ellsmere's bodyguard is a retired Secret Service agent named Hugh McKenna."

"Find out all that you can about Mr. Hugh McKenna," Simon said with a slight frown, his intuition telling him this unwelcome intruder might be a problem. "I'll pass your information about Bishop Martin on to Archbishop Montaldo. He, in turn," Ashley rose deliberately from his chair like a judge rising from the bench, "will see to it that the right people at the Congregation for Bishops understand what the new Bishop of Cleveland is up to. And of course, our brother Sentinels working in the Vatican will be informed."

"And wouldn't it be sad," Trace whispered with feigned gravitas, "if our new bishop had a very, very short reign?"

Simon Ashley ignored Dunmore's comment. He hated all things snide and small, and Dunmore, his breeding as an English gentleman notwithstanding, could be snide indeed. It truly disappointed him. After a moment, he said in a tired voice, "I want you to keep a close eye on Fergus Mann."

"Yes, of course." Trace moved to the door with the air of a man who has done well for himself.

"And really, Dunmore, it would be kind of you to phone before popping in like this."

21

"Ian, I really, really like it." Nora said into her cell phone. The title page of Landers' lecture filled her computer screen in her Johns Hopkins office. "I've read it twice now. It has so many corollaries with my work on contemplative spirituality and psychological well-being."

"I thought so too, Nora."

Landers sat alone in the Tomlinson Hall cafeteria with his cell phone pressed to his ear and the first pages of his lecture spread out before him.

"Are you sticking with your title, "Under Pain of Mortal Sin"?

"I am. In fact, I like the title as much as I like the talk. I know you think it's a bit daunting, but it captures the grave threat of everlasting punishment in hell that gave the medieval church such power."

"I see what you're getting at, Ian. And you're right about the title. 'Under Pain Of Mortal Sin' highlights the threat...if you commit this particular behavior and die without contrition you will suffer the pains of hell. We've talked about this a lot, but for many people, even today, the fear of damnation, the fear of hell, is one of the worst terrors imaginable. What you're doing, brave friend, is exposing an institution's use of fear to control people's behavior. It's kind of like, 'Be good—or else.'"

"You can skip the brave part, Nora. I'm just an historian connecting the dots."

"Yeah, sure. But the way you connect them is fresh, clear,

and...and...liberating. And that's why I think you might get some serious pushback. The institutional church is wary of spiritual freedom. They're convinced it leads to moral laxity. By the way, Bryn and I had a lot of serious conversations about this sort of sin-centered approach to morality when he was in the seminary. He couldn't understand why sins against chastity or purity were always mortal sins. Neither could I."

"It's still right there on the books. Sins of a sexual nature are considered grave sins, mortal sins."

"That was made very clear to me when I was a girl. My time with the Carmelites got me over that. Those years at the monastery were really the most liberating years of my life."

"Listen, I've got to go," Ian said, with just the right tone of regret. "I'm meeting a student, actually a young woman auditing my class, for coffee. She wants to talk about the church's teaching on sex, so wish me luck. But I better go now. Love you."

"Love you, too."

Landers sat still for a few minutes, savoring the moment within. What was it about his relationship with Nora? A blissful mix of gratitude and affection. That and more. Whatever. He loved talking with Nora and he couldn't wait until he could be with her again. He tried to turn his attention to the task at hand—the final edits to his lecture. He looked at the time on his cell phone and was happy to see he had a few minutes before meeting Rachelle Pageotte. He arranged the spread-out pages of his text in correct sequence, still distracted by his conversation with Nora. Where did the bar lie between venial and mortal sins? And whose prerogative was it to decide? Landers remembered his Catholic mother telling him that she was taught it was a mortal sin to eat meat on Fridays. No. 2 pencil in hand, he pulled out the pages to the last section of his lecture. It would be important to put the theme of his talk in historical context. Failing that, it could be dismissed as some kind of anti-Catholic rant.

He rather liked the way he had addressed the question of mortal sin. Yes, the church's strict, even rigid, teaching on the sinfulness of certain behaviors could be understood as classic examples of control and power. But leaving it at that would fail to consider the worldview of the medieval church, especially in the Late Middle Ages. That worldview was held without question by both the hierarchy and the laity: Divine judgment awaited all upon passing from this life to the other side. God was a God of righteous judgment. If you died unrepentant of serious sin you faced an eternity of suffering in the fires of hell. It followed that the ultimate goal of life for both peasant and pope was to avoid damnation and merit the reward of eternal life with God in heaven. And the church had marked out in explicit detail the paths to both. As shepherds, then, the bishops believed they were fulfilling their God-given responsibility to safeguard the faithful from the horrors of damnation.

True enough. But Landers didn't want to downplay one of the main points of his lecture: The church had taken a serious, misguided step when it taught that failure to practice aids to salvation—Mass on Sundays, prayer, abstinence, and the like— could in itself be a mortal sin. In teaching, for example, that missing Mass on Sunday or holydays, or even a priest's missing his obligation to pray his breviary were mortal sins, Ian posited that the church had exceeded its moral authority. And worse, he considered that it greatly compromised the church's moral authority at a time when its enduring wisdom was badly needed to speak to a culture rocked by the Enlightenment and the waves of modernity that followed. Ian believed he made the point as well as he could that while the church's teaching on mortal sins grew out of a legitimate pastoral concern for the salvation of souls, the church had overstepped. Declaring missing Mass on Sunday to be a mortal sin was meant to motivate believers to do what the bishops believed was fundamental and essential to the faithful

114

practice of the faith. But was it helping today's Catholics?

Landers looked up to see Rachelle Pageotte walking toward his table with a Starbuck's in one hand and a notebook in the other.

"I know you suggested I should wait until after your lecture, but I just couldn't."

Fergus Mann stared at the smudged and wrinkled paper napkin Bishop Martin had given him at the Red Chimney. He had read the Blaise Pascal quote over and over. It made him uneasy, but he couldn't forget it, couldn't simply dismiss it out of hand. Seated at his kitchen table, Fergus took the plastic cap off a ballpoint pen and carefully copied Pascal's words onto a clean piece of note paper. *Men never do evil so completely and cheerfully as when they do it from religious conviction.* Was Pascal nuts, or some kind of saint? Fergus honestly didn't know. He folded the note once and placed it into his wallet next to the verses from the psalm Alistair had given him during one of their meetings at The Coffee House. Contrary to his instructions, he wasn't going tell Father Dunmore about the Pascal quote.

The way Fergus figured, he had just one or two more outings with the bishop. The Collinwood area, and maybe the Union Avenue/East 116th Street section on the southeast side. He would miss these drives. If the bishop wanted a few more outings, that would be fine with him. Even when the bishop didn't say much, Fergus seemed to learn something from him. One of the things he was learning from Martin was how to listen. And if Fergus Mann was learning from the bishop, he thought with a smile, maybe the bishop was learning from Fergus Mann. Yes, the bishop was an okay kind of guy. And so was Father Dunmore, of course, though a whole lot more formal. And he sure pressed to know everything Bishop Martin and Fergus talked about. When

Fergus broke it down, he liked Father Dunmore too, for several reasons. He knew priests were set apart from the laity, and was cordial without being too chummy. Another reason, Fergus had to admit, was that Father Dunmore paid attention to him, a retired cop, a nobody.

Mann got up from the kitchen table and went to his refrigerator and took out a beer. Back at the table he took a few swigs from the can, burped, and wondered what Father Dunmore would think if he knew that Fergus Mann was a trusted operative for a secret Vatican network of church loyalists who called themselves the Sentinels of the Supreme Center.

22

G iorgio, it's me," Archbishop Pietro Montaldo said into his desk phone. "Have the car ready in twenty minutes for our drive to Rome."

"It will be ready, Excellency."

Montaldo had come to feel secure and safe when Giorgio was at his side. Officially, Giorgio Grotti was his driver—a very well-paid driver. But he was worth it. And wasn't it providence— divine providence—that allowed Pietro Montaldo to recruit him for service to Holy Mother Church? Grotti was a godsend—he had the temperament, training, and experience to carry out the most dangerous operations of the Sentinels of the Supreme Center. A former seminarian who had entered the Carabinieri after being expelled for repeatedly punching a fellow seminarian who had made a pass at him, he had risen quickly to qualify for the Carabinieri's Special Forces, the GIS. Grotti didn't know it, but Montaldo had obtained a copy of his confidential GIS file. It described his driver as highly intelligent, mentally and physically tough, and fluent in English and Arabic. Moreover, he scored highest in his training group in marksmanship. Montaldo smiled. Giorgio was the network's James Bond.

Grotti opened the back door to the black Audi Montaldo had brought with him from Rome. "It's 180 kilometers to Rome. Traffic should be light. I will have you there in two hours or less."

"Good," Montaldo said curtly, signaling to Giorgio that there would be little conversation on the drive south. "I will be lunching at the Taverna Guilia on Vicolo dell'Ora."

Grotti knew very well where the restaurant was located. He also knew of the many agreements, deals, and conspiracies that were hatched or consummated over its white linen table cloths by certain prelates and art dealers and businessmen with access to the Vatican's private corridors of power. He also thought he knew who his boss's table partners would be, two of Rome's retired cardinals, archconservatives, art aficionados...and not by coincidence very wealthy men.

Cardinals Alessandro Oradini and Andrea Vannucci were already seated when Archbishop Montaldo arrived.

"Eminences," Montaldo said with a slight bow of his head. The nod was returned. Over *rigatoni alla carbonara* the two octogenarians briefed Montaldo on current Vatican gossip, who seemed to be closer to the center and who seemed to have suffered a drop in status, and the various medical problems of senior officials at the Curia. They offered nothing Montaldo didn't already know from his well-placed contacts. The conversation turned serious only after their espressos had been served.

"Your Eminences know why I requested this meeting. And of course I am very grateful that you have agreed to listen to my request." Neither cardinal said a word. "You are aware of the good and prudent reasons our previous fraternity, the Brotherhood of the Sacred Purple, has been disbanded."

"Yes, things got seriously out of hand in Baltimore," Vannucci said with a hint of judgment. "Our brother Wilfred Gunnison failed us terribly and caused serious scandal by taking his own life. May God have mercy on his soul."

"I still can't believe it," Oradini said in a whisper. "The retired

Archbishop of Baltimore, an abuser of young boys."

Pietro Montaldo swallowed hard at their hypocrisy. Both prelates knew he had given the order to do what was necessary for the good of the church. Officially, Archbishop Wilfred Gunnison's tragic death was a suicide. A much better story for the church than the truth. Their world, Montaldo could see, was often necessarily clouded by denial and self-deception.

"Let me give you a brief overview of where we are at the present time," he told them.

Oradini and Vannucci knew that the center of the Sentinels network moved from Rome to Perugia with the appointment of Montaldo as its archbishop. He remained the unquestioned leader of their network, just as he had been of the Brotherhood of the Sacred Purple. And both prelates understood that the Brotherhood had played a role in their own appointments as bishops, and perhaps even in their appointments as cardinals. Their brother Pietro deserved their attention.

Montaldo took a sip of his mineral water. "As with the Brotherhood, the Sentinels have no records, no files, no register of members. We leave no paper trail. We communicate, when necessary, by phone, without mention of the name 'Sentinels.' Our emails are carefully edited to assure our privacy...and safety... from those who might be suspicious of our work."

"We are depending on you, Pietro, to keep the network as small as possible," Vannucci said, as if speaking to an inferior.

"With every new recruit there is added risk of exposure," Oradini added.

Montaldo nodded patiently. "Yes I agree, it is prudent to keep the number of Sentinels at just a few dozen. Perhaps thirty—no more. Mostly clergy, but with capable, well-placed laymen—men like Simon Ashley, whom we now have in Cleveland."

"Yes," Vannucci said impatiently, "isn't that where your beloved *Caporali Missal* is located?"

"For the time being, Eminence. For the time being."

"In addition to Ashley, the chancellor and moderator of the curia of the Cleveland diocese is one of ours. He moved in your social circles while he was here in Rome looking for a diocese. Do you remember Father Trace Dunmore, a convert from a rather aristocratic British family?"

Oradini mumbled, "Vaguely."

"It's because of Ashley and Dunmore that I chose Cleveland to begin our operation to halt once and for all the ordination of women. Of course it's not as strategic a city as, say, Vienna or Munich, but the growing number of women priests in Cleveland invited its consideration. And as I've said, with two of our own in place there, it was the wise choice, the right place to begin our...our crusade."

Vannucci cut in. "Tell me, dear Pietro, is our initiative proving successful?"

"It's too early to say, Eminence. Infiltrating the women's formation programs, laughable as they are, has not been easy. But we take careful note of the pseudo-ordinations that are reported in the media."

Vannucci lifted his napkin to his lips as he raised an eyebrow at what he had just heard.

"I believe," Montaldo continued, "we will have a good idea of how effective our initiative has been within a few months."

"Let us hope so," Oradini said piously. "However, the boldness of our plan continues to unsettle me." Then glancing at Vannucci but letting his gaze settle on Montaldo, "I'm not sure I have the fierce resolve I see in you, Pietro, but I agree that we had to counter this sacrilegious disobedience to church teaching, a teaching from the supreme center itself."

The three churchmen fell silent for a moment, staring at the plates before them.

"You may remember," Montaldo said, "that at our last meeting I told you they had recruited an operative, a retired police-man. Ashley believes he can be relied on to carry out our...our righteous action. So far, he has imposed the ultimate punish-ment on two of the heretics and is ready to continue his mission when given the signal."

Both cardinals looked uneasy.

"A retired policeman? Is that wise?" Oradini said. "And not just a Sentinel, but an operative?"

"He has been very malleable. He is in good hands."

"What do you know about the Bishop of Cleveland?" Van-nucci asked.

"His name is Peter Bryn Martin. He's recently appointed and is still adjusting. He came from Baltimore where he was an auxiliary to Archbishop Cullen and as a young priest served as master of ceremonies to Archbishop Gunnison."

"I assume Bishop Martin was given a push by Archbishop Cullen," Vannucci said dryly.

"Not at all, Eminence." Montaldo took secret pleasure in what he was about to say. "It was Gunnison, not Cullen, who pressed for Martin being named a bishop."

Oradini and Vannucci exchanged a quick glance. This bit of episcopal gossip was likely true. But why did Pietro trust it to be reliable? He was not a member of the Congregation of Bishops, the Vatican department that made the final, highly confidential, recommendations to the Holy Father on candidates for the office of bishop. Both Oradini and Vannucci assumed their brother Pietro had something on one or more of the members of the Congregation of Bishops.

"And," Montaldo continued, "Bishop Martin is definitely not one of ours. Father Dunmore, of course, is in a very good posi-tion to keep us informed."

Vannucci, to Montaldo's surprise, called a waiter to the table and ordered a grappa, a strong *digestivo* for this time of the day.

Oradini signaled he wanted one too.

"Tell us, Pietro, what do you know about Archbishop Cullen?" Cardinal Oradini asked.

"We understand him to be something of a centrist, Eminence, with leanings toward the liberal Vatican II mentality we all find so troubling. Cullen himself described his manner of shepherding as 'pastoral.'"

"*Pastoral!*" Cardinal Vannucci sneered, his watery eyes hard with contempt. "That's code for relativism, and we know what that's all about. Moral laxity, situation ethics—just do whatever you please as long as you feel good about it." Vannucci caught his breath, seeming surprised himself at the fire in his words. "So tell us, Pietro, what's the state of our network?"

"As you know, we have three Sentinels in Cleveland, if you count the operative. There are two other Sentinels in the U.S., each a bishop of a major diocese. There are seven of us here in Italy, including one layman, my driver Giorgio. Germany and Spain each have a Sentinel bishop. So, as you can see, we are just a handful of loyalists. But with God on our side..."

A handful of loyalists, true enough. But all three men at the table knew the Sentinels had an army of allies—bishops, priests, religious, and laity—who shared their fear for the future of a church faced with powerful enemies both outside and inside her fold. More than the other two prelates, Montaldo appreciated the far-reaching influence of conservative journalists, bloggers, and self-appointed watchdog groups who daily pointed to the heresies eating away at the church like a cancer. This is what made him confident that the Sentinels could indeed protect the church's supreme center.

Before their grappa glasses were half-empty, it was time for Archbishop Montaldo to ask Cardinals Vannucci and Oradini for money, money to support the work of the Sentinels and their allies.

"Deeply grateful for your past support, your Eminences, I ask that you each forward to my residence in Perugia twenty-five thousand euros by Friday of next week."

Their lined faces expressionless, both cardinals instinctively touched their jeweled episcopal rings as if taking comfort in their status as princes of the church. Like twins, they looked down at the table as if stalling for time. After a minute, Oradini lifted his head and nodded his consent. A second later, Vannucci did the same.

The two cardinals seated across from Archbishop Pietro Montaldo reached for their napkins, perhaps thinking they had just finished two very expensive plates of rigatoni. They were long ago made aware that Montaldo knew that most of their wealth had been passed on to them by their fathers, revered figures in Rome's aristocracy. And that he had discovered something else—their fathers had been two of Rome's most discreet launderers of money for Italy's organized crime syndicates and for Nazi's fleeing to South America. Such a long time ago. Hardly anyone knew. And no one spoke of such things.

23

Terry Reeves, coffee in hand, studied Bishop Bryn Martin's agenda for the day. It was a few minutes after eight and the chancery was just coming to life. Seated across from Martin in his office, she wondered if he hadn't slept well.

"Not too bad today, Bishop. You have a ten o'clock meeting with the religious superiors of women who, by the way, have heard nothing but good things about you from the nuns they know in Baltimore. The meeting's in your conference room. They will stay for lunch in the rectory."

Martin looked forward to the meeting. Like the religious superiors he had come to know in Baltimore, these elected leaders were well-read theologically and mature spiritually—way ahead of many of their ordained brothers.

"I see I have the clergy personnel board at two. That will be interesting, Terry."

Getting to know the priests of Cleveland was going more slowly than he wished. In addition to an average age in the high sixties, his priests seemed weary and, understandably, a bit wary of him. A few of the pastors he had met seemed emotionally off balance, and like the Baltimore priests he knew much better, unsettled by the realization that to a growing number of Catholics they were more or less irrelevant. "We'll call you when we need you, Father," people seemed to imply, as if priests were spiritual plumbers or electricians whose services were required from time to time for baptisms, weddings, and funerals. On top of that the mostly older Vatican II priests and the mostly younger John Paul II priests were painfully divided. It often came down to renewal versus retrenchment. If he couldn't unite them, Martin hoped at least to get them to respect one another.

Reeves wished she could read the bishop's mind. She decided to wait out the silence that had come over Martin.

Bryn soon came back to the moment. "How is Ann Marie Ellsmere doing?"

"Better by the day, Bishop. She's less nervous and sleeping pretty well."

"Tell her I asked about her, and that I'm praying for her."

Reeves smiled. "There's something else you should know, Bishop. Ann Marie told me that the organization Roman Catholic Women Priests is still accepting candidates into formation. That makes her nervous. I think with good reason."

Martin nodded. "If the man who murdered Laura Spivak and Frances Hellerman or the people who ordered their murder hear this it could put Ann Marie and others in real danger."

"Ann Marie and her husband feel the same way."

Martin was still for a minute. "Terry, I'd like to visit Ann Marie and her husband…Richard, I believe. And I'd like to have you and Hugh join me if you would. Can you arrange that, please?"

The request took her by surprise. "I'd be happy to, Bishop." She judged that this was not the time to tell her boss that she and Hugh were seeing each other. She got up to leave.

"I'll be leaving the office right after the personnel board meeting," Martin said casually. "Fergus Mann is going to drive me to the park where Laura Spivak was murdered."

"We got a nice day, Bishop. Warm for early November, and the leaves are still really somethin'." They rode east on the Shoreway and took the I-90 exit that would take them by the Center for

Pastoral Leadership, the ministry training center that housed the undergraduate seminary, Borromeo, the graduate seminary, Saint Mary, the permanent diaconate program, the lay ministry training program, and a few other diocesan offices. Martin needed more time to get to know the faculty, but he was beginning to think Saint Mary Seminary had the potential to be one of the stronger seminaries in the country. The faculty—which now included women scholars—were capable for the most part, and the library held one of the best collections of books on theology, scripture, spirituality, and ministry in any U.S. seminary's library. And the seminarians, the rector had told him, were likable, rather mature men.

Mann thought the bishop seemed preoccupied. "Do you want to stop at the CPL, Bishop?"

"No, but on the way back drive me through the campus. I want to get the feel of the place."

The North Chagrin Reservation, just a five minute drive from the CPL, was one of about two dozen public parks and golf courses known as the "Emerald Necklace" that ringed the greater Cleveland area. Terry Reeves had described the Emerald Necklace to Martin soon after his arrival as one of the more charming aspects of life in Cleveland. Mann turned the car into the Chardon Road entrance and moved slowly around the runners and bikers hugging the edge of the paved road. Older adult couples, some holding hands, had taken to the walking paths. Once in the park, Mann drove directly to the Intergrove Lodge, a rustic, large, heated cabin that could be reserved for family reunions and other private events...like a Mass celebrated by a woman priest. Fergus pulled onto a gravel drive that he followed to a locked wrought-iron gate thirty feet from the road.

"They keep the lodge locked when it's not rented," Mann said. "But we can leave the car here and walk up to the lodge. You won't be able to get in, but the view you'll get through the windows will give you an idea of the place."

Mann at first lingered by the car, then followed Martin up to the lodge.

"If you want, Bishop, I can drive over to the Rangers' Office and have someone come out and open it for you."

"Thanks, Fergus, this will do." Martin could see a large, rectangular room with a floor-to-ceiling stone fireplace and a stack of what looked like dry firewood along the opposite wall.

"I'll go wait in the car, Bishop," Fergus said suddenly. "Take your time."

Martin understood why the lodge would be almost ideal for celebrating Mass with Spivak's small congregation. Still standing close to the window with his hands cupped at the sides of his eyes to block the afternoon sunlight, he made out a long kitchen counter with plenty of space for a buffet meal, numerous electrical outlets for coffee urns and the like, and a full-size refrigerator. In the middle of the lodge he counted six long portable tables and dozens of folding chairs stacked along one wall. One of the tables, he guessed, would have been covered with an altar cloth and the chairs placed in semi-circles around the makeshift altar. He imagined what a fireside Mass, officiated by a woman, would be like for the small assembly. Martin backed away from the window and began a slow walk around the lodge. It was a perfect chapel in the woods. The stately trees, mostly tall maples ready to shed their yellow and orange leaves, reminded Bryn of the Gothic cathedrals of Europe. He remembered Beethoven writing that in the forest every tree seemed to say, "Holy, Holy." *Yes, Martin*, said to himself, *nature reveals the glory of God*. Here in this park, at this lodge, he was standing on holy ground, a ground made sacred by a cold-blooded murder.

Back at the front of the lodge, Bryn looked again through the large window next to the front door and tried to picture Laura Spivak removing her vestments when her murderer must

127

have startled her. Did he say anything to her before he took her cincture and strangled her? Did she cry out? What—or who—in God's name was behind her violent death? He turned and walked slowly back to the car.

Fergus was seated in the driver's seat when Martin got back in the car, clutching the steering wheel with both hands. The engine was running. Without saying a word, he backed out of the lodge's driveway and headed for I-90.

"Thanks for taking the time to show me the lodge, Fergus. For some reason I don't fully understand, it was important for me to see the place where Laura Spivak was murdered."

Mann suddenly stiffened but nodded his "You're welcome," his eyes fixed on the road ahead. They drove in silence until they reached the Bishop Road entrance to the Center for Pastoral Leadership and Fergus began driving around the seminary property like a cop patrolling a college campus.

"I understand the first institution here was a boarding school for young girls in trouble," Martin said to a strangely quiet Mann. "When the diocese took it over it became Borromeo Seminary High School." Martin chuckled, "Some said it went from a school for young girls in trouble to a school for young boys in trouble." Mann didn't even smile at the joke. *That's not like him*, Martin thought. "The rector told me that back in the 1950s there were about 300 high school seminarians here and about 200 in the college program. Our major seminary, Saint Mary's, was located in the city then, with another 120 or so seminarians."

"Really...that many," Mann said with feigned interest.

"Yes, well over six hundred men studying for the priesthood for our diocese alone. It's true that most of the high school seminarians, well over ninety percent of them, dropped out. We, Fergus, and by 'we' I mean all of us Catholics, need to wrestle with the drastic drop we're witnessing in the number of seminarians. What's it telling us?"

"When I was a server, Bishop, back in the seventh grade, I thought of going to Borromeo. But my grades weren't good enough. Anyway, I don't think I would have lasted a week." He paused just as he was ready to pull out onto Euclid Avenue and said with a nervous edge in his voice, "Would you mind, Bishop, if we stopped for a drink? I really need a drink."

They sat in a booth at The Wright Place, a pub a few miles from the seminary. Fergus ordered a shot and a beer. The shot had disappeared as soon as it was set before him. "I've been doing a lot of thinking about what we talked about at the Red Chimney," he began carefully.

Martin sipped a scotch and soda…and waited.

"For me, being a Catholic was basically about two things—being loyal to the pope, to the church, and avoiding mortal sin, so that when I died I'd go to heaven, not hell. But you say that being Christian, being a Catholic, is more than avoiding mortal sin. You're saying it's more like having a good heart. Like taking Jesus' teachings and making them your own. I always thought obeying the commandments was enough, but I hear you saying we shouldn't judge other people's heart or their intentions. Heck, Bishop, judging other people is one thing I'm really good at. I can tell you what's wrong with almost everybody." Fergus went silent and took a deep swallow from his beer. Martin remained silent.

"For me religion has always been about fear. Fearing God, fearing mortal sin, fearing punishment." Mann's eyes seemed to water and his face tightened, almost as if he was in some kind of pain. "And do you know what, Bishop? As much as I feared punishment, I wanted to punish people who did bad things, people who didn't obey. And I wanted to punish them…severely."

A short time later Mann eased his Ford Focus to a stop under the archway at the side of the cathedral rectory. The two men sat without speaking for a while. Then awkwardly, Fergus said, with a voice on the edge of cracking, "Thanks for listening to me, Bishop. Sometimes I think I'm really screwed up. Our little talks are helpful. I think I might be too old-school for my own good. I'll try to remember what you said, that our God is a God of mercy. That our sins are forgiven even before we commit them. That's a load."

Fergus Mann's mind was spinning. What Bishop Martin had told him in the bar was the opposite of what Alistair said again and again at The Coffee House, that the righteous, the faithful, have not just the right but the duty to punish the sinner.

Martin put his hand on the door handle but didn't open it. "Do you remember me telling you about my friend Ian Landers who is a guest professor at Case-Western?"

Mann squinted trying to remember. "I think so."

"I'm going to a talk he's giving at the university on how mortal sin became a hallmark, like a chief pillar, of Catholic teaching. You might want to attend." Bryn reached into his pocket for a pen and on the back of the receipt from The Wright Place wrote the date, time, and place of the lecture. "It's in the Strosacker Auditorium in the main quad of the Case campus."

"Yeah, I know the place. I've seen a few movies there."

"You won't be sorry if you're able to make it."

24

Ann Marie and Rich Ellsmere had prepared thoughtfully for their guests—coffee, tea, cookies, and a bottle of white wine in the refrigerator, along with a bottle of good single malt on the buffet in case the bishop, Terry, and Hugh were so inclined. They gathered in the family room of the Ellsmeres' Brecksville home on Whitewood Road. Rich lit a fire just as Terry and Hugh arrived. Bishop Martin was the last to get there, dressed in black slacks, an oxford shirt, and a dark maroon wool sweater.

"Thanks for this little gathering," he said, as they settled in the family room. "I thought it would be good for us to get together to see where things were. Terry has told me that there is no real progress on the FBI and police investigations."

Hugh nodded, "That's the last word I've had from the authorities. They're aware of my Secret Service background and I think they're being as candid as they can be with me."

"I really don't have an agenda today," Martin said, "other than to see how you two are getting on. So tell me...how are you two doing?"

"Your being here, Bishop, means more than I can say," Ann Marie said. "Rich and I feel like we're living under surveillance. We're a bit on edge. Nervous if an unfamiliar car parks across the street, bothered if someone holds our glance at a restaurant or the supermarket."

"Terry has been great," Rich added. "She visits as often as she can and she calls regularly."

"And you, Hugh," Ann Marie said with a hitch in her voice, "you seem to be there, quietly in the background just when I'm feeling a little anxious...a bit unnerved. I don't know how you do it."

Hugh glanced at Bryn, and raised his eyebrows, lowering his chin in a bow to the bishop.

"But to your question, Bishop," Ann Marie said, "I have to say I'm doing pretty well. I've told Terry that I feel a bit more okay, a little safer, each day." She rose and walked to the kitchen. "There's coffee too," she said over her shoulder.

"I think she really is doing well," Rich said with obvious regard for his wife's courage. "We think we made the right decision to stay right here. Not to run."

As Ann Marie served coffee the muted firelight and the family-room's soft lighting seemed to draw the five individuals into a soothing circle, like a band of travelers finding comfort and support in the face of some unexpected threat. They fell silent for a while.

Terry leaned back in her chair and sipped her coffee, proud of her high school friend, and with a growing sense of pride in the steadfastness of her boss, Bishop Martin.

In spite of the warmth of the fire and the spirits, the conversation that evening remained careful, almost like the conversation at a wake. Finally, Ann Marie caught Terry's eye and saw her say—without a word spoken—*Go ahead, tell the bishop.*

"I thought you should know, Bishop, that in spite of the murders, there are a few Cleveland women in formation, preparing to be ordained. I'm sure there're at least tentative dates set for their ordinations to the diaconate and priesthood."

A heavy silence seemed to suck the air out of the room. Finally Bryn said, "If the person who murdered Laura and Frances wanted to send a message to Roman Catholic women priests, he's likely to think his message wasn't received. If the assassin was an agent of some radical reactionary group, the group's resolve will likely be strengthened when they hear they haven't halted the ordination of women. And we have to assume they will hear."

"Rich and I...and Terry...we've talked about that, Bishop. We agree, of course, that this puts us—the Cleveland area women priests—in a bad situation. But I can tell you there is a consensus among the women preparing for ordination that going ahead is the right thing to do."

"Ann Marie and I wish they would take a hiatus, Bishop, but we weren't able to persuade the majority." Rich looked at his wife. "The leaders, if you can call them that, are somewhat sympathetic with Ann Marie's decision not to celebrate Eucharist for the time being, but they seem to think she's caving in to fear."

"That's totally unfair," Terry said sharply. "I'm sorry, Ann Marie, but I think some of your...your colleagues are really being terribly self-righteous."

"A few of them might come across that way," Ann Marie said. "But most of the women priests I know aren't like that at all."

"You understand, Ann Marie, that as your bishop, I can't support your ordination. But I will say this. I suspect your colleagues are neither more nor less self-righteous than many of my male colleagues. And it seems that the higher people's degree of moral certainty, the more likely they are to believe that any means are permissible."

"Ann Marie," Hugh said, "Understanding that should put you on guard. You really have to consider carrying a handgun with you whenever you leave the house."

Rich swallowed, hesitated briefly, then whispered, "I've told her the same thing."

"Rich and I have talked about it," Ann Marie admitted. "But

I have always abhorred guns and gun violence. And I don't know anything about them. I've never even held a gun, let alone fired one. They scare me to death."

"Would you have been afraid to touch one the night you were attacked?" Hugh asked.

"No, I guess you're right."

"I'll teach you how to handle one safely," Hugh said in a tone of quiet encouragement. "And I know the gun that would be just right for you, it's small and light, it's very reliable and easy to operate. It's a Smith & Wesson hammerless revolver."

Terry shot a quick glance at Bryn but couldn't read what he was thinking. Rich, on the other hand, was holding Ann Marie's hand, silently urging her to agree to Hugh's advice to arm herself.

"Okay," she said. "I'll give it a try."

25

Father Trace Dunmore closed the door to his chancery office but didn't sit at his desk. Instead he plopped down in one of his visitor chairs and felt his irritation, his restlessness, mount in his chest. Anxiety about his precarious post as chancellor and moderator of the curia had become a constant companion, distracting him from the tedious work of the day: pending assignment changes for priests, audit reports on half a dozen parishes, a list of pastors to call regarding late assessments. Bishop Martin had to be thinking about naming his own team of close associates, and Dunmore assumed he wasn't on the roster, not by a long shot. Moreover, his relationship with Simon Ashley had been testy of late and Ashley was his sole link to Montaldo, the prelate of hidden power who was the only person likely to find a spot for him in the Vatican Curia. Trace smiled... maybe even have him named a bishop. The thought seemed to brighten his dark mood.

Then there was Fergus Mann. Their recent whispered little talks after Sunday Mass at the cathedral had produced only scraps of scuttlebutt on Bryn Martin. At first Mann had taken a certain pleasure in reporting back on his conversations with the bishop. Not so much of late. Ashley needed to keep Fergus on track. Perhaps it was time for another try on Ann Marie Ellsmere. But the recent news from an informant that Martin and Reeves had met with Ellsmere and her husband had left Dunmore off balance. What was that about? Reeves never mentioned the meeting to him. But he would find out more. Such little intrigues spiced his carefully scripted public life as the chancellor of the diocese.

Dunmore stood, stretched, and walked around to his desk chair. Yes, he would find out. "Remember," his mother had told him again and again, "you are always the smartest person in the room, and you are destined to do great things." The thought of his mum—she despised the term—brought a half-smile to his lips. Mother, Trace knew well, thought of herself as *Lady* Elizabeth and her husband as *Sir* Roger Dunmore. "You, my dear Trace, are magnanimous. You have been blessed with a great soul." And like his mother, Trace Dunmore believed it so. The half-smile broadened. Hadn't he learned early on from his upper-class Oxford mates that great-souled men operate beyond morality?

Terry Reeves closed Martin's office door before sitting down. "I have some upsetting news, Bishop. Somehow Trace Dunmore heard that you met with the Ellsmeres." As the bishop's administrative assistant, Reeves took this news as a personal affront. She had been charged to set up a private, off-the-books, off-their-calendars, meeting with Ann Marie and Rich. She had done so. "How did he find out?"

"Let's not waste time trying to figure it out, Terry." Martin had spent a good deal of his time as a priest in the Baltimore chancery and knew all too well the dynamics of clerical office politics. What he had discerned in Baltimore was clearly in play here in Cleveland. Where the bishop was, who he spent time with, and for how long, what was discussed—such information became the coin of the clerical realm. The widely accepted perception was that the more any administrative assistant knew, the closer he or she was to the bishop. "We've never tried to hide from Trace the fact that you and Ann Marie are friends. He's known that from the beginning. It's true I'd prefer he didn't know about our fireside chat with the Ellsmeres, but so what if he does? We need to stay focused on the bigger picture. There's someone out there who has murdered two Catholic women who believed they were called to be priests. I want to know who murdered them, on whose behalf, and whether or not other murders are being plotted."

Reeves shook her head. "Yes, of course. I just feel like I let you down."

"Not at all, Terry. Listen, I know Trace has taken the point on keeping up with the investigations, but I'd like you to follow up too."

The look in Bryn Martin's eyes, for some reason she didn't understand, gave her comfort. Terry nodded.

"It's getting close to five. I hope you have a good evening, Bishop."

"Well, it should be interesting. Fergus Mann is taking me out for a last ride."

26

Bryn Martin found Fergus Mann unusually quiet as they drove east on St. Clair Avenue, toward Cleveland's Collinwood area. In fact, both men were preoccupied, each in his own world, but worlds that somehow coupled well. Mann had remained unsettled since their visit to the Intergrove Lodge. Martin continued to try to unpack his driver's recent edgy behavior—and his sudden need for a drink—the last time they were out.

"Look to your left here, Bishop." They were moving slowly in the curb lane just past East 35th. "See that boarded-up building that looks like a storefront was attached to the front of a house?" Martin nodded. "Years ago it was a real den of iniquity." Fergus seemed pleased with his 'den of iniquity.' "This was my district for a while, and you could expect trouble if you were working the midnight-to-eight shift." Mann gave Martin a nervous glance, hesitated a few seconds, and continued. "It was a seedy gay bar, really heavy into S&M. Studded belts, chains, ropes, lots of leather. The dominants were really ripped. Must have spent their days at the gym and their nights cruising. It was all there: sex, booze, drugs...lots of drugs. The place smelled of beer, spilled whiskey, cigarette smoke, and you can guess what else. All kinds of dark alcoves and booths."

Martin didn't say anything.

"Our drug unit finally sent in some undercover guys. Their written reports made the rounds of the district locker rooms, like X-rated stuff. Eventually, they shut the place down for the drugs, and that was more or less the end of it."

"I know there's a very dark side to the gay culture," the bishop said, "but you know, Fergus, people in that kind of lifestyle are a small percentage of the gay population. And if you want to think of straight culture, you will find a small percentage pretty much into the same kind of things."

"I don't know, Bishop, I really haven't seen that many straight guys behaving like that. But, yeah, I've heard of some really wild parties."

When they were a mile or so past East 55th Street, Fergus said, "There's a fair amount of prostitution around here. Believe it or not, there's a nun who is trying to minister to the hookers. She's wasting her time, if you ask me."

"Yes, I read about her. The reporter who interviewed me for the *Plain Dealer* did a story about her. Sister Celine, I think." Bryn planned to meet with her. She deserved some encouragement.

"You can see St. Aloysius ahead, Bishop. It was merged with St. Agatha…oh, I don't know…maybe twenty years ago. It's got a good elementary school. But I think most of the kids are Protestant or whatever. Maybe just a handful of Catholics. But they say it's good for the neighborhood and they do a lot of what Father Dunmore calls 'outreach.'"

"I know a bit about St. Aloysius-St. Agatha. I am scheduled to do the confirmation there in January."

Mann pulled to the curb in front of a small deli that Martin thought looked closed. "How about some coffee?"

"Sure."

"You wait here, Bishop. I'll be right back." He climbed out and before closing the door said, "You might want to lock the door."

It was a full ten minutes later when Mann returned with

two cups of coffee. "Did a little catching up on the neighborhood news."

Martin slipped his coffee into the cup holder in the console. It was hot and Mann hadn't bothered with the corrugated sleeves.

"The hood's pretty tense right now," Fergus said. "The officers working this area have been pretty tough and have made some enemies. A couple of them are rookies." Mann sipped his coffee but didn't start the car. "This is a pretty rough area, Bishop. If I had to live here I think I'd go crazy. A lot of scum bags is what they are. I'd arrest almost all of them and send 'em to jail. They'd just as soon shoot you as give you the time of day. They have no respect for anything. The few good folks still around here are really scared. It's a hell of a way to live."

Bryn reached for his coffee, holding it carefully by the rim. "Sometimes I think if I had grown up in a tough section of Baltimore or Cleveland, like this area, I'm not sure I would have made it…how I would have lived…how I would have behaved. I think I would have been very angry. And when we're angry we can do very stupid things. Things we wouldn't do if our circumstances were better."

"You starting to sound like a preacher, Bishop." Fergus caught himself and smiled. "I guess that's what you are." Martin smiled too and sipped his coffee.

"Come on," Fergus said starting the car. "Let's get going. I want to show you Holy Redeemer parish and then we'll head back downtown."

The autumn night was cold, but not cold enough to turn the heat on. Bryn zipped his black nylon jacket up close to the open collar of his black clergy shirt. They did a drive-by of Holy Redeemer and the small, nicely kept bungalows around the church and were soon back on St. Clair heading west. They were riding in silence, but Fergus was afraid to turn the radio on. The bishop probably liked classical music and Fergus didn't know where to find that stuff on the dial. *What the hell*, he thought.

"Would you like some—"

Before he could finish the thought, his attention was drawn to the flashing blue and red lights of a squad car angled at the curb about fifty yards ahead of them. "What's this now?" As they got closer, it looked like a dozen or so young men were standing around a figure slumped on the sidewalk against a dark two-story office building that looked locked up for the night. A police officer was holding a flashlight at his left shoulder, lighting up the figure's face. Mann pulled to the curb a safe distance behind the police car.

"Stay in the car, Bishop, and lock the door."

Before getting out, to Martin's surprise, Mann reached under his seat and pulled out a small automatic pistol, tucking it inside his belt and under his jacket. "Stay in the car," he repeated. It was an order.

Martin's stomach tightened as he watched Fergus approach the group—mostly teenagers it seemed—who were yelling at the officer, whose right hand was close to the holster of his sidearm. The shouting stopped as Mann walked up, but only for a second or two. One of the leaders, a man who looked older than the others, was immediately in Mann's face, challenging his intrusion on their turf. His language, even muffled by the closed windows of Fergus's car, was violent and obscene.

The officer appeared to look unsteady, unsure of himself. It was always bad to show any sign of weakness, Fergus thought. He walked up to the cop and, holding his gaze for a second, said out of the side of his mouth, "I'm an RIP." The cop's expression didn't change but Mann caught a glimmer of recognition, maybe even respect, in his eyes. "RIP" is police jargon for "Retired Irish Police."

"We need to get some Narcan into this kid, stat," the cop

said, "and these guys are all up in my face."

The young men standing around their overdosed friend had stepped forward, forming two tight circles, one around Mann and the other around the officer. Their number had increased. It looked now like twenty or so.

Back in the car, Bryn could see that Fergus and the officer were in a tough spot. "Stay in the car," Mann had said. As if on autopilot, Bryn buttoned the top button of his clerical shirt and slid the plastic tab he often carried with him into place. He thought better than to walk up on the situation unannounced, invisible as he would be, clad in black from head to foot, so he popped open the glove compartment hoping that Fergus kept a flashlight there that he could use to make them all aware of his approach. He found an LCD pocket penlight among a clutter of plastic gloves, a beaten owner's manual, a few maps, and a coiled piece of rope. Bryn flicked the light on, slammed the glove box shut, and reached for the door handle with a silent prayer on his lips.

Martin waved the light at the growing crowd and was ten feet or so from the circle when he was first noticed. He turned the light on himself so they could see the clerical collar. His priestly uniform seemed to take the young men by surprise and they looked at him with a kind of bewilderment that said, *Preacher, what are you doing here?*

"What's the problem, guys?" Martin said in an even voice. "How can we help?" Mann's glare back seemed to say, *You're really making the situation worse.*

"Nobody's taking our brother to the hospital, or anywhere else." The raised voice came from a young man wearing a hooded maroon Cavs sweatshirt. Bryn simply nodded and walked slowly over to the sprawled kid. He was clearly a teen. His jeans were urine stained and caked with layers of dirt. Leaning down with his hands on his knees, Bryn asked the boy his name.

The young man's half-closed eyes went completely shut but his cracked lips parted. "Maaar...cus," he slurred.

"How do you feel, Marcus? Are you in pain? We need to get you to a hospital."

His glassy eyes opened but didn't focus. "No, man, no hospital."

Bryn straightened and looked squarely at the young men around him. "He needs help, and right now."

Another kid, not much older than the boy on the ground, leaned toward Bryn aggressively. "Just who the hell do you think you are, telling us what to do?"

"He's Bishop Martin. The new Catholic Bishop of Cleveland," Mann said clearly, loud enough for everyone to hear. A few in the crowd must have gone to school at St. Aloysius and it seemed to register that a Catholic bishop had some kind of clout. The muttering quieted a little.

"My friend here," Martin said with a quick look at Mann, "his name is Fergus. We'll go with your friend to a hospital or an emergency center. If one or two of you want to come with us, that's fine. But he needs medical attention and he needs it now."

The officer, whose name-badge read "Lismore," finally spoke. "I've already called for an ambulance. The bishop's right, your friend Marcus could die if he doesn't get help."

"Think about it," Fergus added. "Officer Lismore and the bishop know what they're talkin' about." Mann held their gaze. "Nothing bad is going to happen to Marcus." The streetwise young men standing in their now-broken circles looked at one another and then to the guy in the Cavs hoodie as if waiting for his signal. It would be easy enough for them to jump the cop and the wanna-be hero who couldn't mind his own business. The bishop would be no problem either.

Without a word, Marcus' friends retightened their two circles, one crowding around Mann and the other around Lismore.

No one blinked.

Martin broke the silence. "If you guys don't mind, I'm going to say a prayer for Marcus."

Without waiting for a response, Bryn went down on one knee next to the young addict deep in his own dark world of dreamy delusion. The bishop's quiet poise and his kneeling next to Marcus ratcheted the tension down a little.

Martin spoke softly. Only the leader and those standing close could hear him. "Dear God, be with your servant and our brother, Marcus. He's broken in body and soul and needs your healing hand to rest upon him...to protect him. May God bless you, Marcus, in the name of the Father, Son, and Holy Spirit."

Fergus alone said, "Amen."

Martin reached out and traced the sign of the cross on Marcus's forehead. The young men seemed to back off a little. Maybe their friend wouldn't just be dumped into some drunk tank and charged. And what kind of priest, or bishop, would care enough about some poor druggy to leave the safety of his car in this neighborhood? Then in the chill of the evening, they heard the too-familiar wavering strains of sirens approaching from the center of the city. The small crowd of men and boys suddenly had somewhere important to go.

27

Bryn Martin was getting to know his new home. To a large extent that was to the credit of Fergus Mann. But the bishop was also getting to know Fergus. And that was the source of his unease. Over and over, Martin played back his last two outings with his retired police driver and, it was fair to say, his new old-school Catholic friend. Replaying the mental tapes of their rides kept him awake at night and distracted him from his ministry during the day. Bryn found himself thinking like a detective, trying to fit disjointed pieces of a puzzle together. Was he making too much out of what he remembered? No, what he observed first hand was real, and too compelling to dismiss as misperceptions on his part.

Bryn gripped his umbrella tightly as he encountered the natural wind tunnel on East Ninth Street. The icy rain off the lake hit the right side of his face like pinpricks as he made the short walk to his office in the Cathedral Square Plaza building to begin his day. In the elevator taking him to his sixth floor office, Martin finally admitted he needed help. He needed to talk to his sister, Nora, and to Ian Landers. And soon.

Bryn shook the water from his umbrella and opened it to dry. Both Terry Reeves and Trace Dunmore were in their offices and it wasn't yet 7:30. Dunmore's door was closed, but as he passed Reeves' office she looked up from her desk. "Stop over when you can, would you, Terry?

"I can come over shortly."

"The sooner the better."

The windswept rain streaked the windows of Martin's office, making it impossible to see much at all beyond the blurred outline of the cathedral just across the street. Most of the time, he loved the rain, loved the patter of it on the roof of his car or its lash against the windows, loved its transforming power to change his perception. It was the Irish in him. Rain often made him feel like a monk in a windblown abbey in Connemara. But not this rain. Not this time. It felt to Bryn now like a harbinger of trouble, even danger. Without looking over his shoulder, Bryn sensed Terry standing in the door of his office.

"My sister Nora will be in town next week. She's coming to hear Ian Landers' lecture. I think I mentioned that she and Ian are colleagues at Johns Hopkins. Actually, they're much more than colleagues. I'd like to treat them to dinner after his talk. Would you make reservations for next Thursday at 9:15 at the Blue Point Grille?"

"For three then?"

Martin hesitated. "Yes, for three." He had considered seeing if Terry and Hugh might join them, but then had thought it better to leave that situation alone.

"Will do." Reeves turned to leave. "By the way, I'm afraid I'm having no luck finding out who informed Father Dunmore of our visit to the Ellsmeres. That still bothers me."

Martin raised his eyebrows in a gesture that said, *I understand.*

"Tell Trace I'd like to see him, if you would, Terry."

Dunmore hadn't yet taken a seat when Martin said, "How well do you know Fergus Mann?"

"Not that well, really," Dunmore demurred. "He's always at Sunday Mass at the cathedral, usually the early Mass. He likes to talk a bit afterwards either in the cathedral or downstairs where there is coffee and pastries. I knew he was a retired police officer and thought that he would make a safe companion for your tours."

Martin suspected it was Dunmore who initiated these chats after Mass.

"And I thought, being retired, he has time on his hands. He likes to be helpful, likes to volunteer. The St. Vincent de Paul Society in particular." Dunmore paused before going on. "By this time you know firsthand what a traditionalist he is. He'd love to have the Mass back in Latin and thinks Vatican II is the cause of everything wrong with the church, from the drop in Mass attendance to the leaks in the roof."

And so do you, Father, Martin thought.

Dunmore studied Martin's face. "Is there some problem?" He didn't wait for an answer. "Is he still driving you around the city?"

"I think we've pretty much completed my grand tour of the city. Fergus has been quite generous with his time." Dunmore looked relieved. "Have the comptroller draw up a check for three hundred dollars I can put in a thank you note to him. Charge it to the bishop's discretionary fund," he said, answering Dunmore's unposed question.

As Dunmore left his office Bryn went back to the window. It was still pouring. He felt anything but its usual blessing of warmth and intimacy. Quite the opposite—he felt chilled and troubled, and quite alone.

28

The Archbishop of Perugia felt like a weary warrior. The battle to save the One, True, Holy, Roman Catholic Church from forces both within and without was never ending. It could be no other way. A cease fire would be a shameful, sinful compromise with the demonic forces of liberalism and secularism. Since his years in Rome when he had quietly yet efficiently directed the now self-suppressed Brotherhood of the Sacred Purple, Montaldo had mastered the skills and strategies of clerical power. These he would employ without hesitation, even ruthlessly when necessary, to fulfill his sacred mission. Yes, he had come to believe, humbly but firmly, that God had chosen him to protect the supreme center, the absolute authority and sovereignty of the papacy. Now, as Supreme Sentinel, he would continue to direct a network of holy soldiers, his Sentinels of the Supreme Center. With comrades like the aging-but-wealthy Cardinals Oradini and Vannucci, the orthodox bishops of Italy, Spain, and Germany, and the countless lay allies supporting their mission, he would carry on. Montaldo sipped from the cup of coffee on the table before him. His thoughts turned to the States and to Simon Ashley and Father Trace Dunmore. For the present, he had to trust them. But in his heart, more than any of these learned men, he trusted without a sliver of doubt his personal assistant and the Sentinel's chief operative, Giorgio Grotti. The archbishop understood perfectly that his gossamer-like network would always be vulnerable, especially in its weakest members.

And Simon Ashley's American recruit, this retired policeman, Fergus Mann, might well be the weak link that threatened the chain's strength. Pietro was tempted to smile, but his cunning willfulness overrode that impulse. In spite of himself, Montaldo couldn't help imagining this retired policeman as an American Lone Ranger, riding down and punishing the enemies of the church.

The Archbishop of Perugia, as chief Sentinel, considered himself ordained by God to save his Holy Church. God's holy angels—Michael, Raphael, and Gabriel—had his back. *Be firm, be strong,* he whispered. And with that thought, there it was, front and center, the dream that fueled his beleaguered spirit, that one day soon he would be rewarded with a cardinal's red biretta. And beyond that, who knew?

Montaldo picked at his breakfast of eggs, a link of pork sausage, and black olives. His appetite had been dampened by a new threat to the integrity of the church—actually an age-old threat that was gathering new force, spreading like a silent virus into the unsuspecting souls of the Catholic faithful. The archbishop sat alone in the elegant dining room of his episcopal palace. Directly in his line of sight as he sat at the head of his fourteen-foot, hand-crafted Bavarian table hung a striking panel painting titled *Crucifix* by Bartolomeo Caporali, created here in Perugia in the fifteenth century. Until recently, it had hung over the main altar of the island church of San Michele Arcangelo, in the middle of Umbria's Lake Trasimeno. The pastor of San Michele, Montaldo wanted to believe, would eventually get over his resentment at the loss of Caporali's masterful painting. With the anticipated addition of the *Caporali Missal*, still in the Cleveland museum, his collection of works by Perugia's masters would be the envy of his episcopal peers. Montaldo gazed at the painting, imploring the crucified Christ for strength and wisdom. In the moment of his prayer, the archbishop confessed to God his two sins of lust—his lust for ecclesiastical power, and his lust for the transcendent, soul-lifting pleasure of great religious art. *Forgive me, Most Holy One. All this passion is for your glory alone.*

The threat the Sentinels had to counter with urgency and skill was a growing movement both within and beyond the church toward the vacuous, self-deceiving indulgence known as "contemplative spirituality." Orthodoxy firmly established that experience of the divine has to be channeled through the church's sacraments, not through subjective, pseudo-mystical experience. Pietro's stomach tightened. Modernity's great sin, he had long held, was its ineluctable turning to human experience, honoring it ahead of essence, the sole repository of authentic truth. Hadn't the church, in her wisdom down through the centuries, been wary of contemplatives and mystics? And of their dangerous concept of spiritual freedom? In their pride, these "seekers," as they called themselves, downplayed the importance of sacred dogma and the magisterium, the teaching office of the church. Worse still, many of the movement's leaders were priests and nuns—even bishops. The movement embraced Buddhists, Jews, Muslims, Hindus, Unitarians—even non-believers.

The archbishop rang the small bell next to his water glass. A middle-aged nun entered the dining room with fresh coffee. Neither the archbishop nor the nun spoke. Montaldo's mind was racing. His genius was to see before any of his fellow bishops the specific dangers inherent in movements like contemplative spirituality. It reeked of relativism, claiming there was a common spiritual path to the divine. Perhaps, worse, it promised a kind of spiritual communion, based on a pernicious insistence on the fundamental oneness of creation. His thoughts darkened. This turn to contemplative spirituality had the power to undermine the very mission of the church, not to mention its sacred power to channel God's grace through its sacramental ministry to the faithful. This movement must be stopped, would be stopped.

A knock on the dining room door broke Montaldo's thoughts. "Come."

Giorgio Grotti entered and walked to the side of the table, where he remained standing. "Excellency, I've just now received a call from the secretary of Cardinal Oradini. His Eminence and Cardinal Vannucci would like to visit late this afternoon and stay for dinner. I have been told that each will deliver his *busta*."

Montaldo paused. In addition to hand delivering their offering of twenty-five thousand euros, they must have something else on their minds. He felt off kilter and was aware that Grotti was watching him. "Very well," he said evenly, "inform Sister Assumpta two guests will be joining me for dinner this evening. And Giorgio, have a silver tray available for their Eminences' envelopes, their *bustas*." Yes, a little ritual, a touch of *Romanita*, would be appropriate.

29

Cardinals Alessandro Oradini and Andrea Vannucci arrived at Perugia's episcopal palace shortly after 6:00 in the evening. Giorgio, dressed in formal evening attire, opened the massive main door and bowed slightly. "Good evening, Your Eminences. His Excellency is waiting for you in his study."

They followed Giorgio down a marble hallway lined with paintings by some of Italy's most renowned artists. Oradini slowed as he passed works by the Florentine masters Giotto and Botticelli and raised his eyebrows—a nod to his host's sense of place—as he recognized a rare panel painting by the Umbrian painter, Perugino.

The archbishop was standing by the fire trying to hide his concern over this unusual visit by two princes of the church who were, on the surface, simply delivering necessary financial support for the important, though hidden, work of the Sentinels. Why, he wondered, had they not simply dispatched a trusted servant, as was customary? Montaldo moved a bit too quickly to his guests, greeting them with the clergy's ritual *embrazio* and brushed kisses to their now slightly stubby cheeks. Giorgio remained at the door, his white-gloved hands holding a silver tray. As soon as the cardinals placed their envelopes on it he withdrew, closing the door behind him.

"Please, sit." Montaldo said, gesturing to brocaded chairs near the fire. "A glass of brandy, perhaps?"

"Thank you, Pietro, but I think it best we move to your dining room for our meal. We are faced with a long drive back to Rome, and at our age, well, we hope you understand."

Montaldo, forcing a false smile, moved to an inlaid oak writing table that cradled a large illuminated bible. "Of course, Alessandro." He then pressed a small button on the side of the table. Within seconds Giorgio stood at the door of the study. "Please inform Sister Assumpta that we wish to dine as soon as possible."

After the final dinner plate was removed and espressos poured, Oradini and Vannucci, without explanation, stood abruptly. "Please join us, Pietro." With their espressos in hand, the two cardinals led Montaldo to the far end of the candle-lit dining table. They stood now on each side of Montaldo beneath Caporali's *Crucifix*.

Montaldo pressed the palms of his hands against the skirt of his crimson cassock.

Oradini whispered, "It's quite extraordinary, don't you think?"

Sensing what was coming, Montaldo remained silent.

"Of course, Andrea and I have no need to speak to you of its beauty, of its power to inflame our hearts with love for our suffering Savior."

Montaldo's anxiety abruptly hardened—transformed by some spiritual alchemy—into the ice of anger. *So this is why my friends are here. I am to be humiliated for requesting funds to sustain the Sentinels' crusade.*

Vannucci turned and placed his espresso cup and saucer on an end table next to an elaborately embroidered eighteenth-century chair. Turning back to Montaldo, he placed his hand on the archbishop's left forearm and without taking his eyes from the painting, said in the cultured, measured voice of a Vatican diplomat, "You understand, Pietro, this masterpiece of Christ's crucifixion must be returned to the parish church of San Michele Arcangelo. And it must be returned *pronto.*"

Montaldo understood all too well, and strained to repress an appropriate response to the insult to his dignity and authority. He said nothing, only lifted his chin and tightened his jaw.

Breaking the heavy silence, Cardinal Oradini made explicit what Cardinal Vannucci's unctuous declaration had implied, "Until Caporali's *Crucifix* is returned, with an appropriate apology to the pastor of San Michele, you have no hope of being named to the College of Cardinals."

30

Ian Landers stood at the left edge of the stage, next to Dr. Graham Moore, chair of the religious studies department.

"Let's give the crowd another five minutes to settle in, Ian. You should be pleased. This is a wonderful turnout."

"Fine. I'll be ready when you are." Landers was pleased. Nora, looking great, was in the fifth row next to her brother, Bryn, now the twelfth Bishop of Cleveland. In a few hours he would be having a late dinner with them at the Blue Point Grille. A perfect way to unwind. The stage lights made seeing beyond the first dozen or so rows difficult. Still, he spotted Simon Ashley and Trace Dunmore a third of the way back. *Good of them to come,* he thought. Spread throughout the auditorium, Landers recognized a number of Catholic nuns and faculty he had met over the past months from the religious studies and history departments at Case, John Carroll, and Ursuline College. Earlier Bryn had warned him not to expect any faculty or students from the diocesan seminaries. He was right, as far as Ian could tell.

Fifteen minutes earlier, as he had walked into the hall, a reporter from the *Plain Dealer* named Christina Tomasso introduced herself and asked for a copy of his text. She sat now in the first row with Ian's twenty-page text on her lap under her reporter's notebook. Ian had heard that a stringer from the *National Catholic Reporter* would also be covering his talk. That bit of news had surprised him. And sitting just a few seats down from Tomasso was his audit student, Rachelle Pageotte. But no Nick.

Dr. Moore moved to the lectern on the stage of the Strosacker Auditorium. He was pleased and a bit surprised at the large turnout for Landers' lecture. He estimated there were at least three hundred in the hall—a good mix of students, faculty, and clergy. Most of the audience, however, appeared to be non-academics—gray-haired Catholic laity Moore assumed were hoping to rid themselves of what he thought of, perhaps unkindly, as "Catholic guilt." His introduction was warm and sincere: a welcome to all, and specifically to the new Bishop of Cleveland, Bryn Martin, and his sister, Dr. Nora Martin, an associate professor of psychology at Johns Hopkins; a brief information point about the Hallinan Chair of Catholic Studies; Landers' credentials, with emphasis on his doctorate in medieval history from Oxford University and his appointment after several impressive publications to the history department of Johns Hopkins University.

That brought Graham Moore to the title of the evening's lecture. "I should mention," he said smiling, "that Dr. Landers' lecture is closely linked to the course he is teaching this semester here at Case-Western Reserve. The course title is 'Sin in the Medieval Church.' And I'm hearing rave reviews from his students. There isn't an open seat in his classroom. On his syllabus, however, he has added a subtitle: 'The Fear of Hell Fire in Medieval Christendom.' So, I dare to say, with a nod to Saint Augustine, fellow saints and sinners, join me in giving a warm welcome to Professor Ian Landers, whose lecture this evening is titled 'Under Pain of Mortal Sin.'"

Precisely forty minutes later, Ian Landers moved to his conclusion. "Let me begin this final section of my talk with a personal note, and then I'll offer a brief summary of my remarks. After that, your questions and comments are welcome.

"Dr. Moore," Landers gave his chairman a nod, "as a Presbyterian minister you might be surprised to know that when I was a teenager in Leeds, England, I secretly wished I were a Protestant. In my Catholic world then, the ultimate goal was getting to heaven after leading a faithful, moral life here on earth. It looked to me like there was a kind of mathematical formula that went something like this: Moral Rectitude + Believing the Creed and the Church's Teachings = Salvation. It was the moral living part that caused me considerable anguish. The big goal, to my adolescent mind, was to not die in mortal sin, for that meant eternal separation from God. Die in the state of mortal sin, and…hello hell!" Landers saw the older people in the hall smile in recognition.

"As I mentioned earlier, the Catholic Church has held for centuries that willful sexual desires or behaviors outside of marriage are all mortal sins. No misdemeanors here. This was a hard teaching for my teenage Catholic mates and me to swallow. Now it happened that I had a crush on a girl named Sarah from the time I was ten until I left Leeds for Oxford. Sarah was a Protestant, and my Protestant friends didn't seem as troubled as I was by their church's teachings on sexual morality. So, I admit, I wished, as a young British teenager, that I were a Protestant." Landers paused. "But not for long. For I soon came to believe that leaving the Catholic Church could itself be a mortal sin. That is, a further distancing of myself from God.

"So, with that being said, let me summarize my major points. Today the Catholic Church's teaching relating to sexual morality is, in this historian's judgment, much healthier than it was in the medieval era. Our theologians and clergy are helping us lay Catholics see that human sexuality is fundamentally good—and even holy—in the committed relationship of marriage. The message today is not so much on avoiding sin, but living in right relationships—with God, others, creation, and oneself. That's what Saint Augustine meant when he said, 'Love God, and do what you will.' It's what Pope Benedict XVI meant when he told us that Christianity was not a law to be obeyed but a presence to be embraced. Healthy Christianity is about the transformation of our hearts through loving relationships, it's about letting God's Spirit expand our minds to see that ultimately all creation is holy and *all* creation is somehow one.

"Yes, the church did have a long roster of behaviors that were to be avoided 'under pain of mortal sin.' And the roster was not, as I said, as capricious or arbitrary as is sometimes thought. The intention of church authorities was to motivate Christ's followers to do what was judged at the time to be essential or at least important for the salvation of their souls.

"You remember, of course, that missing Mass on Sunday has long been considered a mortal sin. Eating a hot dog on Friday was considered a mortal sin until the Second Vatican Council. Here's one I didn't mention earlier. One Irish theologian reported that some Catholic moralists held it a mortal sin to watch animals mate, unless there was a sufficient distance—never authoritatively defined by the magisterium—separating the viewer from the rutting animals." When the laughter faded Ian added, "I'd like to believe this was a moral instruction limited to the back bogs of Ireland."

Landers paused to take a breath. "Fear. Fear of punishment. Fear of hell was, in the medieval period and to some extent in our own time, used as a means of control and as a means to motivate people to lead good and holy lives. In the medieval world, fear of damnation by a loving but just and all-knowing God was, for most clergy and laity, beyond question. As I argued in the final section of my talk, that common if not universal perception of reality and the moral life has changed. Religious leaders and educators today understand that the use of fear to motivate parishioners to do what is right and good simply doesn't work.

"It's no longer *do this* or *don't do that* 'under pain of mortal sin.' Rather, healthy religion invites us to respond to God's grace out of love for what is good and right.

"I believe that many of you here tonight have read or at least heard of the Trappist monk, Thomas Merton. He and many other spiritual masters today believe that it is fear that is at the root of war, aggression, and violence. The medieval mystics and our contemporary writers like Merton all understood that, in the end, there are two basic ways to go through life—we either are 'in love' or 'in fear.' And they urge each of us, as I urge each of you, to choose love.

"Thank you."

Graham Moore moved to the podium as sustained applause greeted the spent but grateful speaker. "Dr. Landers told me earlier this evening that he would speak for forty-five minutes. And he did...to the minute. Ian, on behalf of everyone here this evening, our sincere thanks for a stimulating, informative, and uplifting presentation...on sin. Your speech was pure pleasure. No pain whatsoever." He waited for the second round of applause to die down. "And now for your questions and comments..."

Seated alone in the back of the auditorium, dressed in his usual dark pants and black jacket, Fergus Mann stood to leave. He was quite pleased with himself. This was the first academic lecture he had ever attended, and he had hung on every word. He looked forward to discussing it with Bishop Martin. Suddenly he froze in disbelief. About ten rows ahead of him on the opposite side of the hall, chatting like old friends, still seated, were Father Dunmore and his mentor Alistair. What could this mean? He felt like he had just taken a punch to his stomach. Confident that neither Dunmore nor Alistair had seen him, Mann turned quickly away and moved as fast as he could to the lobby of the auditorium and out into the night.

31

The hostess seated the three of them at a table next to a large window with a good view of the young people bar-hopping in the St. Clair/West 7th Street section of downtown Cleveland. While they waited for their drinks, the group's conversation returned to Ian's talk.

"A hit for sure," Bryn said.

"A home run," Nora corrected amiably.

"Thanks," Ian said. "I did feel good about it. I was hoping for a hundred or so and I think Graham Moore was right, maybe three hundred turned out. And the questions were good—especially from the faculty and students." Landers sat back and took a long look at Nora and then a slightly embarrassed glance at Bryn. "It was wonderful having you both at my talk."

Bryn smiled at Nora, "It almost made me feel like I was back in Baltimore."

Returning her brother's smile, Nora asked, "What's the adjustment been like? Ian and I know it's been rather tough for you, especially with the two murders."

Bryn was quiet while their server distributed drinks.

"I never thought it would be as hard as it has been, to be honest. The murders have been the worst of it, of course, but there's something off balance at the Catholic Center. Just what's wrong, I'm not sure. I plan to make some changes in the chancery staff sooner rather than later. That should help. On the surface, it's pretty much the same culture I knew at the Catholic Center in Baltimore. But I'm picking up negative vibes both in the cathedral rectory and in the offices across the street."

Nora frowned, thinking there was something more that her brother was choosing not to share.

"It's getting late," Bryn said, picking up his menu. "Why don't we order."

Over decaf coffee and Drambuie, Nora announced the happy coincidence that Ian's talk fell just before her fall break. "I'll be staying here in Cleveland for the next nine days! I hope your schedule will be open for a few more dinners, Bryn."

"Of course. That's a promise."

"I'm still surprised by the good fortune of it all," Ian said. "This appointment as Hallinan Chair has been in the works for two years. And just after I arrive, you're named Bishop of Cleveland…and it gets better." Landers passed the conversation to Nora with a glance.

"I'm partly here on business," she said. "Business that involves you."

"This is getting interesting. What have you two been holding back from me?"

"I've been working with members of international groups promoting contemplative living. Groups like Global Peace Initiative of Women and the Contemplative Alliance. When I was in Japan last year I attended a conference in Kyoto sponsored by those groups. We're planning another international conference and we'd like to hold it here in Cleveland."

"That sounds wonderful. How can I help?"

Ian said, "I've suggested the Glidden House for the conference working sessions. But there will be a major convocation on contemplative living open to the public. Isn't that right, Nora?"

Nora nodded. "I'd love to have the open session in the atrium of the Cleveland Museum of Art. It's such a wonderful, contemplative space."

"It is," Bryn said. "I've only been to the museum once, but the atrium alone is worth a visit."

With an approving nod, Ian said, "It's only a five minute walk from my office, and I try to get over there at least once a week. I really think Cleveland would be a great location for this conference. I'm hoping Case Western Reserve might sign on as a co-sponsor."

"Cleveland's our first choice right now. We're thinking of December of next year. I've always found Advent a very contemplative time. So, I'm going to do some scouting while I'm here. Ian has promised to help."

Ian smiled. "I can be really generous with my time when it comes to Nora."

Bryn looked at his watch. It was almost 10:30 and most of the tables had been cleared. He looked at his two dinner guests with a feeling of heaviness in his heart. "Ian, I don't know your teaching schedule, but if it's possible I'd like to meet with you and Nora at my office for lunch tomorrow. It's important."

"I don't have an afternoon class on Friday," Ian said. "So I'm free by noon."

"Works for me," Nora said. "*I'm* on vacation."

Fergus Mann sat alone in the kitchen of his Fulton Road bungalow. The only light came from a naked sixty-watt bulb above the sink cluttered with three days of dishes enduring their indignity in patient silence. He was sipping Jim Beam, which seemed to calm his nerves but somehow sharpen his thinking. He found himself on full alert. His priest friend from the cathedral, his Sunday morning pastor, always so ready to talk about anything and everything, from the Indians, Browns, and Cavs, to the horrors of the Catholic Church's slide into liberalism, was a friend of Alistair. What the hell did that mean? Just a coincidence? Don't be stupid, he told himself. He had to face it. He had been played. He remembered now that Father Dunmore knew he stopped for coffee and a pastry on most Saturdays at The Coffee House at University Circle. It was clear to him now that his chance meeting with Alistair was anything but chance. *Fergus, you dumb ass, you were set up.*

The former cop took a deep breath and made a last light pour of whiskey into his glass. *Think this through,* he told himself. Dunmore was likely a Sentinel. The weight of this possibility confused him. Why didn't he, not Alistair, invite him into this select group of fighters for the church? Maybe Dunmore himself couldn't ask him to be an operative for the Sentinels because he worked so closely with the bishop. So Dunmore had passed him off to Alistair? *Yeah, maybe that was it.* He would think about it, sleep on it. One thing he knew for sure. He wouldn't let Dunmore know that he had seen him with Alistair. And if Alistair contacted him, he wouldn't let on that he knew he and Dunmore were friends. He had a card to play now, and he would play it well.

Fergus looked up at the wall clock. A little after 11:30. His joints ached, his eyes burned, but he was wide awake, on full alert. It would be a long night. He put the Jim Beam in the cupboard and his glass in the sink and was about to turn off the kitchen light when, in spite of himself, he began to wash the pile of crusty dishes and cups, glasses and cereal bowls, knives and forks. Fergus's late night decision to do his dishes—what he thought of as woman's work—somehow calmed him. As if in slow motion, he washed each dish carefully, even reverently. Then, Fergus stood awash under a sensation he had never, ever experienced before. From where it came he had no idea. He struggled to name it. Finally it came to him, as if spoken by a voice both within and without. It was...mercy. Fergus stood still at the sink for a long moment, then reached for the dish towel and brought it to his eyes.

32

Bryn Martin gave Nora a quick hug and directed her and Ian to the sitting area of his office. "Make yourselves comfortable. I'll be back in a minute."

Terry Reeves rose as Bishop Martin entered her office. "Food should be here shortly," she said. "Is there anything else I can do?"

"Thanks, Terry. Coffee for me and tea for Nora and Ian. And once we're settled in, hold any calls."

Reeves sensed that this was more than a casual lunch. Something was up. In less than five minutes, she predicted to herself, Trace Dunmore would be standing at her door wanting to know what was going on. She looked forward to telling him that she had no idea.

Once Terry closed the door to his office after delivering the tea and coffee, Bryn sat down and took a deep breath. "Thanks for coming."

Nora asked, "Bryn, are you okay?"

"Yes, really, I'm fine. I want to talk to you about the murders of Laura Spivak and Frances Hellerman." Bryn paused. "In fact, I *need* to talk to you about them. I can't think of any two people more likely to help me sort the whole mess out. So bear with me."

"I thought this might be about the murders," Nora said.

"I think I know who murdered them."

Nora and Ian stared at Bryn in stunned silence.

"He's someone I know personally. A regular at the cathedral. A retired policeman who attends the early Sunday Mass. And for the past few weeks he's been showing me around the city. He was recommended to me by Trace Dunmore."

"Are you serious?" Bryn heard Ian whisper.

"I was looking for someone who knew Cleveland well and had the time to show me her neighborhoods. I wanted to get a feel for the city as soon as I could. Trace Dunmore was quick to offer a suggestion, a retired cop named Fergus Mann. So, a couple times a week I've been riding around the city with him, getting an up-close look at Cleveland's neighborhoods. We've had some rather significant conversations. A few were highly personal. Heartfelt, I thought, on his part." He shook his head. "How is it that I feel like *I* am betraying *him?*"

Ian said, "Discussing your suspicions with people you trust is the responsible thing to do. You're not betraying anyone."

"I guess." Bryn sat silently for a minute before continuing. "Fergus is a very conservative, old-school Catholic who has been saddled all his life with a rigid, moralistic understanding of his faith. Being a Catholic has meant little more to him than avoiding mortal sin, obeying the church, and dying in the state of grace. And he told me sinners should be punished…and punished severely. I think that's an exact quote. He's capable, I believe, of wreaking terrible vengeance upon anyone he thinks has harmed the church."

"You're beginning to paint an interesting clinical picture." Nora's said. "When did you first start to connect the dots?"

"My first thought that something wasn't right occurred when I asked Fergus to drive me to the lodge where Laura Spivak was murdered. It's a good half an hour east of downtown. Fergus drove directly to the place where Spivak was killed, the Intergrove Lodge in North Chagrin. He knew precisely where it was located. No map, no directions, no GPS. Rather unusual for a Westsider. The Reservation is huge. And the name of the particular lodge was never mentioned in the media's coverage of the murder. And Fergus, usually a very cool customer, was visibly unnerved by our visit to the lodge. Not like him at all."

"Did he explain why he was shaken by the visit?"

"Not really, Ian. But he was upset enough that he asked if we could stop for a drink before heading back into town. Over drinks he repeated something he told me earlier…that he was a very judgmental person and that he wanted to punish people who did things that hurt the church. That's when he said, 'and I want to punish them severely.'"

"Dear God," Nora said.

"But here's when the dime dropped for me. Just a few nights ago, Fergus was driving me back to the cathedral rectory when we saw the flashing lights of a squad car parked at the curb along St. Clair Avenue. We could see that an officer had his flashlight on a man on the sidewalk, propped up against a wall—over-dosed, it turns out. A group of young men, mostly teenagers it seemed, had gathered and were shouting at the officer.

"Fergus pulled to the curb. We both sensed the officer was in some danger. Fergus took a gun from under the seat and told me to stay in the car. He got out and approached the young men and the officer. I couldn't hear much of what was said, but it wasn't friendly, that was clear.

"In spite of what Fergus had told me about staying in the car, I decided to join him. Walking up on a volatile situation, in the dark, dressed in black, seemed like a bad idea, so I opened the glove compartment hoping to find a flashlight. I found one all right, but that wasn't all I found. There was a pair of latex gloves in there—the kind doctors wear—and a length of coiled white rope wrapped in cellophane. You'll remember that Laura Spivak was strangled with the cincture she had worn celebrating Mass. I was pretty involved in the moment when I opened the glove box.

It only occurred to me later that the coiled rope I saw in Fergus's glove compartment may have been a cincture."

Nora and Ian stared at Bryn, eyes wide with alarm. There was a chill in Nora's voice. "What happened when you got out of the car? When you joined Fergus?"

"Fergus was furious with me, but I think my presence helped defuse the situation. I spoke to the young victim. I said a prayer. Before anything got out of hand, we heard sirens, and the gang disappeared into the side streets."

A soft knock on the door startled all three of them. Bryn walked to the door and opened it few inches. It was Terry Reeves.

"I've set up place mats in your conference room. There are sandwiches, pickles, coffee, tea, soft drinks, and water. Let me know if you need anything else."

"Thanks, Terry." He turned to Ian and Nora. "There's some lunch for us in my conference room, but let me first tell you where I'm going with this. Then I want to hear what you think. What I've just told you is strictly circumstantial. But I think it is pretty compelling. I'm going to talk to Fergus and see what he has to say for himself. Maybe I'm missing something."

Nora rose and hugged her brother. "I'm so worried, for you, Bryn. You've got to be careful around this guy."

Landers' thoughts had turned to the dark intrigues of the Brotherhood of the Sacred Purple. When faith becomes ideology, he had learned, anything, even murder, can be justified to "safeguard the faith."

"Let's continue over some lunch." Bryn led Nora and Ian to his conference room where Reeves had arranged a nice spread. They were all strangely very hungry.

Later that afternoon Father Trace Dunmore looked up from his desk to see his Oxford classmate Ian Landers and a professional-looking woman pass his open door. The woman, he assumed, was the bishop's sister, Nora. So those were the two that Martin had been holed up with for the last two hours. Why didn't Ian stop to say hello? And what was the meeting with Martin all about? Reeves hadn't known. But Dunmore understood one thing for certain: It was about something important, even urgent. He walked down the hall to Reeves' office for a second try.

"What was that all about? It certainly seemed more than a simple visit from the bishop's sister and her significant other."

"What I know, Trace, I already told you. The bishop wanted some private time with his sister and her friend. And yes, I'm sure it was important." Reeves lowered her head to the papers on her desk, the hint of her smile suggesting, much to Dunmore's annoyance, that it was really none of his business.

Later that afternoon, Bryn stood at the window of his office as the first signs of rush hour slowed the traffic below. Over lunch, both Nora and Ian had been adamant: Don't wait until you talk to Fergus, go to the authorities with what you have now. That was certainly the prudent thing to do. Bryn moved back to his desk but before he could sit down, his cell phone chimed. It was Fergus Mann.

"Bishop, it's Fergus. I need to talk to you. I need to talk to you now. It's really important. And I can't come to your office."

"Are you okay?"

Mann didn't answer. "There's one more place I want to show you. And something I need to tell you."

Bryn hesitated for a moment, then said, "I'll be under the arch at 7:00."

33

Where are you taking me?"

"I have a favorite spot I go to think, Bishop. It's a marina, Wildwood Marina on the lake. It's a part of the Euclid Creek Reservation. Sometimes on Saturday mornings I like to drive out there to sit by the lake and...and just think. Edgewater Park on the West Side is closer to home, but this place is more private. And now that it gets dark early, hardly anyone will be there."

"I'm glad we'll be able to talk, Fergus. Ever since we visited the lodge where Laura Spivak was murdered, you really haven't been yourself."

Mann nodded, then squeezed his eyes shut as if to say, *Yeah, there's something on my mind.* But he remained silent for a few minutes before saying, "Let's wait till we get to the marina." They drove east on Lakeshore Boulevard in silence.

Except for one other car, the marina parking lot was empty. As soon as Bryn opened the passenger door, he heard the soft slapping of waves against the shoreline. It was a clear night, cool but not yet cold, and for a moment he thought he saw faint lights on the Canadian side of the lake. A tipped slice of moon hung low over the barren branches of the tree line to the east. The vacant park felt like an empty church without a roof.

Fergus headed to a picnic area nestled in a cluster of trees to the east of the parking lot, just far enough from the lighted lot to guarantee privacy. Bryn looked casually up and down the shore line, and across the lot, hoping to find occupants in the other car, but Fergus had all the privacy he needed for whatever he had in mind.

The two of them, dressed alike as usual, dark pants and similar dark jackets, sat across from each other on the wood benches of a picnic table. Fergus sat with his back to the lake. Bryn sat on the side of the table farther from the car. In the dim light he could barely read the features of Fergus's face.

"It's time for us to talk, Fergus."

"Yes it is, Bishop." Fergus rested his elbows on the table and squeezed the fingers of his right hand in the palm of his left. He stared at Bryn, his eyes watering.

"You've given me so much to think about, Bishop. I've become involved in some things that I really think you need to know about. On most Saturdays I drive to a place on the campus of Case Western Reserve. The Coffee House at University Circle. It's a big old house with a fireplace in the main room. Not one of those trendy places like Starbucks. I stopped there often when I was assigned to the Third District. It's homey. Good coffee and really great homemade pastries and I have a chance to catch up with some old buddies on the force who stop there."

Bryn strained to read Fergus's eyes in the failing light.

"One Saturday, this guy strikes up a conversation. He's dressed like a professor or somebody who worked at the museum. You could say he was very refined. He even had an English accent. But he wasn't stuffy at all. On top of that, it turns out he isn't an Anglican or whatever else the English tend to be—but a Catholic. Even better, an old-school Catholic like me. We talked about how the church was going to hell in a handbasket. No more Latin Masses, girls as altar servers, Catholics not going to Mass or confession, priests leaving to get married or to live with their boyfriends…"

"I think I get the picture."

"But what sickened us both the most was women being ordained priests by some crazy retired bishops. Unthinkable. So this guy, he told me his name was Alistair, and for the next two or three Saturdays we talked about a lot of things, but especially about the craziness that happened after Vatican II.

"Maybe about a month after we got to know each other, Alistair tells me there are some highly placed people in the church who feel just the way we do. He said they made up a small network of bishops, priests, and some lay people who would do whatever was necessary to save the church from the liberal reformers trying to destroy it. This was all very interesting to me, even exciting. A welcome relief. After all those years on the job, and now I just watch TV and hang out alone in coffee shops."

Bryn brought the zipper of his jacket up to his chin and thought of the Baltimore group of priests who, with their retired archbishop, had made up the Brotherhood of the Sacred Purple. He shivered.

"This network turns out to be very secret. They call themselves the Sentinels of the Supreme Center." He paused before going on. "Alistair is one of them. He has a direct line to the chief Sentinel, some bishop in Italy." Fergus smiled. "I knew right away 'Alistair' wasn't his real name. It was like code. Well, Alistair tells me he thinks I would make a good Sentinel. That I was right-thinking like them. This made me feel pretty good. I said to myself, 'Yeah, I do think like these guys in this secret network.' Does this sound crazy, Bishop?"

"No, Fergus. I'm afraid it doesn't sound crazy. There have been groups like these Sentinels throughout the church's history."

Bryn forced himself to keep quiet and listen. He needed to give Fergus space to let him tell his story. A story he apparently wanted badly to tell.

Mann suddenly stood up and turned his back on Bryn. "Give me a minute, Bishop." Fergus took a few steps toward the marina's ramp then stopped, peering into the water's darkness. "This isn't easy for me to talk about, Bishop. But to be honest, you've really messed with my mind. I've learned a lot from our conversations. From just being with you. What I've learned from you about God and our faith has made me look at things differently—a lot differently."

Martin found himself saying a prayer. *Be with him, Holy Spirit.*

Fergus suddenly turned back, sat down on the bench and said, "I want to go to confession." He reached into his jacket pocket and pulled out a rosary. "Holding the rosary will help. I guess you can see, I'm pretty nervous about this."

Martin nodded but remained silent.

"Bless me, Father…Bishop…for I have sinned. It's been since Lent, maybe six, seven months since my last confession. I need to tell you the circumstances of my sins, my mortal sins. I don't think I'm trying to minimize what I did. What I did, I now see as truly horrible. But you need to know there's something pretty sick going on in Rome, or maybe I should say in the Vatican.

"Here's what I want to tell you, the mortal sins I need to confess. Alistair not only asked me to be a Sentinel, he said I had the background and temperament to be an operative for the Sentinels. You know, like the Army's special ops, like a secret agent who has a license to kill. And then he goes on to say he had an assignment for me from this chief Sentinel in Italy, from this archbishop. I was to be God's avenger to those women who had attempted ordination. Alistair drummed it into me that they were heretics and the harm they were doing to the church couldn't be overstated. I was to bring God's judgment to them. I was to execute a sentence of death against them."

Martin squinted at Mann as if trying to see into his soul.

Was it possible to feel horror and compassion at the same time? Bryn found himself suddenly shivering, but not from the cold air off the lake.

"Alistair told me that bringing God's judgment to the women priests would put an end to other women preparing for ordination. And that Cleveland had maybe a half-dozen women getting ready to be ordained. The Sentinels were determined to stop this scandal, and I was to be their instrument of retribution. I was, for the good of the church, to put the fear of God in them." Mann half turned on the bench and looked out into the blackness of the lake as if he couldn't bear to meet Bryn's eyes. "I see things differently now."

Martin didn't move a muscle. For a long time, he and Mann sat as if hypnotized by the weight of Fergus's confession. Slowly, the creeping grace of truth invaded their pores and seeped deep into their bones.

Fergus, now breathing more easily, broke the silence. "The turning point for me, Bishop, came when I took your suggestion to attend Professor Landers' lecture. I got there a little late and sat in the back row. Once he got into his talk, I knew why you wanted me to go. He was kind of saying what you were saying to me at the Red Chimney. But that's not what I meant when I said I had a turning point." Mann held Bryn's eyes for a moment. "The jolt I had was seeing Alistair at the lecture. And the man he was with…was Father Dunmore."

Bryn tried to hide his shock and his mounting anger. What he had just heard was unthinkable. It complicated everything— and clarified everything. Simon Ashley was Alistair? Trace Dunmore was a Sentinel? *Holy Mother of God!*

"Dunmore set me up, Bishop! It was all an act. All the attention he paid me after Mass on Sundays was bull. Chatting me up over coffee like we were friends. Agreeing with me that the church was screwed up, that it was going down the toilet. All bull. And he wanted to know everything you and I talked about when I was driving you around the city. And I pretty much told him everything he wanted to hear."

"Did Dunmore or Alistair see you at the lecture?"

"No, they were about ten or twelve rows ahead of me and way across the auditorium. I'm sure they didn't see me. I turned tail and got the hell out of there. It really shook me up. I've decided not to tell Father Dunmore that I know he set me up with Alistair. Not until the time is right."

Another silence followed. Bryn found the air heavy with… with what? With reality. But it was also light with mercy.

"These are my mortal sins, Bishop. There's an ocean of venial sins, but you've just heard the worst sins of my life. I am really sorry for these sins and all the sins of my past life."

Bryn thought for a few moments, "I'm not trying to minimize what you did, Fergus, but you were seduced."

"Okay, but there's a big part of me that wanted to be seduced. That's how they get you. Your own weakness."

"Let's leave that to the mercy of God."

Fergus Mann reached into his back pocket for his handkerchief.

"You're a new man, Fergus. A different man by this act of confession. God's mercy is God's love. Let it sink in. I know you believe in the power of this sacrament. I know you believe God forgives you your mortal sins. My prayer, Fergus Mann, is that you will be able to forgive yourself."

Then, in the darkness of the marina, the light of truth worked its healing powers as Bishop Bryn Martin prayed the transforming prayer of absolution.

34

Trace Dunmore knew it would be futile to make another try at prying information from Terry Reeves about Ian Landers' visit to his boss. He considered that she might really not know anything, but doubted it in his bones. Her smugness betrayed her. It's time, he told himself, to go to the source itself. Trace swiveled his chair so his back was to his office door and called Landers' cell.

"Ian. It's Trace. How are you?"

"Good, but busy. It's midterm exam time here."

"Let me say again how much I liked your lecture the other night."

Landers found himself smiling. He knew very well that Dunmore didn't like it at all. For Father Dunmore, the threat of sin was the only way to keep most Catholics in line. The fear of falling "under pain of mortal sin" had, in Dunmore's way of thinking, saved the souls of countless believers.

"Listen, I saw you walk by my office yesterday with the bishop's sister. Why, for God's sake, didn't you stop and say hello?"

"I was in a hurry to get back on campus for…a faculty meeting."

Dunmore rose and started pacing. *Don't jerk me around, Ian.* "You were with the bishop for more than two hours. That's a big chunk of his day." Landers, saying nothing, refused the bait. "Well, listen, the next time you're down here stick your head in my office."

"Yes, of course, if your door is open."

"Better yet, how about a drink? Say 5:00 at Valerio's?"

"I'd like that, but I'm afraid I can't today. Things should lighten up in a few days. I'll give you a call."

Turning back to his desk, Dunmore wondered who called the two-hour-long private meeting. If it was the bishop, that made it all the more urgent for Trace to figure out what the hell was going on. He feared it had something to do with Fergus Mann. But why would Martin want to discuss Mann with his sister and Ian? It didn't make sense. Maybe Mann had told the bishop on one of their sorties into the city that Father Dunmore was interested in what they talked about. That shouldn't be a problem. Understandable enough. And Fergus was in way too deep to say anything about the Sentinels. Then a chilling thought tightened his stomach. What if he had made a huge mistake in proposing Fergus Mann to be Martin's guide? He dismissed the thought. Mother would harshly disapprove of such self-doubt. Maybe the bishop's sister or Ian had asked for the meeting. Maybe they wanted no more than to tell him they were going to be married. Upon reflection he thought that unlikely. There would have been more smiles. In fact there were no smiles as they walked past his office. Whatever the meeting was about, it was a deadly serious matter.

Dr. Nora Martin sat across from the special events director of the Cleveland Museum of Art with an open notebook on her lap. So far, so good. The museum's atrium was available for the closing event of her conference—the evening of the Second Sunday of Advent. The director had smiled when Nora mentioned the gathering's international dimension.

"Your conference on contemplative living is just the kind of event that resonates with the museum's mission," he had remarked. They went on to discuss the rental fee, food services, space for exhibitors, parking, and security issues. The conference itself, Nora explained, would be held at a nearby hotel, possibly the Glidden House, for about fifty invited participants. The climax of the meeting would be this public convocation in the atrium. Nora estimated that four to five hundred might attend the closing session, which would feature short presentations by contemplative masters from the Americas, Europe, and Asia.

"We will send you a contract at your Johns Hopkins address. Feel free to call if you have any questions, Dr. Martin."

Before leaving the museum, Nora ordered an espresso from the Provenance Café and sat for a few moments of quiet enjoyment, letting the atrium's natural light wash over her. It was the perfect venue for the final, public session to the conference. As she let her gaze scan the atrium's empty, transcendent space, Nora's thoughts turned to her brother. What if Bryn was right about Fergus Mann? Had the murderer of the two women been under his nose all along? But what left her sick with worry was the possibility that her brother was in danger. Nora hoped Bryn was right to want to talk to Mann before going to the authorities with his suspicions. *Let this go,* she told herself, *for the time being.* She picked up her briefcase and headed for her rental car in the parking garage one level down. There was plenty of time to stop at Ian's Thomlinson Hall office for a brief visit before heading back to her room at the monastery.

As Nora approached the glass doors of the main entrance to the museum, she saw a man walking toward her who looked vaguely familiar. He caught her eye.

"Pardon me, but are you Nora Martin?"

"Yes, I am."

"I'm Simon Ashley. We met after Ian's lecture at the university. Ian and I were classmates at Oxford. Balliol College."

Nora smiled. "Yes, and if I'm not mistaken, don't you teach

art history at John Carroll?"

Ashley seemed pleased that she remembered. "So good to see you, Nora. But I must hurry off to pick up a special visitor's pass at the office of the curator of medieval art. The security is really something here, but I guess it has to be." As he ran off he looked over his shoulder and said, "My best to Ian."

Late that night Ashley sent an email to the Archbishop of Perugia from a private account.

> I met with the curator of medieval art at the Cleveland Museum today. Finally, after numerous calls requesting an appointment. The good news is that he believes a loan of the *Caporali Missal* and other works created in Perugia is a distinct possibility. Have your chancellor send a follow-up letter repeating your request. Unfortunately, the curator was unable to give me a time-line relating to the loan. Now that I have made contact with him, I will do my best to keep things moving forward. Father Dunmore reports worries about our agent. I'll investigate. I have my own serious concerns about the shepherd here.
>
> S.A.

In the morning, Ashley would make arrangements to meet Fergus Mann at The Coffee House. It was time to find out what was troubling the small mind of his American operative.

35

Bryn Martin stood under the archway next to the cathedral rectory. It looked like rain, but he needed a walk. He needed to get out of the rectory that more and more seemed like an isolated fortress to him. With his collar up and his Orioles cap low on his forehead, Martin strode west on Superior Avenue, his mind numb from processing all that had come to light at the Wildwood Marina the night before. It was Baltimore all over again. The Brotherhood of the Sacred Purple emerging now as the Sentinels of the Supreme Center, self-appointed guardians of orthodoxy, justifying any means, even murder, for the good of the church. It made him sick.

As Martin passed the main branch of the Cleveland Public Library, he thought of a few words by the Jesuit theologian, Walter Burghardt, that always gave him solace. "In the course of half a century, I have seen more Catholic corruption than you have read of. I have tasted it. I have been reasonably corrupt myself." Bryn hoped his own corruption was of a different order, a different kind than what he had heard sitting across a picnic table from Fergus Mann. Burghardt knew what all great reformers knew—that the church had pockets of corruption in her mantel of holiness—*simul justus et peccator.* Are we not all simultaneously righteous and sinful? *And so am I,* Bryn reminded himself, *so am I.*

It started to drizzle as he turned onto Ontario. Street lights were on and the people he passed were as silent as monks, each bearing in disguised dignity their own goodness, their own wounds. Bryn thought of what Thomas Merton had said about the anonymous office workers he passed in downtown Louisville one day, that each was "shining like the sun!" *Yes, I guess even Ashley, even Dunmore, even the killer, his friend Fergus Mann.*

Merton's mystical insight aside, Bryn understood that he had things to do. Ann Marie Ellsmere needed to know that she wasn't in immediate danger of another attempt on her life. Trace Dunmore needed to be dismissed as chancellor and moderator of the curia—and soon. Martin wasn't sure what to do about Simon Ashley. Neither did he know what to do about the Sentinels of the Supreme Center. Perhaps there was nothing to be done about them. And Fergus Mann needed a good therapist and a wise spiritual counselor. And a good lawyer.

He made another right on Lakeside and headed back to the rectory. The drizzle had turned to a light but steady rain. *Blessed rain, wash me clean.*

As on so many other Saturday mornings, Fergus Mann sat across from Alistair at The Coffee House. But this one was different. The man seated across from him was no longer his mentor, and hardly his hero. Maybe this Sentinel so committed to saving the Catholic Church wasn't even a real Catholic. Fergus had made up his mind while driving to the meeting not to confront Alistair. Not yet at least. *See what he wants*, he told himself, *and wait for the best moment to strike.*

"I thought it was time for us to meet again, Fergus. You have been a very effective agent for us. But the assignments you've carried out can take a toll on a man—even when they're done for the best possible reasons."

"I'm doing okay, if that's what you're asking." Fergus stared into Alistair's eyes and could tell his former mentor was a bit unnerved. Strange for a man accustomed to being in control. "One thing you gotta know though, no more assignments."

"I understand," Alistair said lowering his head and giving Fergus an assuring glance over the top of his reading glasses.

"I'm finished as your special-ops man. Is that clear?"

Alistair didn't say a word, his eyes seemingly soft with sincerity and concern. *Dunmore was right to be alarmed,* he thought. Fergus was no longer reliable. Worse, he could no longer be trusted. And what he knew could do unthinkable damage to the mission of the Sentinels. Alistair didn't know what was at the core of this sudden change in the man, but determined that it didn't matter for the moment.

"Yes, of course. That's perfectly clear. All the Sentinels want from you is for you to be the Catholic, loyal to the papacy, that you are. There need be no more assignments. You have already proven yourself beyond measure."

Fergus nodded as if he understood. As if what he had told Alistair was perfectly clear and could bear no contradiction. But Mann's jaw remained set and his eyes were cold, as cold as the eyes of a killer.

Alistair's strategy was simple. Make Fergus feel needed, feel important. "So, my good man, there will be no further assignments. Still," Alistair leaned across the table, "we are worried about the bishop here. He is the kind of parasite that is destroying the church from the inside. I hope you will be willing to help us with this matter."

Fergus tightened his fists under the table and told himself to remain cool. He resented the British "my good man" crap. *You're being played,* he reminded himself. With a half-smile that he hoped would convince Alistair that he was still a Sentinel, Fergus said dryly, "I'll do what I can."

Alistair felt a slight wave of relief. "Good. I'm counting on you."

"By the way," Fergus said without expression, "do you happen to know a Father Dunmore—he's one of the cathedral priests who works in the bishop's office?"

Mann's casually put question seemed to catch Alistair off guard—but only for a split second. "Why…yes, I do know him. We were in college together." He waited for Fergus to continue. But he didn't. "Why do you ask?"

"No reason. Just thought we might have a friend in common." With that, Fergus Mann, with only a nod for goodbye, stood and left Alistair sitting alone at the table.

Ashley lingered at the table for a long time after Fergus left, pondering their conversation. Of course there was a reason for the question about Trace. He didn't like at all this apparent turn in Mann and stared blankly at the cold cup of coffee before him, trying to read Fergus's new attitude. It was true that Dunmore had established a friendly relationship with Fergus over the past months based on their common old-school Catholicism. Could the question about knowing Dunmore be innocent? He would be a fool to believe that. Dunmore was right. Fergus Mann was a changed man. And that changed everything.

Fergus turned left onto Juniper, then made another left onto Ford, pulling into the circular drive in front of the Glidden House under a sign that read "Registration Parking Only." He cut the engine and waited. Ten minutes later he watched Alistair walk with hurried steps to a car parked at the curb on Wade Oval, not far from the main entrance to the Cleveland Museum. It was time to find out who this guy really was.

36

The tension on the sixth floor of Cathedral Plaza hung like a low cloud over the suite of offices closest to the bishop's corner office on Monday morning. The chancellor's subtle inquiries about the nature of the bishop's long meeting with his sister and Ian Landers had been met with blank stares. Even the usually steady Terry Reeves appeared slightly off balance. Dunmore's hopeful explanation for the chill in the air was the anticipated changes Martin was about to make in his core staff, but his worst fear was the possibility that Fergus Mann had betrayed him. Mann's recent coolness was a clear signal that something fundamental had changed. And Mann hadn't been at Mass the day before. Very unlike him. Fergus understood that missing Mass on Sunday was a mortal sin. Maybe Simon Ashley, who had just had a Coffee House rendezvous with Fergus, would shed some light on what was going on. From Simon's recent phone message, insisting they meet at Valerio's tonight, Dunmore inferred that their whole enterprise might be going off the rails. His anxiety level had risen to the point of nausea. He would have to muddle through until connecting with Simon. Dunmore shook his head as a sardonic smile, almost a grimace, tightened his lips. All he needed right now was for Bryn Martin to call him into his office to tell him he was out as chancellor and moderator of the curia.

Terry Reeves sat a little nervously after being summoned to Bishop Martin's office. Odd, because the bishop never made her feel nervous. Something in his manner this morning told her this would be no ordinary meeting.

"This is a little awkward, Terry, and I don't want you to make any suppositions regarding what I am about to say. And I don't want you to think I don't trust you to keep anything I tell you confidential. But I have some information that ought to be conveyed to the Ellsmeres. Good news actually. Information that has been brought to my attention proves she is no longer in any danger from the man who attacked Laura Spivak and Francis Hellerman. If I could tell you more I would, but I cannot. I just want you to tell your friend that I believe she is safe, and she and Rich can put their hearts to rest."

"She is going to ask—"

"What I have learned was shared in absolute confidence. Just tell her not to worry. Please. That's all."

Terry nodded and left, a little piqued at Bishop Martin's abruptness, perhaps, but certain of one thing: Bishop Bryn Martin knew the identity of the man who murdered Laura Spivak and Frances Hellerman.

The trio from Baltimore—all veterans of the dramatic fall from grace of their home city's retired archbishop—gathered in Ian's kitchen that evening.

"Bryn, are you telling us you haven't gone to the authorities with your suspicions?" There was an unusual edge of anger in Nora's voice.

Ian, who was at the kitchen counter making coffee, turned to see how Bryn would answer his sister's pointed question.

"No, I haven't talked to the authorities. I am still struggling with what I can and cannot say about Fergus Mann. He called me yesterday and said he needed to talk to me. He drove me out to a marina on the lake he likes to visit when he's in the mood for solitude. After I tell you what I can share, I think you two will put two and two together."

Ian poured three decaf coffees, went to the refrigerator for a pint carton of half and half, served the coffee, and sat down next to Nora. Bryn sat facing them.

"Fergus, an old fashioned Baltimore Catechism Catholic, afraid of going to hell for a single mortal sin, was befriended by your classmate, Trace Dunmore."

Ian nodded. "And your esteemed chancellor and moderator of the curia."

"Fast forward a bit. Fergus Mann gets to know a man at an east side coffee house who sees the Catholic Church as he does—as being corrupted by evil forces both inside and outside the church. The man said his name was Alistair. Fergus was sure that wasn't his real name. Well, this Alistair belongs to a small, secret, international network of true believers who have a patron bishop who is highly placed in the Vatican." Bryn looked at Ian, "Sound familiar?"

"The Brotherhood of the Sacred Purple," Landers said.

"Mann told me the network calls itself the Sentinels of the Supreme Center. And their mission is to safeguard the divinely instituted sovereign authority of the papacy, *by whatever means necessary.*"

Nora said, "I think I see where this is going. The name Alistair is no coincidence. It's an anglicized form of 'Alastor,' a Greek god of vengeance." Nora went silent, then added, "It suggests the mission of the Sentinels is not just to protect, but to bring down God's vengeance on those who disobey the supreme authority."

Bryn locked eyes with Nora. "That fits perfectly with what I know. Mann told me he was invited into the Sentinels as their 'special-operations' man. And as such he was told that the Sentinels gave operatives like him a license to kill, to punish sinners who were destroying the church."

They sat in silence for a while, letting the implications of their late night talk sink in. Ian refilled their coffee cups before breaking the silence. "That perverse pattern of vengeance and murder was common enough among secret groups in the late Middle Ages. Nora and I have talked a good deal about it. From the secret society known as the *Fideli d'Amore*—the Faithful of Love—down through the centuries to the Brotherhood of the Sacred Purple. And if your friend, Fergus Mann, is right, to the Sentinels of the Supreme Center."

"By the way, Ian, it was at your lecture that Fergus discerned that Trace had set him up to meet Alistair."

"How's that?"

"Well, Fergus and I had been talking a lot about sin on our drives around the city. He was terrified of committing a mortal sin and dying outside of God's grace. He was terrified of going to hell. His God was a God of strict justice. Slowly, I think he began to see things a bit differently. It was hard for him. The final judgment of the church in matters of heaven or hell was deeply, deeply ingrained in him."

Nora added, "Couple that moralistic approach to Catholicism with his keen desire to punish wrong-doers, and you have a perfect candidate to be the enforcer for the Sentinels."

"I was thinking along those lines myself even before my last conversation with Fergus," Bryn said. "Well, to get back to your talk, Ian, I suggested to Fergus that he would find your lecture interesting. Your title, 'Under Pain of Mortal Sin,' caught his interest. I encouraged him to attend. And to my surprise, he did."

"Did you spot him in the audience?" Nora asked.

"No, no I didn't. He said he came in just after the introduction and sat in the back of the auditorium. But at the end of the lecture, as people were standing to leave, Fergus spotted his buddy, Father Trace Dunmore, sitting next to Alistair. It was apparent that the two had come to the talk together. That changed everything for Fergus. He was furious, feeling stupid and played. I think he is waiting for the right time to confront Dunmore. And his 'Alistair' as well. And by this time, I'm fairly certain he knows his 'Alistair' is Simon Ashley."

"My God, Bryn!" Ian said shaking his head. "Dunmore and Ashley, members of the Sentinels of the Supreme Center? I had dinner with them a few weeks ago!"

Nora put her arm around Ian's shoulder and, after a minute, raised her head and looked into Bryn's eyes. "Did Fergus admit he murdered the two women priests?"

Bryn let the question hang. The reason for his silence seemed to dawn on Nora and Ian simultaneously: Bryn could neither answer Nora's question nor go to the authorities. Fergus Mann had gone to confession!

Bryn wanted to weep at their understanding, and their love.

37

After an early dinner at Pizzazz, Nora and Ian took a break from the tension that had embraced them to enjoy an evening of Mozart and Tchaikovsky at Severance Hall. During the intermission, Nora stood by herself in the marbled main lobby while Ian queued up for two glasses of chardonnay. The crowd of couples and small islands of acquaintances moved slowly, as if dancing in place to the various rhythms of refined conversation. An evening at the orchestra was just what Nora needed. She let her eye rise to the balcony level that led to the private loges. She caught her breath. Standing at the rail in quiet splendor looking down at the milling patrons below were Simon Ashley and a handsome priest in a dark gray suit. The priest, wearing a formal collar, not a plastic tab tucked into the neck band of a clerical shirt, looked familiar.

Nora felt Ian's presence at her side. She accepted a paper cocktail napkin and a clear plastic cup of white wine.

"Guess who's here?" she said. "Simon Ashley." Ian followed her eyes to the balcony. "Do you want to duck back inside?"

"Oh, no. Let's stroll upstairs and say hello."

"This should be interesting," Nora said under her breath as they climbed the curved, carpeted steps.

Simon and Trace turned as they approached. Had Simon spotted her?

Ian spoke first. "What a nice surprise."

With a practiced smile, Simon responded, "Yes, isn't it?"

"Nora," Ian said, "this is Father Trace Dunmore, Bryn's chancellor. I don't think I had an opportunity to introduce you to him after my lecture. But I do remember introducing you to Simon. And Trace, this is Nora Martin, Bishop Martin's sister."

Trace gave Nora a brief smile. "Of course. I'm happy to meet you, Dr. Martin."

Dunmore seemed to expect Nora to extend her hand. She didn't.

There was a very slight pause before Ian said, "Nora is a professor of psychology at Johns Hopkins. This week is their fall break."

Leaning into Ian's shoulder, Nora said, "Ian tells me the three of you are Oxford classmates. And here you all are in Cleveland."

"Yes," Dunmore said flatly, "Simon and I were happy to hear that Ian was the Hallinan Professor for the year." Before he could go on, a chime signaled it was time to return to their seats.

"Why don't you two join us for a drink after the program? At Valerio's."

Ian glanced quickly at Nora. "That might be nice. We'll see. It's been a long day."

Ian had parked in the faculty spaces behind Tomlinson Hall, sparing them the long wait getting out of Severance Hall's underground garage. The Mozart/Tchaikovsky program already a blur, they drove up the Cedar Road hill in silence.

Nora finally spoke, "They know that we suspect them."

"Yes, but they don't know precisely what we know. That could be dangerous for Bryn, Fergus Mann, and God knows who else. I'm half-thinking of joining them at Valerio's after I drop you off."

Nora said with a smile, "That might be interesting."

After a bit of reflection, Ian said, "I think I'll let events play out a bit longer before I meet up with my two classmates."

Nora didn't say it, but she felt for the first time that what was unfolding could be dangerous not only for Bryn and Fergus Mann. It could also prove dangerous for Ian.

Ashley and Dunmore sat at a table in the empty dining area of Valerio's. The only action in the small restaurant was at the bar. They had chosen a table for two reasons: Dunmore was in his clerical collar, and they wanted privacy.

"This, my dear Trace, could be a disaster. If we lose control of Fergus Mann, our entire mission is in jeopardy."

"My dear Simon," Trace said testily, "I believe we have already lost control of our man. He's always been eager to chat me up after Mass. But not recently. He's rebuffed my polite questions about what he and the bishop talk about when driving about the city. Fergus has been close to rude with me. That's very unlike him." Dunmore sipped his fifteen-year-old single malt. "He's been turned, Simon, and there is no doubt in my mind that Bryn Martin turned him."

"I'm afraid I agree with you. At our last meeting Mann was adamant about not accepting any more assignments. And he was abrupt. I could see a cold anger in his eyes. But not at those fools who attempted ordination. He was angry with me."

The two Sentinels of the Supreme Center looked into their glasses, calculating the implications of the sudden change in their operative.

Ashley broke the pause in their conversation. "Last Saturday when I met with Fergus he asked if I happened to know a Father Dunmore. It was more than idle curiosity."

Dunmore shivered as if taking a sudden chill.

Ashley continued his analysis, "Fergus has connected us somehow."

Dunmore said, sounding thoughtful, "My name may have come up often in his drives around the city with Martin. It would have been a natural point of conversation for Martin to mention that Landers went to college with me—that we go way back. But that hardly explains how our rather thick-headed Fergus Mann put the two of us together."

Ashley was impatient to get to the deeper issue. "For the time being, we need to put that question aside—sooner or later we'll get the answer. Right now we have to assume that Fergus Mann has told our dear bishop about the Sentinels."

Dunmore's handsome face appeared drawn. Worse, his customary confidence seemed to have deserted him. "What if Mann told Martin that he killed those women? And did it at your direction?"

"Rather unlikely, don't you think? The man's not really stupid enough to incriminate himself."

"Unless he made Martin his confessor..."

Ashley stared into Dunmore's frightened eyes. The two Oxford grads sat frozen in place, as if caught by a wave of mutual terror as the consequences of this possibility sank in.

The bartender's raised voice startled them from their revery. "Last call, gentlemen."

38

Archbishop Pietro Montaldo pushed his high-back leather chair away from the working desk in his private study. He looked again at the screen of his personal computer. What he saw disturbed him. Things were getting out of hand at his base in the United States. He read for the third time an email from Simon Ashley, his Sentinel in charge of operations in North America. He smiled briefly. Ashley was a master at saying what needed to be said without saying anything that would put the Sentinels of the Supreme Center at risk of discovery. It was easy to read between the lines of Ashley's email. Their operative, a retired policeman, had been turned. Not to be concerned, Ashley had advised. After carrying out two deadly assignments, he had his own secrets to keep. The American operative was hardly a threat to the mission of the Sentinels. But it was probable that the newly appointed Bishop of Cleveland, Peter Bryn Martin, was aware of the presence of the Sentinels in his diocese and suspected their role in confronting the heretical action of the attempted ordination of women.

Ashley's message had made it clear that the real threat to the Sentinels was not this retired policeman, but the recently appointed Bishop of Cleveland. Tomorrow, the Archbishop of Perugia would take the necessary action—for the good of the church.

Giorgio Grotti walked swiftly to Archbishop Montaldo's private study. His Excellency's summons this early in the morning was a sure signal that the archbishop had something important on his mind. Giorgio rapped twice on the closed door and entered without waiting for a response. Montaldo pointed to the chair across from his desk.

"Good morning, Excellency."

"Good morning, Giorgio. I hope you slept well."

"Yes, very well." The casual personal question put him on full alert. The archbishop, he had learned early on in his service, feigned a certain thoughtfulness and concern when he was about to order the taking of another man's life.

"I am sending you, dear Giorgio, on another mission to the United States. Not to Baltimore, of course, but to Cleveland. You will travel as my personal representative to the officials of the Cleveland Museum of Art. As you know, I have requested a loan of the *Caporali Missal* and other Perugian artifacts in the museum's collection. Alas, the museum moves even more slowly than our holy church. You will coordinate your efforts to expedite the loan with Professor Simon Ashley, a trusted colleague of mine. Ashley is on the faculty of John Carroll University. The university is in University Heights, a suburb of Cleveland. I will have his contact information ready for you this afternoon. I have instructed Professor Ashley to pick you up upon your arrival in Cleveland. You will travel under your own name using your Vatican passport. But of course, carry with you your Italian passport and one other passport for your lodging."

Giorgio's pulse leapt. At last another assignment worthy of the training, experience, and skills he had honed in the elite guard of the Carabinieri. He understood immediately that his role in expediting the loan of the *Caporali Missal* was a cover for something more pressing. Grotti's face was expressionless. He remained silent and alert, waiting for Montaldo to go on.

Montaldo paused and fingered the pectoral cross on his chest just above the sash girding the jelly-soft flesh of his stomach. When he spoke next his voice was soft and solemn. "While you are in Cleveland, you will have an additional assignment, a most delicate and dangerous one."

Giorgio Grotti locked eyes with Montaldo, a sly smile on his lips.

"I trust you remember Bishop Bryn Martin," the archbishop said. "He was the auxiliary bishop in Baltimore when we had to deal with the tragic matter of Archbishop Gunnison's fall from grace."

"I do, Excellency."

"Bishop Martin was recently appointed Bishop of Cleveland." Montaldo's face turned solemn, even pained. "He is proving, I'm afraid, to be a very lax and a very secular bishop, a dangerous wolf dressed in shepherd's robes." Montaldo paused and rose slowly from his desk and turned his back on Grotti. He stood motionless for a good ten seconds as if in prayer. Then he turned, dramatically he thought, and faced his trusted assassin. "For the good of the church, for the good of our sacred mission to preserve the church in her purity and integrity, Bishop Martin must not be allowed to continue his treachery."

Grotti abruptly stood and approached Montaldo. "I am ready and willing," he said, his words soft but firm. Then, just feet from the archbishop, he fell to his knees. "Your blessing, Excellency."

39

Terry Reeves studied the strained face of her boss. She thought he needed a vacation. While still alert and personable as ever, he was definitely preoccupied. How could he not be?

"Hugh and I met with the Ellsmeres last night, Bishop. I'm not sure they feel much better after receiving our assurances that she is safe." Bryn Martin nodded that he understood. "Before we left, Ann Marie and Rich both said they trust you. They want to believe you, but there are so many unanswered questions."

Martin leaned back in his desk chair. "And I suspect, Terry, that you, the Ellsmeres, and Hugh think that I have some of the answers to those questions."

Terry's face remained respectful, but her squinted eyes said softly, *yes*.

Martin leaned forward, his elbows on his desk now. "It would help me, Terry, if you, Hugh, and the Ellsmeres would understand I'm not playing some kind of game with you. I know it might seem like that, but it isn't at all."

"No, Bishop, we don't think that. It's just very hard..." An awkward silence followed until Terry smoothly relieved the tension. "I've made reservations for you to fly to Baltimore on Thanksgiving Day. You leave on Southwest at 1:20, arriving in Baltimore at 2:40. Ian Landers is on the same flight."

Martin said, "That should work. I have the 10:00 Mass here at the cathedral. It might be a little tight, but I should be able to make it to the airport in time."

"You and Ian will return the following Monday on an early afternoon flight. I guess this will be your first visit home since you came to Cleveland."

Martin flashed a weak smile, "Don't repeat this, Terry, but I do need to get away, even if just for a long weekend. What else do you have for me?"

Reeves reached across the desk and handed Martin a manila folder. "Here's the tentative agenda for your core staff meeting tomorrow. Next year's budget for the chancery and diocesan offices is the big item, really the only item you have. I'm sure Father Dunmore will raise some issues. He always does."

This might be as good a time as ever, Martin thought. He stood and pointed Terry to the chairs around the coffee table in the carpeted corner of his office. Reeves followed, bracing herself for what was to follow.

"Last evening, Terry, after a rather tedious dinner at the cathedral rectory, I had a frank, private conversation with Father Dunmore. He will no longer be serving as chancellor and moderator of the curia."

Terry sat upright. The news wasn't surprising. The chancery staff knew changes were coming, but the abruptness of the decision caught her by surprise. Along with Dunmore and most of the staff, she thought the changes would not be announced until after the holidays. She simply nodded and, after taking a deep breath, asked, "When will the change take effect?"

Martin said deliberately, "It's already taken effect. Trace will be moving out of his office tonight."

Reeves was still at the edge of her seat, absorbing the news of a summary firing of the bishop's right-hand man. Her stomach knotted and she was suddenly cold. She averted her eyes from Martin's and waited for him to go on.

"I'll send a personal email to the staff announcing Trace's departure this afternoon. And I'll work up a statement for the Diocesan Memorandum. I think it better if I do this myself, Terry."

Reeves nodded gratefully. Her boss, she had learned early on, was good at this kind of thing. He would say what needed to be said directly, but as kindly as possible. Then the bishop's two-hour meeting with his sister and Ian Landers sprang to mind. There must be a connection. She was sure of it. Terry tried to stay focused, but her mind was racing—the murdered women, Ann Marie, Fergus Mann, Dunmore's sneaky pursuit of office gossip. "I can't really say I am sorry. I believe you know very well, Bishop, that working with Father Dunmore hasn't been easy."

Bryn gave her the briefest of nods. Terry finally sat back in her chair. So, the days and weeks ahead would be charged with the muted excitement that accompanies a major change. Her colleagues would be doing their best to find out what was behind Dunmore's firing, wondering who would be next, tabulating the winners and losers.

Bryn held her gaze for a minute. "There's something I'd like you to think about, Terry."

His comment put her back on the edge of her chair.

"I would like to appoint you chancellor. I'd also appoint you moderator of the curia if that position didn't have to be filled by a priest."

Reeves felt herself blushing. She was still cold but somehow she could feel heat rising up through her neck to her cheeks. She didn't quite know what to do with her hands. More than a dozen U.S. bishops had named lay men and women as their chancellors. And there were another dozen or so chancellors who were deacons or vowed religious. Still, Terry was surprised—even shocked—at the invitation to become the chancellor of the Diocese of Cleveland, akin to being the bishop's chief of staff and overseer of documents, records, and diocesan archives. Reeves' mind raced. She sat back again feeling the weight of her silence.

Then she spoke quietly and confidently. "You've really caught me off guard, Bishop, but I don't have to think about it. I'd be honored to serve as your chancellor."

Her boss exhaled through closed lips, his cheeks coloring slightly.

"Good," he said, smiling. "I'll make the announcement of your appointment in a few weeks. Let's hope the dust will have settled by then."

Reeves stood and asked, "Will that be all, Bishop?"

"Isn't that enough?" he laughed, and she joined him.

40

I knew it was coming, Simon. But not like this."

Father Trace Dunmore sat uncomfortably in the visitor's chair in Simon Ashley's office in the Dolan Center of John Carroll University. "Martin came to my room after dinner. He didn't even sit down. 'I'm making a change,' he said. 'You're no longer chancellor or moderator of the curia.' Just like that. I asked him when this change was to take effect. 'As we speak,' he responded. It was bloody awful! So...I'm out."

Ashley had little patience for the hurt feelings of Trace Dunmore. "What made Martin fire you now and with such, shall we say...abruptness? Did he offer any explanation?"

"There was no explanation. Once he announced his decision our conversation lasted less than five minutes. I was told to vacate my office immediately and to move out of the cathedral rectory as soon as possible. I'm on a three month leave of absence."

"There was no mention of Fergus Mann?"

"None."

"But we both know that it was Mann who turned Martin against you."

Dunmore said wryly, "I was so sure that Mann would prove a good source of information on where our new bishop stood on the supreme office of the papacy, on orthodoxy, on renewal. For a time, he was. You've been able to pass on to Archbishop Montaldo a meaty file on Bishop Bryn Martin's scandalous presence at the funeral of a woman priest, and his heretical views of sin, hell, and salvation. But that dumb cop has betrayed me."

Ashley was annoyed at Dunmore's self-absorption. "He has betrayed *us*," Simon corrected. "And he has put the Sentinels of the Supreme Center in grave danger."

Dunmore gritted his teeth. As he often did when faced with a challenge, he thought of his mother. Elizabeth Dunmore was the source of his confidence, his intelligence. "Never doubt yourself," she had always said, without a hint of affection. "Never doubt your breeding, your destiny for greatness." But Ashley was right. The concern now had to be the mission of the Sentinels. He would wait for the right moment to square things with Bishop Bryn Martin.

"Yes," Dunmore said with color rushing to his cheeks, "Fergus Mann has betrayed *us*."

Ashley rolled his chair back from his small desk. "We can take care of Mann later if we must, but right now we should turn our attention to Bryn Martin. What might Fergus have told him about the Sentinels? And how did Mann connect the two of us?" Ashley sat thoughtfully for a moment. "I've told Archbishop Montaldo that we must assume Martin knows it was the Sentinels who wrought God's judgment against the women priests."

"Martin knows far too much about us," Dunmore offered lamely. "But he never even alluded to Mann or the Sentinels when he fired me. I think we can infer from that that he isn't quite sure of what he knows, or what to do with what he thinks he knows. That ought to give us some time."

Ashley nodded his agreement. Then turned Dunmore's blood cold by turning back to Fergus Mann: "We must tread carefully, Trace. What if our avenging assassin turns his sights on us?"

Fergus Mann had followed Dunmore's gray Passat from the cathedral garage to the John Carroll campus. He had figured out just where Dunmore was going when they got to within a few blocks of Ashley's apartment, just a short walk from his art history department office. He ducked into Sweet Melissa's for a cup of coffee to go, parked where he had a good view of the Passat, and sat with a cop's patience, waiting for Dunmore to return to his car. He took an occasional sip of coffee, and every quarter hour rolled his head, his neck slightly stiff from sitting too long in one position. Then, compulsively, Fergus reached below the seat to make sure his Glock 43 was still there. This was but stage one of the plan he would put in play. Learn the comings and goings of Trace Dunmore and Simon Ashley, aka, Alistair. He was stalking his prey, just as he had before assaulting the women priests.

The only thing that could distract him from his inner anguish, from the terrifying darkness that clouded his soul, was his steely will to get even with Alistair—to Fergus he would always remain "Alistair"—and Dunmore. He said a silent prayer that Laura Spivak and Frances Hellerman would forgive him. And he prayed the Ellsmere woman would forgive his thwarted attempt on her life. He had confessed his mortal sins to Bishop Martin. He prayed that he would discern an appropriate penance for his sins. He clung to his faith that God had forgiven him. He trusted in God's mercy, he believed with his whole heart that God had forgiven him. But he was afraid that he couldn't forgive himself, not now...not ever.

41

Fergus Mann sat in the cab of a non-descript pickup truck in the BP gas station lot across from the Corinthian Apartments. The night before, right after his supper in his Fulton Road house, he had walked across the street to the Catholic Worker house and asked if he could borrow their truck for a few days. They agreed and he had left the keys to his Focus. If he was still following Alistair when he had to return the truck, he would borrow a neighbor's car. Both Alistair and Dunmore knew his Focus. He would be difficult to spot in an unfamiliar vehicle.

The previous day he had watched as Dunmore pulled into the circular drive in front of the Corinthian and removed two large suitcases from his trunk. It looked like he would be staying with Alistair. Fergus wondered if Bishop Martin had kicked Dunmore out of the cathedral rectory. He knew for sure he wouldn't want to live under the same roof with the guy. Fighting his own guilt, Mann felt more and more like a shell of the man he once was. Tailing Alistair didn't help—too much time alone, too much time sitting and waiting. On the other hand, getting ready to play his hole card gave him just enough energy to keep at it.

Suddenly alert, Fergus turned the ignition key. Alistair was pulling out of his underground parking garage in his dark blue Volvo. He turned right onto Warrensville, heading south. Mann stayed about fifty yards back. Alistair was alone. That meant Dunmore was alone in the apartment. Fergus thought of turning around and heading back to the Corinthian. He wanted to see the look on Dunmore's face when he confronted the bastard. *Stay with Alistair,* he told himself. Once they passed Chagrin Boulevard, Fergus reasoned they might be heading toward I-480. He was right. Alistair pulled onto the entrance and headed west. Fifteen minutes later Fergus followed Alistair into the Cleveland Hopkins International Airport where he pulled to the curb in front of the United Airlines baggage area. Mann pulled in about five car lengths back and cut the engine. As soon as he did, a police officer walked purposefully toward him.

"Sir, you can't park—Fergus, is that you?"

Mann reached his hand out the window. "It is, you old snake. How are you?"

"Good." The officer flashed Mann a snarky smile, "Patiently waiting for the day I can retire like you, you old bastard."

"Listen, let me sit here for a while. And see that Volvo up there? Can you let him alone too? I gotta see who he's picking up."

The cop nodded warily. "You know you're supposed to have a license for this, Fergus."

"I left it in my other suit."

Fergus slipped out of the truck and into the airport, looking for the arrival board. Four United flights had arrived or were expected within thirty minutes of Ashley's arrival: Chicago/O'Hare, Nashville, Indianapolis, New York/JFK. He returned to the truck and waited.

It wasn't more than ten minutes before a fit-looking man, maybe in his late thirties, wearing a tailored topcoat, headed for Alistair's car. Alistair opened his trunk from inside, then got out and put the guy's roller bag in and closed it. They neither shook hands nor even nodded to each other.

Instead of heading back east on I-480, Alistair drove north

toward the city on I-71. Mann kept the Volvo in sight. The early afternoon traffic was light and moving at a good pace. The passenger Alistair had picked up was olive-skinned and wore a trimmed dark beard, with dark hair combed straight back, and was wearing sunglasses on one of Cleveland's typically gray fall days. He walked ramrod straight, with a purposeful stride, with the bearing of a military man—a military man on a mission. There was something odd about the cut of his overcoat. And JFK was a likely connector for European flights. Fergus speculated that he might be Italian. A Sentinel. His replacement, perhaps.

As they made their way through downtown, Mann thought Alistair might be taking his passenger to St. John's Cathedral. He was dropped instead at the Hampton Inn directly across from the cathedral, on the northwest corner of East Ninth and Superior. Strange, Fergus thought. Why not one of the classier hotels near Public Square? He looked like he could afford it. Alistair left him at the main entrance to the hotel and pulled away without looking back. Mann decided not to follow him. Better to focus on this new player.

Giorgio Grotti checked into the room Dunmore had reserved for him, a corner room on the third floor with an unobstructed view of the cathedral rectory. He opened a package that had been waiting for him at the front desk before unpacking and found inside a coiled length of white rope—a cincture—along with a printed note: *He takes a walk on most evenings shortly after seven.* Grotti smiled. All the information he needed. He slipped the note into his coat pocket. Tomorrow, Ashley would take him to the Cleveland Museum of Art where they would iron out the details regarding the museum's loan of the *Caporali Missal* to the cathedral of his employer, the Archbishop of Perugia. After completing that tedious errand, Giorgio would get down to work.

42

Bishop Bryn Martin left the cathedral rectory at a little after seven as he did most weeknights when he wasn't scheduled for a confirmation. His after-supper walks helped clear his head and soothe his nerves. The move to Cleveland had proven much harder than he anticipated. Bryn smiled at the understatement. He still knew only a few of the priests on a personal level, but he sensed that many, if not most, were overworked and discouraged, if not outright depressed. His meetings with the personnel board had so far left him feeling unsettled. Martin blocked out the financial challenges, the law suits, the parishes and schools struggling to survive. All this and dozens of other issues amounted to a ton of work. What he couldn't block from his consciousness was the murder of two of his people, his flock, and the near murder of a third. Nor could he block out the jolt of discovering the identity of the assassin, and that his own chancellor and a professor at the Jesuit university in town were members of a network of self-appointed, self-righteous guardians of the church's orthodoxy, willing to kill to achieve their ends. He remembered reading somewhere that the Austrian philosopher, Ludwig Wittgenstein once said, "Don't think. Just look." That's what he needed to do, stop thinking and just look. Martin then made his own little paraphrase of the maxim: Don't even pray; just look. Nora had remarked more than once that during her years in the monastery there were times when she had to stop thinking, stop praying, and just look, just be.

He stood below the traffic light at Ninth and Superior wearing his black windbreaker over his clerical shirt and sweater vest, on his head his favored Orioles baseball cap. The days were short now, and the damp fall darkness brought him a strange sense of comfort. The people waiting for the light with him were perfect strangers. Yet somehow, Bryn felt very much like he was one of them. Good, tired, burdened, they were all these things, mysteries of grace and weakness, small triumphs, and hidden wounds. Spiritually speaking, Thomas Merton wrote, we are all bodies of broken bones. And how painful even a broken finger can be. Bryn liked to think of priests as setters of broken spiritual bones.

If Martin had raised his eyes to the third-floor corner suite of the Hampton Inn across Ninth Street he would have seen a man staring down at him. But the bishop didn't raise his eyes. He crossed the street unaware that he was under surveillance, unaware that he was in mortal danger.

But across the street, on the south side of Superior, standing in the semi-darkness of the entrance to the former East Ohio Gas building, Fergus Mann did raise his eyes to the corner suite of the hotel. There he was, just as he had been yesterday, the man Alistair had picked up at the airport. Mann knew a setup when he saw one. And he knew, without a sliver of doubt, that Bishop Martin was targeted for assassination.

Giorgio Grotti had followed Martin on two of his previous walks. The route was the same—he walked to Public Square, turned right, then walked north on Ontario to Lakeside and back to Ninth Street. He always crossed Ninth Street at the light at Rockwell and turned into the paved alleyway between the cathedral and the diocesan parking garage. An attempt had been made to dress up the alleyway with a wrought-iron bench and well-tended shrubbery, but the passage, Giorgio had noted, was poorly lit. This is where he would end the life of the heretic Bryn Martin.

Grotti glanced at the white cincture on his bed. Next to it lay a length of iron pipe, five centimeters in diameter, that he had obtained the day before at a plumbing supply store. All was ready. When Martin went for his usual walk on Friday, the day after tomorrow, it would be his last.

Fergus Mann curled his ankles around the front legs of his kitchen chair and twisted his head from side to side in an effort to loosen the stiffness in his neck. All his life he had lived by the rules of his church. He couldn't remember ever missing Sunday Mass. But his talks with Bishop Martin made him feel like he really didn't get what it meant to be a Catholic. All these years he had been off target. It wasn't really about fighting temptations and avoiding mortal sins, it was about finding a new heart, a heart that didn't judge others, a heart that was humble and open, a heart that trusted in God's loving mercy. It made him sick to his stomach that he hadn't met the bishop before he met Dunmore and Alistair. Laura Spivak and Frances Hellerman would still be alive. He had been putty in the hands of a slick priest and a self-righteous professor. But he was putty no longer.

Fergus shook his head. He had to put these thoughts aside for now. He had to focus all his energy on the man in the third-floor window of the Hampton Inn. His every instinct told him this guy was big trouble. He could be mistaken, but he didn't think so. The snappy dresser was the Sentinels' hit man, and his target was Bishop Martin. Fergus stared at the glass of Jim Beam in front of him. *Yes. That was it. He had been sent to kill the bishop. The Sentinels suspect I told Bishop Martin all about them.* He cursed Dunmore and Alistair and their mysterious leader somewhere in Italy. Then, as if receiving an answer to a prayer, he understood what he had to do. And the weight of his hellish guilt seemed to lift.

43

Giorgio Grotti laced up his new black cross-training shoes, double-tying the knots. He would have to run only a very short distance, but at full speed, and with his topcoat slowing him a bit. The shoes were important and would be discarded after he had brought down the bishop. And by this time he knew where to find a woman later in the evening. He always needed a woman after his assignments. Always. Now, unlike his first assassination as a Carabinieri when he found himself unable to perform, his virility peaked whenever he was called upon to execute a sentence against the enemies of the church. But first things first. Grotto tightened the knots of the laces, stood up slowly, and walked to the full-length mirror. Dark pants, dark shirt, midnight-gray topcoat, and a black watchman's cap. A black cashmere scarf completed his dress. He thought he resembled a priest. Of course, a priest ready to make a sacrifice.

Grotti turned off the lights in his suite and moved to the window overlooking Ninth and Superior. The illuminated digits of the bedside alarm clock read 6:55 p.m. Invisible to anyone looking into his suite from the street below, Giorgio Grotti stood alert, muscles tensed, like a warrior anticipating the rush of battle. The minutes passed slowly. The city below was shutting down except for the bars and restaurants close to Public Square, where the action was. Cleveland's real night life would begin hours later—and Giorgio Grotti would be a part of it. *Pray for patience*, he told himself, waiting for Bishop Bryn Martin to appear. And finally, there he stood, at the corner waiting for the light to change so he could begin his evening walk. He was dressed as usual—black pants, black jacket, and Orioles baseball cap. Grotti moved from the window to the king-size bed where he had laid his instruments of retribution. He put the cincture in his left coat pocket, pulled on his calfskin gloves, and wrapped the length of pipe in the Friday edition of the *Plain Dealer*. To passers-by, he would look like just another lonely man taking an evening walk with a rolled up newspaper in his hand.

Grotti stuck the end of a strip of black duct tape to the inside of the left sleeve of his topcoat. He would leave the hotel by the stairwell at the end of his corridor and exit through a service entrance he had scouted two days before. He would tape the door lock open so he could return to his room without going through the hotel's lobby. The whole operation should take less than fifteen, maybe twenty, minutes. Grotti slipped out of the hotel into the service alley behind it at precisely 7:15. He would wait there until he saw Martin cross Ninth Street at the Rockwell light and head toward the passage between the parking garage and the cathedral. How fitting, he thought, to end the life of this heretic in the shadow of his own cathedral.

Giorgio waited in a dark corner just beyond the hotel's service entrance. Only a few pedestrians walked briskly on either side of Ninth Street in the early evening darkness. They walked with their heads down, hurrying to catch a bus or to their cars in one of the nearby parking garages. So far so good. Then he picked up his target. Martin was right on schedule, waiting for the light to change. Then, as he did each night, he walked across Ninth Street, turned right, and headed for the passage between the parking garage and the cathedral.

Grotti emerged from the shadows of the service alley and crossed Ninth Street about twenty paces behind his target. He picked up his pace as Martin passed through the open gate of the passageway, took two deep breaths, and sprinted after his target. Running at full speed from behind Martin he struck him on the back of his head with all the force he could muster. He heard the skull crack and a soft groan escape from Martin's mouth as he drove the heretic down to the concrete sidewalk. Martin's nose broke and spurted blood. Grotti knelt with one knee in the middle of the bishop's back and wrapped the cincture around his neck and pulled with all his might, squeezing the last gasps of life from the heretic. Martin's face lay in a spreading puddle of blood. The execution completed, Grotti stood, feeling the rush of adrenaline coursing through his taut body. He glanced over his shoulder. The Ninth Street sidewalk in front of the passageway was empty. He had checked for surveillance cameras on his practice run the night before, but looked again now for any sign of a camera he may have missed. None. Picking up the pipe but leaving the cincture behind, Grotti walked straight ahead to the surface parking lot behind the former chancery building and walked deliberately to Rockwell where he headed east to East Twelfth Street. There he turned right toward Superior Avenue. Once south of Superior he looked for a sewer grate. He approached it casually and bent down as if to pick up something he had dropped. Without a wasted motion he slid the heavy length of pipe into the sewer. As it splashed into the black water below, Grotti straightened up and continued his walk. At the trash bin at the corner of East Twelfth and Chester Avenue, he stuffed the newspaper deep into its covered mouth.

He turned right at Chester to finish his wide route back to the Hampton Inn. He entered the hotel from the service entrance and made his way up the back stairs to his third-floor suite.

Back in his room, with the lights still out, Grotti went to the window and watched the first responders and the flashing blue and red lights of police cars turn the face of St. John's Cathedral and the corner of Ninth and Superior into a circus of activity befitting an executed prelate of the church. He counted three squad cars and one ambulance. Then more squad cars and finally a fire engine arrived. Ninth Street was quickly closed to through traffic from Superior Avenue to St. Clair Avenue as officers strung yellow crime-scene tape cordoning off the area. Among the police and other emergency personnel, Grotti spotted at least two priests talking to men in suits. A television news truck pulled up to the barricade across Ninth Street and a camera crew and reporters pressed against the yellow police tape. The police seemed to ignore them.

Giorgio turned away from the window and went into his suite's bathroom and washed his hands and face. *May God have mercy on the heretic's soul,* he prayed. Then he changed into a fresh white shirt, anointed himself with his favorite cologne, and made ready for his well-merited ritual of carnal indulgence.

Early the next morning, Giorgio Grotti rode the RTA train from Public Square to the Cleveland Hopkins Airport. Once through the security checkpoint he moved coolly toward a Hudson News store along the C Concourse to buy a copy of the *Plain Dealer*. He had imagined the headline reading "Cleveland bishop murdered in the shadow of his cathedral." But to his surprise, the main headline was about economic growth in northern Ohio. Beneath the fold, Grotti saw a story that made him shiver with shock and disbelief. The heading read, "Retired Cleveland police officer murdered." In a daze, Grotti moved to a chair in front of the gate closest to the newsstand. In disbelief, he read that a Fergus Mann, a retired Cleveland policeman, was killed by a blow to the head with a blunt instrument according to a preliminary report released from the medical examiner's office. The actual cause of death would not be confirmed until an autopsy was completed. The motive for the attack was unclear. Giorgio skimmed the rest of the story. Mann, a native Clevelander, who lived alone on the near West Side, was a widower who often attended Mass at St. John's Cathedral where the attack took place. There was little else to the story.

Grotti stood up and moved without purpose to a wall-to-ceiling window and stared blankly at a parked United Airlines plane. He was positive he had identified his target. Somehow, he had made a terrible mistake. He decided not to call Archbishop Montaldo until he reached JFK. He wanted to distance himself from Cleveland—and from Simon Ashley and Trace Dunmore—as quickly as possible. That was his first objective. Get to New York, he told himself, and you will know what to do. But of course, he already knew what he had to do. He had to fly to Rome, catch the first train to Perugia, and face the acute disappointment of his Excellency, Pietro Montaldo.

44

W ell, folks," the casual yet professional voice from the flight deck announced on the hastily arranged Saturday flight back to Ohio, "we're beginning our initial descent into the Cleveland area. We're about eighty miles out and should be touching down in about twenty minutes. Cleveland reports a temperature of forty-two degrees with winds from the southwest at eighteen miles per hour. Make sure your seatbelt is fastened. It might be a little bumpy ahead. As always, thanks for flying Southwest Airlines."

Numb, that's how Bishop Martin felt. Numb in body and to the core of his soul. He couldn't concentrate, but knew he had to sort out multiple, confounding questions: why Fergus Mann had been murdered, who murdered him, and at whose order? Martin looked without seeing out the window of the descending 737. Banks of gray, heavy clouds waited to swallow the descending plane, and Martin felt like he had been swallowed himself into the belly of Jonah's whale.

Without turning, Martin said to Ian Landers in the seat next to him, "Thanks for flying back with me. Can you come with me to the office when we get in? The police want to talk to me."

"Of course, Bryn."

Martin said, "I'm glad Nora will be flying in next Friday. Having you two here will make a big difference." Bryn remembered the role both Ian and Nora played in helping him through the ordeal of Archbishop Gunnison's death—his murder, actually—

215

and the secret role played by the Brotherhood of Sacred Purple during his time as auxiliary bishop in Baltimore. "I'll need you both to help me figure out what the hell is going on."

Ian was quiet for a moment. "If there is, as we suspect, a link between the Brotherhood and the Sentinels, then we are dealing with some very dark powers. Dark powers that think of themselves as protectors of the church."

"And as avengers against the church's enemies." Bryn said. The plane shuddered in the turbulent air as it approached the runway. "Has there ever been a time in the church's history when we haven't had groups or networks like the Brotherhood and the Sentinels?"

"We can go back to the end of the fourth century. In 385 Priscillian of Avila was beheaded for heresy—the first Christian to be executed by fellow Christians for his religious views."

"And," Bryn added, "not the last by a long shot."

The bump and screech of the plane's landing gear on the tarmac seemed to punctuate Martin's comment.

During the taxi to the B Concourse, Ian said, "Seven popes were murdered during their reign."

"That we know of."

"Most likely for political reasons, but the political and religious spheres were so tightly entwined that the killers may well have believed they did their grisly work in the name of God."

Martin thought of the murder of countless children, women, and men during the crusades, the torture and execution of alleged heretics during the years of the Inquisition, the bloody religious wars of the sixteenth and seventeenth centuries that resulted in the death of millions. He thought of the priests and the conquistadors, who came to the New World to serve God and get rich, and of recent, unspeakable violence against Christians, Muslims, and Jews in the Middle East. The Brotherhood of the Sacred Purple, the Sentinels of the Supreme Center, they were

216

all of a piece. Bryn Martin was wrestling with the dark side of religion that had persisted through the ages.

"You know, Ian, I think Fergus Mann may have been one more person who died for his faith."

45

Terry Reeves joined Martin and Ian Landers in the bishop's office a few minutes before the police were expected to arrive.

"Bishop, I'm so sorry for your loss," Terry said. "I know how much you came to like Fergus."

"I did, Terry. Your call really took the wind out of my sails." With a gesture Bryn directed Terry and Ian to the conversation corner of his office. "We don't have much time, and my interview with the police will be tricky."

Landers and Reeves held Bryn's eyes. They both understood where this was going.

"I'm not going to be able to fully answer their questions. I'll do my best, but I'm sure they'll suspect I'm being evasive. I'm going to ask if they will agree to question me with you two present. You might be able to say things that I can't. Trust your judgment." Bryn took a deep breath and prayed aloud, "Spirit of Wisdom, be with us."

Outside the office, the elevator door chimed. Martin rose and went to his desk but remained standing. "Ask them to come in, Terry."

Detectives Janusz Kaczmarek and Timothy Lismore approached Martin's desk, introduced themselves, and displayed their gold shields. Martin came from behind his desk and directed them to the chairs around the coffee table. "Detective Kaczmarek and Detective Lismore, this is Dr. Ian Landers, a good friend of mine teaching at Case Western for the year. I'd like to have Dr. Landers and Therese sit in on our meeting, if that's all right."

Kaczmarek hesitated but shrugged. "Okay. This will likely be the first of a number of interviews we will be having with you, Bishop."

Martin moved one of the guest chairs in front of his desk to the conversation area of his office and they settled in—rather uncomfortably.

"Actually, Bishop," Lismore said, "we met a few weeks ago, when I was still in uniform. Fergus Mann stopped to give me some assistance with a small crowd on St. Clair."

Bryn nodded. "I remember that evening very well, Detective. Congratulations on your promotion."

Kaczmarek said, "Both Detective Lismore and I knew Fergus from his years on the force. He was a straight-by-the-book kind of guy. We understand that you recently spent a good deal of time with him."

"Yes I did. Fergus volunteered to help me get to know the city. He was very generous with his time."

"How did you come to meet Fergus, Bishop?" Lismore asked.

"Father Trace Dunmore, who was on my staff at the time, introduced us. Father Dunmore thought he would be just the right person to drive me around."

"You say, 'at the time'?"

"Father Dunmore has taken a leave of absence. He's no longer in residence at the cathedral rectory. I'm not sure we have current contact information."

He looked at Terry, who shook her head. Both Lismore and Kaczmarek scribbled in their tablets.

"Did he leave voluntarily?" Lismore asked.

"It is customary for a predecessor's chancellor to stay on just long enough for a new bishop to settle on his own staff. Father Dunmore was the first of a number of staff changes I'll be making. Can you tell us anything more about the attack on Fergus? We know nothing more than what was in the newspaper."

Lismore began. "Fergus Mann suffered a severe blow to the back of his head by a blunt, heavy instrument. His body was discovered around 7:35 p.m. on the concrete walkway between the cathedral and the garage. The overhand blow was inflicted with considerable force. From the angle of the blow, it was likely struck by a right-handed man, taller than Fergus. His skull was literally cracked open. There was a white rope around his neck and the ligature marks on his throat indicate he was strangled after falling to the sidewalk. The blow alone would have been ultimately fatal. He was alive, but probably not conscious, during the strangulation."

Martin, Landers, and Reeves sat motionless, their faces drained of color, their eyes narrowed.

Kaczmarek continued, "The attack wasn't a robbery. Mann had forty dollars in his pocket, a set of keys to his home and car, and a rosary. He carried no wallet, no identification. But the first officers on the scene recognized him."

It was Lismore's turn. "Do any of you know any reason why someone would want to murder Fergus Mann?"

"No," Martin hesitated, then shook his head, "No I don't." Bryn's mind was racing. As long as he took Lismore's question literally, he could honestly answer as he did. The so-called Sentinels may have seen Fergus as a threat to their perverted mission. But Bryn didn't *know* that. After all, the Sentinels probably reasoned Fergus couldn't go to the police without implicating himself, so they should have had no reason to kill him.

Landers and Reeves both shook their heads. They were taking Bryn's lead, but not doing a very good job of disguising their lack of ease.

"The media doesn't know this, Bishop," Kaczmarek said, "and I would not want to see it in print, but the rope around Mann's neck was a cincture. Laura Spivak and, we believe, Frances Hellerman were strangled with cinctures. So was Ann Marie Ellsmere. So, there is a plausible link between those attacks and Fergus's murder." Janusz Kaczmarek paused, locking eyes with Martin, then Landers, then Reeves. "Do you think there is a connection between Fergus's killing and those murders?"

Again Martin's mind raced. His ability to think logically, chronologically, and clearly was lost. *Yes, there was indeed a connection.* Mann had attacked those three women! But Fergus was dead. Didn't he have some claim—even in death—to his reputation? Martin nodded thoughtfully, "Yes, it certainly looks like there's a connection."

"Let's assume," Lismore said, "that the two women were murdered because they had attempted ordination as Catholic priests. Mann was known to his police buddies as a very strict, even rigid, Catholic. If the motive for murdering Spivak and Hellerman was to inhibit other women from seeking ordination, or to render some kind of divine vengeance on them, then murdering Mann, whom we assume was also scandalized by the ordination of women, makes no sense."

A momentary silence followed Lismore's analysis.

"There's another line of thought we're considering, Bishop," Kaczmarek said. "A priest in the rectory heard the sirens last Friday evening, and he was at the scene just after the police arrived. The officers allowed him to get close to the body, thinking he wanted to anoint him. The priest stiffened and said something like 'Oh, God, no!' He thought it was you, Bishop, who had been murdered."

Ian and Terry glanced at Bryn, whose face remained expressionless, both stunned at what they had just heard. Martin looked at Kaczmarek and Lismore as if to say, *Go on.*

"The priest," Kaczmarek looked at his notebook, "a Father George Smyth, said that you more or less regularly went for a short walk after watching the 6:30 news. Fergus Mann was murdered around 7:30. We received a 911 call at 7:41."

"That's right. I do take a walk after the news when I'm home in the evening. I'm usually back at the rectory by 7:30."

"What do you wear on these walks, Bishop?" Lismore asked.

"I wear a black windbreaker and an Orioles baseball cap," Bryn said, confused by the question.

"And black pants, I assume?

"Yes, black pants."

Kaczmarek asked, "How tall are you, Bishop?"

"About five ten."

"Fergus Mann is about five ten." Lismore said slowly. "You are about the same weight... and with similar builds."

"Fergus was wearing a black jacket and black pants...and a Baltimore Orioles cap," Kaczmarek added with emphasis on the cap.

Her voice tight, Terry asked, "Are you suggesting that Bishop Martin was the intended target of the killer?"

"We have to consider that possibility," Kaczmarek answered carefully. "What reason would Fergus Mann have for being just outside the cathedral, at just that time, dressed just as the bishop dresses?"

Bishop Martin stood suddenly and walked to the windows overlooking East Ninth Street and leaned forward slightly, bowing to the weight of what he had just heard. He pressed his palms against the window's inner ledge. He felt tears in his eyes. He couldn't speak. He was slowly shaking his head from side to side when he felt the presence of Terry Reeves at his elbow.

"Can I get you anything, Bishop? A glass of water?"

Bryn declined with a slight shake of his head and returned to his chair, fighting for control. "Fergus knew I would be away over

Thanksgiving. Had I been home last night, I would probably have taken my usual walk." Martin shook his head in disbelief at the possibility...no, the probability...that Fergus Mann anticipated that he was in danger, then took the steps that he did.

Ian asked, "How would Fergus Mann know if the bishop was in danger? And why would he dress like the bishop did on his evening walks? Why didn't he just let Bishop Martin know he was in danger?"

"We think he was acting as a decoy," Lismore said.

"Whether he intended to fight off the assailant or meant for things to happen just as they did is something we are still working on," Kaczmarek said. "Six days ago, a policeman on duty at the airport talked to Fergus briefly. Not much of a conversation. Fergus just asked to be allowed to sit in his car for a bit. He was parked in a no-parking zone outside the United baggage area. He appeared to have a man in a blue Volvo under surveillance. A few minutes later, our man remembers a well-dressed male, probably in his late thirties, getting into the Volvo. Fergus followed the car out of the airport. The officer didn't get the license plate but we're checking the surveillance cameras at the airport. We're hoping we will be able to ID the driver and his passenger."

Kaczmarek added, "We've subpoenaed passenger manifests from flights arriving around the time Fergus was out there."

"Bishop," Lismore asked, "do you have any idea who the driver Mann was following might be, or who his passenger was?"

"No. No, I don't. I spent a good deal of time in Fergus's Ford Focus, but I don't know anyone who drives a Volvo." Martin remembered with relief that Dunmore drove a gray Passat. He wondered what kind of car Simon Ashley drove. "But there is more," he said. Kaczmarek and Lismore exchanged a glance. Bryn Martin swallowed and said, "There's something that Fergus told me on our outings that you should know. He spoke of someone he met in a coffee house who belonged to some kind of international network of laymen, priests, and bishops who were fiercely committed to 'saving' the Catholic Church from any kind of renewal or reform. Fergus told me in confidence that they called themselves the Sentinels of the Supreme Center." Martin gave the two detectives a wry smile. "You won't find this group or organization in the Catholic Directory. They're very private, Fergus said. Secret, in fact."

Bryn gave Ian a "go ahead" nod.

"I teach medieval church history at Johns Hopkins in Baltimore. We know that since the Middle Ages, at least, secret societies or groups take form from time to time. And it often has been a major objective of these societies to protect the Catholic Church from any significant renewal or reform. These secret networks had members in the upper levels of the clergy, including Vatican bishops and cardinals—some wielding great power and influence."

"You're saying Fergus may have gotten himself tangled up with this group, these Sentinels?" Kaczmarek asked.

"We know very little about groups like the Sentinels. There is no concrete evidence, no records or rosters of members, no minutes from meetings. But we are certain they exist. From time to time similar groups have taken overt action that betrays their existence." Ian took a breath. He was walking a delicate line around the still-secret murder of Wilfred Gunnison. "The men who make up these secret societies are so self-righteous, so convinced of the absolute correctness of their orthodoxy, that they believe they have the right to use any means necessary in the defense of the church. Such means have included murder."

"Bishop Martin," Kaczmarek said haltingly, but emphatically, while holding Bryn's gaze, "you need to be careful, very careful. We think that whoever murdered Laura Spivak and Frances Hellerman intended to kill you, but instead murdered Fergus Mann. The killer's motive appears to us to be his belief that the women priests were heretics—and in his mind—deserved to die. So, I need to ask you, do you know of anyone who might think of you as a heretic?"

The stark question was logical enough, but it raised the eyebrows of Landers and Reeves.

"Not really," Bryn answered. "But in our polarized church, there are countless Catholics, including bishops and priests, who believe that those of us who have embraced the renewal and reform of the Second Vatican Council have sold out to a morally lax secular culture. In their eyes, I guess I might be judged a heretic. And a tiny few, taking Ian's point, might consider that I should be sentenced to death. For the good of the church, of course."

The four men and Terry Reeves sat in silence for a moment.

"So our murderer," Lismore said, "might think of himself as some kind of holy warrior, doing the work of God."

Landers said, "Precisely."

Both detectives scribbled in their notebooks.

"We're going to station a squad car outside the rectory. A visible police presence will help."

Martin nodded his acceptance. "Thank you."

Lismore added, "You have to understand, Bishop, that Fergus Mann's murder wasn't a random assault. It wasn't a mugging that went south. It was a carefully plotted assassination."

Martin looked tired and slightly dazed. Landers and Reeves looked wary and alert.

"That's probably enough for today," Kaczmarek said, rising. "Thank you for your time, Bishop, we'll be getting back to you, probably sooner rather than later." He turned with his hand on the door knob. "And let's suspend your evening walks, eh, Bishop. The world has just become a very dangerous place for you."

46

Trace Dunmore and Simon Ashley finished a simple break-fast of toasted English muffins in Ashley's apartment across the street from the university. Neither had much of an appetite and their coffees were cold and scarcely touched. Both men were badly shaken by the terrible mistake Montaldo's avenging angel had made. Mann they could live with. Martin was another matter. They had to assume Mann had told the bishop everything. And that meant they were both in danger.

Dunmore shoved the Sunday *Plain Dealer* aside. There was nothing more on Mann's murder. That was good. And tomorrow Trace would be flying home to his mother.

"My flight's at 10:50. So let's leave here at 7:00 or a little after. 480 will be a mess at that hour."

Ashley said, "That should work."

"You should get out of the country too." Dunmore's voice was flat.

"I know. But the archbishop insists that we act deliber-ately, without raising any alarm. Once we get back to England, he wants us to stay there until things quiet down here. A few months, he said. I'll return to England at the end of the semester. It is just a few weeks more. Once back in London, I'll send my resignation to the dean."

"I don't think you should wait. What if that special-ops man Montaldo sent is still lurking around somewhere? Have we be-come liabilities?"

Ashley shook his head and said, "He's back safe and sound in Perugia. I'll take my time, but believe me, I will get the bloody hell out of here."

Therese Reeves sat across from Bishop Martin with a manila folder open on her lap early Monday morning.

"The funeral's set for Wednesday at 10:00, Bishop. The pastor of St. Pat's was relieved to hear that you would be presiding and preaching—and that the funeral would be at the cathedral. He thought that was very appropriate. He added that he hasn't seen much of Fergus the last few years."

Her bishop and boss looked defeated. No, that was too strong. He looked preoccupied. Not at all focused on the business at hand as he usually was. She could only imagine what he was thinking, how he was feeling.

Martin forced a weak smile. "Tell me things will get better, Terry."

"It's hard to think of things getting worse," Terry responded. "I spoke with Hugh McKenna last night. He'd like to stop by this afternoon to see you, just to check in, if you have the time."

Martin looked at the typed *horarium* for the day. "Ask him to come in at 3:30. And, Terry, sit in if you can. And see if Ian can join us."

"Of course." Reeves sat still for a moment. "We're all pretty shaken by what happened, Bishop. Such a brutal crime, and so close to home. A uniformed Cleveland policeman was sitting next to the receptionist when I came in this morning. It is too much to be believed."

Bishop Martin sat at the head of his conference table with Terry Reeves and Hugh McKenna to his right and Ian Landers to his left. Reeves had briefed McKenna on the recent visit of Detectives Kaczmarek and Lismore.

"Thanks for coming in, Hugh. There's still so much we don't know, don't understand, about the murder of Fergus Mann." Even with these trusted confidants Martin knew he had to be careful. "The cincture around Fergus's neck is significant." Martin paused. "The wrath of God visits the heretic."

"How could anyone possibly consider you a heretic?" Hugh McKenna asked.

"You might be surprised at the things that pass for heresy these days."

"They crucified a guy for less," Terry said.

"Bryn," Ian said, "we're at this table because it's almost certain that the attacker left the scene thinking he had killed you."

The bishop nodded. "I'm going to be careful. And I'm open to any suggestions—especially yours, Hugh—about security, but I've told Terry that I'm going to carry on as usual. Which reminds me, where are we with the funeral for Fergus?"

Reeves said, "He doesn't have much family. He has an older brother, Brian, who has four children, but they're not really close. We've contacted two cousins here in Cleveland. There are others living out of state, but they haven't been in touch with the Cleveland branch of the family in years."

"Beyond mentioning that his wife passed on a few years ago, I don't remember Fergus speaking much of his family," Martin added. "Terry, let's see if the cathedral choir will be available for the funeral."

McKenna said, "You can count on his police colleagues being well represented. The retired cops who knew him will be there in force. They'll have at least one bagpiper. And be ready for a very long procession of police cars on the way to the cemetery. It will be a sendoff Fergus would have been proud of."

"I owe this man my life," Martin said in a whisper.

Landers turned the conversation. "Bryn, we need to talk about your safety. Someone has found the nerve to try to murder the Catholic bishop of a major American city. That someone has the resources to try again."

"More likely those some*ones*," Terry said heavily.

"I do think about that, believe me," Martin said. "But there's only so much we can do. I can do. I won't be taking any solo walks. I'll be watchful in going from the garage to the rectory. But I won't be looking over my shoulder every time I go out. Nor will I wear a bullet-proof vest."

Terry looked up at Hugh and smiled to herself. She knew he would try to do for Bryn Martin what he had done for Ann Marie Ellsmere.

Martin looked slightly embarrassed. "I really didn't need to drag you in to talk about Fergus's funeral and my well-being. But having all of you around me has been a great comfort."

The next morning a student-worker manning the religion department's desk appeared at Landers' door. "Dr. Landers, there are two Cleveland policemen here. They want to talk to you."

Ian Landers rose from his chair as Detectives Kaczmarek and Lismore entered his office.

"Gentlemen, I've been expecting you."

47

Bishop Bryn Martin and Chancellor Therese Reeves sat in the back seat of the funeral director's limousine waiting for the cortege to Calvary Cemetery to begin its slow drive. The roar of four police motorcycles, the flashing lights of a fleet of Cleveland police cars, and a dozen or so cars from suburban police forces had all but halted pedestrian traffic at Ninth and Superior. The post-funeral pall of emptiness and out-of-time displacement fell like an invisible cloud on the mourners moving to their cars. Martin surrendered to the peculiar yet familiar numbness that accompanied the funeral rites of his beloved church.

"Your homily was perfect, Bishop," Terry said as they settled in the limousine. "You put it so well. An old-school Catholic with rock-solid beliefs and judgments surrenders his biases and prejudices to the mercy of God."

"There was so much that I wanted to say that couldn't be said."

From the corner of her eye, Terry saw a tired and pained man seated next to her.

Martin looked out the window at the office workers standing still—almost at attention, as if ready to salute the fallen former policeman. *Yes, salute him,* he said to himself. *Salute this long time bigoted, self-righteous, traditional Catholic. Salute this man who killed two women and attempted to kill another, all in the name of God, or at least in the name of his church.* Without looking at Terry, Bryn said, "In the last weeks of his life, Fergus Mann woke up, as if from a lifetime of fear and judgment. He wasn't quite free. There was too much guilt." Martin went silent. *Be careful here*, he told himself. He took a deep breath and exhaled slowly. "There is no doubt in my mind that Fergus Mann wanted his murderer to think he was killing me. I owe my life to him."

Terry squeezed her eyes shut. Most of the chancery staff and employees also believed the killer was really after the bishop. They all feared he would try again.

The six white-gloved police pallbearers slid Fergus Mann's coffin into the hearse. A burst of sirens shattered the strained stillness as the funeral procession moved slowly south on Ninth Street. Once across Superior Avenue, the sirens went still as the long line of police cars, lights flashing, led old-school Catholic Fergus Mann to his waiting grave in Calvary Cemetery.

Terry Reeves stuck her head in Bishop Martin's office. Fergus Mann had lain in his grave only a few hours now, and while the late afternoon sun suffused the room with light it offered little comfort. "Bishop, Christina Tomasso is here. She's asking for only a few minutes."

Martin simply nodded.

Tomasso walked through the door in a chalk-stripe pants suit with the air of a woman on a mission, "Thank you for seeing me, Bishop Martin. I know it has been a long day."

"It's all right. Have a seat." Martin pointed to one of the two chairs across from his desk.

"My editor wants to add a little human interest to the story of today's funeral with a bit about your relationship with Fergus Mann. Something like 'new bishop engages with retired cop.' I was at the funeral this morning. It was clear that there was some kind of bond between you and Mr. Mann."

Martin thought, *You have no idea.*

"Yes, there was a bond between Fergus and me. He was helping me get to know the city by driving me around Greater Cleveland. We had some interesting conversations about the Catholic Church's renewal and reform following the Second Vatican Council, about our growing secular culture, about sin, and the transforming power of God's grace. I think you get the picture. Fergus was a serious man. We didn't talk much about the Indians, the Cavs, or the Browns."

Tomasso looked up from her reporter's notebook. "The city desk reporters working on the murder of Mr. Mann are looking into the possibility that the killer was really after you, Bishop. Could that be the case?"

"That's a question you'll have to take to the police. That's speculation at this point." Bryn knew better than to say "No comment."

"Can you tell me about the personal qualities or traits you liked about Mr. Mann?"

"Well, he sure was honest, even blunt, when expressing his opinions, likes, and dislikes."

"Yes," Christina said. "I picked that up from your homily."

"And he was loyal. To his Catholic faith, to his country, to Cleveland, to his brother police officers."

Tomasso made ready to stand. "That should do, Bishop, thank you. I don't want to take any more of your time."

"Let me add this to my list, Christina. Fergus Mann was a very brave man."

"Thank you again, Bishop. This has been very helpful."

She turned at the door when Martin spoke again. "Wait, Christina. There's one more thing…Fergus Mann was my friend."

Alone then Bryn closed his eyes and sat perfectly still…*to lay down one's life for a friend.*

48

Carl Spivak sat in a booth at Mulligan's Pub, a neighborhood spot in Highland Heights, an outer-ring Cleveland suburb. Across the table sat his dead wife's cousin, Janusz Kaczmarek. A couple of tall beers stood sweating on the table in front of them.

"We might finally be making some progress, Carl. I gotta tell you, this is one of the damnedest cases I've ever worked on."

Carl almost took offense. But this was just Janusz.

"The man who murdered Laura might be dead. We're looking into the possibility that she was killed by a former Cleveland cop named Fergus Mann."

"Fergus Mann? Yeah, I read about him. Murdered next to the cathedral. And with a rope around his neck, like Laura."

"We don't know who killed Fergus, but the names of two people who might be connected to Laura's murder have surfaced. One is a priest, a Father Dunmore, who used to work with the bishop. This guy has fallen off the face of the earth. We got eyes on the other suspect, a professor at John Carroll. His name is Simon Ashley. We think they belong to some crazy right-wing group of Catholics who think the ordination of women is a mortal sin that they have to avenge. And we think these guys duped this Fergus Mann into killing Laura."

Spivak shook his head in disgust and silent fury. "I hope you nail these bastards."

"We have some more work to do before we close in on Ashley. We suspect he knows where Dunmore is. What we have right now is circumstantial at best. The critical piece that's missing is who killed the killer."

Carl said, "I guess a little progress is better than nothing."

"Listen, I gotta get going," Kaczmarek said, downing the last of his beer. "And if anyone asks, we never had this conversation."

Simon Ashley put on his raincoat, put the strap of his briefcase over his left shoulder, and walked to the door of his Dolan Center office. He turned out the light and began the five-minute walk to his second-floor apartment in the damp dark of a late November evening. He waited for the light to change at Fairmount Circle, then crossed Warrensville Road and walked toward the main entrance of the Corinthian Apartments. An unfamiliar car was parked on the curved drive immediately in front of the entrance. Two figures were seated in the darkened car. The street lights along Warrensville Road gave him just enough light to make out their features. A man and woman, he thought. They weren't talking to each other. They were looking straight ahead, at him. Ashley looked away and went straight for the door, through the lobby, and pressed the "up" elevator button. Once in his apartment, he locked the door, but left the lights out. He went cautiously to the living room window that overlooked the front entrance and curved drive. The car was gone.

Calm down, he told himself. The car's interior light had been out. Maybe he imagined they were staring at him. Ashley moved into his kitchen to get a glass of wine. Fergus Mann was dead, and it was his testimony Ashley had feared the most. Martin's testimony would be hearsay. And maybe Bryn Martin didn't know as much as he and Dunmore once feared. No one could prove anything. Simon went back and stood at the front window of his dark apartment. The garish lights from the BP gas station

234

directly across the street spoiled his view of the university's main entrance. It had started to rain. Not a heavy rain, but a veil of mist, a soft, English rain. Soon he would be back in England. He would spend a few days with a London art dealer who had once been a "friend with benefits," then, when the dust had settled to Montaldo's satisfaction, fly on to Perugia, where he would be welcomed with gratitude by his Excellency, the archbishop.

Simon Ashley, though hardly hungry, moved through his darkened living room to the kitchen, switched on the ceiling light and prepared a salad for his evening meal. Two hours later, restless but unable to read, he got ready for bed, where he knew he would be unable to sleep.

"Thanks for coming back to Cleveland so quickly, Nora."

Bryn was seated comfortably on the couch in Ian Landers' apartment, just a few hundred yards from Ashley's apartment in the Corinthian. Two large pizzas from Pizzazz that Ian had ordered sat unopened on a coffee table in front of the couch.

"Getting away for a weekend isn't that hard. Ian's filled me in on some of the details." Nora smiled weakly. "He says you're okay, but I need to hear that from you. How *are* you, Bryn?"

"I'm as good as can be expected under the circumstances."

Nora agreed. Her brother looked better than she thought he would. Tired perhaps, but with a characteristic air of imperturbability still about him.

Landers got up and closed the living room blinds. "I had a visit from Detectives Kaczmarek and Lismore. I told them a few things that I don't think you felt free to tell them."

"I was hoping you would. Expecting, actually."

"They're pretty sure Fergus Mann murdered Spivak and Hellerman and attacked Ann Marie Ellsmere. But they're still trying to figure out who murdered him."

"What you mean," Nora said, "is that they're still trying to figure out who tried to kill Bryn. I for one won't sleep easy until they do."

Bryn leaned back into the couch. A knowing expression crossed his face. "I think I know who did it. We've encountered him before."

49

T he name he used the last time our paths crossed," Bryn
continued, "was Monsignor Giancarlo Foscari. We know
he was sent to Baltimore to clean up the Wilfred Gunnison mess by this Brotherhood, a group of self-appointed protectors of the supreme center. Sound familiar? We know he is
capable of murder; Wilfred's suicide was clearly faked. You'll
remember Margaret Comiskey saw Foscari shortly before he
disappeared. He was about six one, and Italian. The police say
Fergus's attacker was taller than him. Fergus was five ten. And
the police are looking for someone who flew in a few days before the attack. I believe Foscari was dispatched to kill me by the
same person who sent him to kill Gunnison: the high-ranking
clergyman at the Vatican we only ever knew as M."

Ian broke in. "For some time I have had an idea who M might
be. One of my Oxford professors has been teaching for the past
ten years at the Dominican's Pontifical University. We keep in
touch. We spoke on the phone not long after your appointment
as Bishop of Cleveland. He mentioned the recent appointment
of a Vatican bishop, Pietro Gonzaga Montaldo, to the archdiocese of Perugia a few months before. He told me that Montaldo
maintains an extremely low profile but is considered by many
to be among the most powerful bishops in the Vatican. He has
a reputation for being unusually influential in the naming of
bishops, a real behind-the-scenes mover and shaker. My source
suggested Montaldo must have something nefarious on half the

political climbers working at the Vatican."

"His mother was a Gonzaga?" Nora said making sure she heard correctly. "As in *the* Gonzagas?"

"I wouldn't be surprised," Ian said, "if the current archbishop of Perugia is a descendent of the Gonzaga line. They hold the record for having the most cardinals in history within a single family. There have been at least ten Cardinal Gonzagas. Even one saint. We don't know nearly as much about the Montaldos. It's a common enough surname in both Italy and Spain. In the late fifteenth century a layman by the name of Montaldo was one of six members of the Council of the Supreme and General Inquisition." He arched an eyebrow and added, "Usually condensed to 'The Council of the Suprema.' He was one of the men who oversaw the actual questioning, torturing, and burning at the stake of witches, heretics, bigamists, homosexuals…anyone the hierarchy sought to persecute for their sins against the church."

"Then Montaldo," Nora said, "could well be from a long line of defenders of the faith. Both the Brotherhood of the Sacred Purple and the Sentinels of the Supreme Center are part of a long string of secret societies—clergy and lay—that surface from time to time to protect the orthodoxy of the church. And I think we can be pretty sure their motives and mission were less than pure. They had to be. There was so much greed, ambition, and power at play."

Ian was in gear. "Historians are still fighting over the influence the Knights Templar had both in the history of the church and in the shaping of the medieval world itself. Their actions ranged far beyond the spiritual. They were everyone's favorite charity in the twelfth century. They managed other people's money, developed a vast empire of land holdings and farms, built cathedrals and castles, had their own fleet of ships, even owned Cyprus at one time. They can rightfully be considered Europe's first financiers. The great Saint Bernard of Clairvaux lent his weight in validating them by writing 'In Praise of the New Knighthood' but it all eventually ended in blood and tears. Then came the *Fideli d'Amore*—the Faithful of Love. They were a secret society of poets, philosophers—also financiers—who thought of themselves as guardians of the supreme center, the papacy, the heart and soul of the Holy Roman Empire. This… I'll call it a society…this society of the faithful was also a major player in shaping the medieval and early modern world. Heck! Dante was a member of the *Fideli*."

"Nora, you're a psychologist. What is it about secrecy that is so alluring?" Bryn said. But without giving her a chance to respond, he blurted, "Our church is obsessed with secrecy. I see a difference between confidentiality and secrecy. There's a place for confidentiality and privacy, of course. But secrecy? Secrecy is the enemy of community. And the Catholic Church must be, at its core, a community."

"Secrecy," Nora explained, "and I speak here more as an anthropologist than a psychologist, is almost always a dynamic of power. Whether power that is threatened, or power that is pursued. When the pursuit of power gets cobbled up with greed, and camouflaged eroticism, and repressed sexuality—remember the Knights Templar were forbidden to marry—then you can expect trouble. Big trouble. Of course, most secret or quasi-secret societies aren't celibate. The Masons, for example, or Yale's Skull and Bones fraternity." Nora paused…then smiled. "Though they are also all male, all elite.

"When claims of a motive of high idealism are added to the mix—defense of God or country, for example, or even something like freedom of thought, any cause worth fighting for— *look out!* You're facing an ideology just waiting to go nuclear."

Bryn and Ian sat in quiet consideration, as if they were in church and had just heard a sermon that was highly enlightening—or really scary. Both men nodded.

"Great power," Nora continued, "breeds great secrecy. And great secrecy poisons power. It's a mean circle. From a psychological perspective, secret societies like the Brotherhood of the Sacred Purple and the Sentinels of the Supreme Center fulfill a fundamental human need—the need for meaning."

"Fergus suffered from that," Bryn said. "He felt important because the Sentinels sought him out."

"Daily life for a lot of people is so often dampened by routine," Nora said. "It's just plain boring. I guess I'm preaching to the choir here, but bear with me. For centuries, some argue from the beginning of human history, religious practice and belief served to address the problem and mystery of meaning. Most people wrestled all their lives with the ordinariness of it all. As awful as war is, you can't say it's boring. As terrible as natural catastrophes can be, survivors aren't suffering from ennui. But between the wars and the earthquakes, the pull of a secret brotherhood or society can be overwhelming. It gives its members a sense of purpose, a sense of adventure, a sense of danger. They even have an opportunity to awaken the hero archetype. All this bolsters their sense of identity. They probably never have the thought, 'Gee, my life now has meaning and I'm no longer bored,' but that's exactly what's going on."

"And in our secular age," Bryn said, "religious faith, really for the first time, is a choice, a choice among a number of ways to find meaning in one's life. For some time now I've thought that the self-appointed zealots for religious orthodoxy are simply trying to repress their own unrelenting doubts."

Nora smiled, and said, "You can say that again."

Ian said, "I expect they'll go underground at this point. The risk of exposure is too great. I believe they take great comfort in knowing there's no hard evidence to prove that the Sentinels of the Supreme Center exist, and will do what is necessary to keep it that way."

240

Bryn glanced at the wall clock.

"We never touched the pizza," Ian said.

"Too much food for thought," Bryn said. "Time for me to get going. Thanks for the company. I really needed to talk through what's been going on. And I really wasn't looking forward to another quiet evening at the cathedral rectory. It can be so ordinary there."

50

Simon Ashley was irritated and distracted as he walked to his 11:00 class on the second floor of the Dolan Center. Trace Dunmore had not returned his carefully drafted emails. Nor had Montaldo contacted him to assure his safe haven in Perugia. While Dunmore could sometimes irritate him, he was usually interesting company. Simon already missed their leisurely meals at Valerio's and Primo Vino. Worse than missing Dunmore was another unfamiliar feeling putting him off balance. He was afraid. The mysterious presence of two strangers in a darkened car the previous evening had shaken him. Just who were those people? In two more weeks the fall semester would be over and he would be gone forever. The only positive had to do with the media. There had been no reported developments in the investigation into the death of Fergus Mann. Archbishop Montaldo's special operative must have been very careful.

In a few minutes, however, Simon Ashley would find himself once again in his element, lecturing on the religious art of Umbria in the late Middle Ages. *Too bad,* he thought, *that Pietro Montaldo couldn't sit in on the class to hear him speak of the Bartolomeo brothers and his coveted Caporali Missal.* Thinking of the missal, Ashley didn't doubt that Montaldo would still do everything he could to get it out of the Cleveland Museum and into his episcopal palace in Perugia. But that was the least of Ashley's concerns now.

The class he had so looked forward to deteriorated into a disaster. And it was Ashley's fault. He had been too preoccupied to muster his usual passion when lecturing about Umbrian art. And his students' questions—only two were asked—had been superficial. On top of that, the class discussion, if you could dignify it with that name, was labored. He was grateful now that Montaldo had not been sitting in on the class.

Back in his office, Ashley put down his lecture notes and put on his belted, double-breasted topcoat. It was still fall, but the wind made it feel like winter. As he passed through the Dolan atrium heading for the university's deli, the Inn-Between, for his usual lunch of soup and salad, he passed a middle-aged man sitting by himself in front of the Dolan Reading Room. At first he thought he must be the father of a student. But then they made brief eye contact and Ashley instantly felt a chill. The man gave him a steely glance, cold and judgmental. Ashley walked as quickly as he could without running, through the Dolan Center's double doors and onto the Hamlin Quad's tree-lined walk. He continued past the Grasselli Library with his head down, avoiding eye contact with anyone else. As he approached the Administration Building, Ashley took a nervous peek over his shoulder. He didn't see the man. But he couldn't really be sure. Maybe he had mingled with the students heading for the university's dining room.

Terry Reeves inched her chair closer to Bryn Martin's desk. "When you were at lunch," she told him, "Detective Kaczmarek called to say they found something in Fergus Mann's house he thought you should know about. On his kitchen table was an envelope containing six-thousand dollars in cash. On the outside of the envelope, Fergus had written 'For the West Side Catholic Center.' Kaczmarek wants to know if you have any idea where the money came from."

Martin didn't say anything for a moment. It likely came from Alistair…Ashley…or even from Dunmore. "If Kaczmarek calls back, tell him I don't know where the money came from. But I'm grateful he let me know about it. Did he say anything else about the investigation?"

"Not really. But on the kitchen table next to the envelope was a small spiral notebook. Apparently, Fergus made some notes after each of your evening drives. And there were two quotes Fergus had underlined. One was from Psalm 149." Terry looked down at her notes. "'Let the praise of God be in their mouths / and a two-edged sword in their hands / to deal out vengeance and punishment upon the peoples.' The other was from Blaise Pascal. 'Men never do evil so completely and cheerfully as when they do it from religious conviction.' Kaczmarek said he was surprised Fergus was into Pascal."

Martin swiveled his chair and looked out the window. *You did some really evil things, Fergus. But I'm glad I got to know you.*

"The money was the only thing out of the ordinary that they found going through his house. His neighbors liked him well enough, but found him to be pretty private. They said the fact that he was a retired cop made them feel safe. No neighbor had ever been inside his house."

Bryn nodded. *Yes, Fergus Mann was a very private person.* "About that money. While I don't *know* who the six thousand dollars came from, I certainly have an idea. And so do you," Bryn said. "I don't know whether sharing that notion with the police would be a good idea. Have you heard from Ann Marie?"

Terry raised her eyebrows just a little. "I had dinner with Hugh McKenna last night," she said, a subtle way to let Bryn Martin know that she and Hugh were spending some time together. "Hugh has stayed in touch with Ann Marie and is encouraged by the change he has seen in her."

"How so?"

"She's feeling pretty much at home with her little gun. Hugh says she has what he called a good concept of trigger control, and having a means of self-defense seems to make her feel like she is back in charge of her situation. The fear that almost crippled her seems to be gone. Hugh put it this way: 'She's not afraid of anyone.' I'm going to call her tonight. I want to hear about the change first hand."

"Tell her I asked about her."

"And one other thing, Bishop. Hugh wanted me to tell you that you are not being followed."

Nervous and tired, Professor Simon Ashley walked slowly back to his office after another disappointing class that afternoon. Outside his office door, a middle-aged couple was waiting for him. Parents of a student was his first thought. Suddenly he stiffened as his mind leapt to the couple he had seen staring at him from the dark car in front of his apartment earlier in the week. He resisted an impulse to simply turn and walk away.

Instead he said as calmly as he could, "May I help you?"

"Are you Simon Ashley?" the woman asked.

"Yes, I am Professor Ashley. What can I do for you?"

The man at her side said, "We would like a private word with you. May we come into your office?"

Another man came up from behind Ashley, forming a semi-circle around him. It was the man Ashley had seen in the atrium of the Dolan Center.

"Unlock the door to your office," he said.

Ashley looked over their shoulders, but saw only a few students at the far end of the hall.

"Unlock the door to your office," the man said again, taking a menacing step towards him.

Ashley saw the same cold look in his eye he had seen earlier. He fumbled for the key and opened the door. The three intruders pushed in behind him, closed the door, and locked it.

"Sit down at your desk," the woman said. "And keep your hands on the desktop."

Ashley did as he was told. He was shaking.

The man from the atrium walked up to his desk and disconnected the line to Ashley's phone. Without taking his eyes off Ashley he backed up so his body blocked the glass panel in the office door. No one outside could now see in. There was no other exit. Ashley was trapped.

The man who had been waiting with the woman went to the window and closed the blinds.

"What are you doing here?" Ashley demanded.

Three pairs of eyes simply stared at him. His question hung in the air.

The couple moved to the chairs in front of his desk. The other man remained like a sentinel at the door of the office. Slowly, deliberately, the woman opened her handbag and as casually as if taking out a pen and pad, withdrew a handgun and pointed it directly at Simon Ashley's chest.

"Keep your hands on top of your desk," she ordered again.

For the longest time, the three intruders simply stared at Ashley, seeming to take a perverse pleasure in his extreme discomfort.

"Let us introduce ourselves," the woman finally said. "My name is Ann Marie Ellsmere. This is my husband, Richard. The gentleman behind me is Carl Spivak. We believe our names are familiar to you, are they not?"

Ashley blinked furiously, his heart racing.

"Tell me, Mr. Ashley, are you familiar with our names?"

Ashley hesitated, then nodded weakly.

"I thought so."

"And are you familiar with the name Laura Spivak?"

Again Ashley hesitated, then nodded.

"And are you familiar with the name Frances Hellerman?"

Ashely whispered, "Yes."

"Our conversation will soon be over, Mr. Ashley," the woman said coolly. "Just a few more questions." She nodded to her husband.

"And are you familiar with Alistair?" Rich asked. "Alistair is an interesting name. It is, I only recently learned, a derivation of Alastor, an ancient Greek god of vengeance."

Without leaving his post at the door, Carl said, "Your three guests, Ashley, are angels of Alastor. We are his messengers of vengeance."

Simon sat as if frozen in a block of ice. *So this is what it's like to face execution.* The Ellsmere woman rose deliberately and walked around behind Ashley's desk, standing over his right shoulder.

"Rich," she said, "please stand over there," indicating with her free hand a point near the door, perpendicular to her line of fire.

Urine rushed down Simon's left leg. "Please, please don't."

Ann Marie pressed the barrel of the Smith & Wesson into Ashley's right ear, and pulled the trigger. Ashley fell back in his chair, in a dead faint. Richard Ellsmere came around behind the desk and slapped Ashley's face. Ashley opened his watery eyes as his three tormentors came back into focus.

"What you did, Mr. Ashley, was so terribly wrong, so terribly cruel," Ann Marie Ellsmere said as she put her unloaded handgun back into her bag.

"You're a smart man, Ashley," Spivak said. "You won't want to report our visit to the police."

"A dozen people know who you are and what you did, so don't even dream about retaliation," Ann Marie added.

They walked out and quietly closed the door to Ashley's office, leaving him shaking with fright. They proceeded unhurriedly to the south entrance to the Dolan Center and out into the piercing sunlight of a clear December day.

Detectives Janusz Kaczmarek and Timothy Lismore took seats across from Bryn Martin in the conversation corner of the bishop's office.

"We thought we'd give you this update in person, Bishop," Kaczmarek said. "We're holding the six-thousand dollars for the time being. As soon as the prosecutor's office gives us the green light, we'll get it to the West Side Catholic Center. We'll be keeping the notebook. I can't tell you when or even if it will be released. There's been no interest in it from Fergus's relatives."

"Our interview with Dr. Landers was helpful," Lismore said. "*He* was very forthcoming." His tone seemed to suggest that Martin had not been.

Martin said, "I'm sure it is difficult for you to understand why I was so guarded when you interviewed me last week. I'm glad Ian Landers was more helpful to you than I could be."

"Don't be too sure," Kaczmarek said. "I'm a Catholic myself. Our Lady of Peace parish. I think I understand why you were so…careful in answering our questions. Lismore here is a Methodist. I've tried to explain the seal of the confessional."

The detective knew that Bishop Martin would never repeat anything Fergus might have confessed, but he had spent a lot of years interviewing suspects and hoped, by confronting the bishop, to somehow confirm his suspicions. Martin nodded slightly and let out a slow breath. It seemed almost a prayer of gratitude. Kaczmarek, suspicion confirmed, was pleased that the bishop had tacitly shown his appreciation for his respect for the sacrament.

"There's another development," Lismore said, "that we find interesting. Do you know a Simon Ashley?"

"He is a friend of Trace Dunmore's. And Ian Landers knows

them both from college."

"Yesterday Simon Ashley resigned his position on the faculty of John Carroll and left his nearby apartment in apparent great haste. He disappeared before dawn. He never spoke to his department chair or the dean—just left a scribbled note. Strange, there's only a week or so left in the semester. And the leasing office of his apartment said he took only a few bags with him. We've got no idea where he went."

"Another mystery," Martin offered.

Kaczmarek leaned forward with his elbows on his knees and looked into Bryn's eyes. He shook his head in bewilderment. "Two murdered women priests, another attempted murder, the murder of a suspected murderer. No clear motive for the murder of the women except that it was a possible hate crime. No clear motive for the murder of Fergus Mann, or for what may have been your own intended murder. Yeah, we got lots of mysteries." Kaczmarek settled back in his chair and said with a wry smile, "Welcome to Cleveland, Bishop Martin."

Late that evening, alone in his chancery office, Bryn Martin felt as if he had just emerged from a nightmarish initiation rite as the twelfth Bishop of Cleveland. He went to the window and looked out on a very quiet East Ninth Street. Quiet was exactly what he needed. Contemplative quiet. He resolved to make a retreat at the Baltimore Carmelite Monastery as soon his responsibilities allowed. He was so desperately tired of turmoil.

Martin looked around his well-appointed office. Rembrandt-era prints and some good original oils passed down by his predecessors. A wall of old books. And his "let's be comfortable" corner for conversation, near the window, where the light was best. But the large ficus plant in a plain terra cotta pot, with a few pale leaves fallen on the floor beneath it, was the only symbol of life in the room. Even it was struggling for light and fresh air. He felt the walls closing in around him. Two innocent women were dead. Fergus was dead. Ashley and Dunmore had fled. His divided church was as polarized as ever. Could all be right with the world? Once again, Bryn Martin told himself that he wasn't sad at all.

EPILOGUE

Three Months Later

B ryn, its Ian. Got a minute?"

Martin, with his cell phone to his ear, walked to the windows overlooking East Ninth Street. "Yes. Good time to call. I'm just looking over recommendations from the clergy personnel board that can wait."

"I just got off the phone with my friend in the Vatican. He's heard from a priest in Perugia that my Oxford classmates have surfaced. You won't believe this. Trace Dunmore has been appointed master of ceremonies to Archbishop Montaldo."

Martin walked from the window to a stuffed chair in the corner of his office and eased himself down. "God almighty!"

"There's more. Simon Ashley is the new curator of religious art for Montaldo's episcopal palace and his cathedral. Apparently, Pietro Montaldo takes care of his own."

"I guess I shouldn't be surprised. What the hell is going on in this church of ours?"

"Business as usual. Nothing more. In a feudal system—and remnants of feudalism are still deeply ingrained in the church's structure—loyalty is the first virtue, the only virtue that matters to a climber and his liege lord. Dunmore and Ashley are being rewarded for their loyalty to Montaldo."

"And to the Sentinels." Martin sat speechless for a moment. "Are you free for dinner tonight? I need a friend to process this news."

Landers said, "Sure. Is six okay?"

"Six is fine."

"I'll pick you up under the arch."

Just two days later, Baltimore's Archbishop Charles Cullen sat at breakfast with two cathedral priests when the cook barged into the dining room.

"Archbishop, it's the nuncio. He's been trying to reach you. You must have your cell phone off."

One of Cullen's personal rules was that cell phones were not allowed at meals. Cullen stood slowly and followed the cook out to use the land line in the kitchen. Five minutes later he returned to the dining room, flushed and straining for composure.

"Well, boys, your archbishop is a cardinal. At two o'clock, Rome time, the Vatican released the names of fifteen new cardinals. I'm on the list."

Both priests stood and with the cook standing in the doorway, all three clapped.

An hour later, Bryn finally got through to the cardinal-elect. "Congratulations, Charles. I'm so very happy for you, for the Catholics of Baltimore, and most of all for the church."

"It's a bit of a madhouse here, Bryn. Television cameramen and reporters tripping over one another. I'm fighting for a few minutes to write a statement to feed the beasts. Let me call you tonight. We can talk about this later, but I want you to accompany me to Rome for the Consistory."

"Absolutely, Charles. Good luck with everything there."

Martin ended the call and walked thoughtfully to the windows of his office. The March day was partly cloudy, the most one could expect for a late winter day in Cleveland. He looked north to the churning gray waters of Lake Erie. The view he had grown to love gave him no comfort this day. Along with Charles' good news was another announcement that spoiled the glow he felt at his friend and mentor's appointment to the College of Cardinals. Also on the list of new cardinals was the name of the recently appointed Archbishop of Perugia, Pietro Gonzaga Montaldo.

Still burdened by the news of Montaldo's red hat, Bryn Martin walked heavily down the hall and stopped at the door of his chancellor. "I'm going out for a walk, Terry. I need some fresh air, some contemplative time."

"The office staff are all delighted that Archbishop Cullen has been named a cardinal."

"Yes, it's wonderful news, isn't it?" Bryn said, knowing his tired smile was forced. "Hold down the fort, huh? I'll be back in less than an hour."

Once out the door of the Cathedral Square's office building, Martin turned north and headed for the Ninth Street Pier. A few of the people he passed recognized him and smiled. Others looked a bit wary at the sight of his Roman collar. Bryn expected the usual strong wind off the lake to water his eyes, but found himself leaning into a light breeze instead.

As he walked onto the pier he got that feeling of serenity that a large body of water always gave him, the moment of calm that inexorably drew him to this point on the lakeshore. Leaning against the pier's guardrail, Bryn stared at a freighter a mile or so out on the water. It was moving, he could see, but at first glance it appeared to be standing still. Not a bad image for his church. God's pilgrim people, sailing against the wind, tacking toward the Promised Land. Full of hope and spite. Full of courage and fear. Full of compassion and greed. Bryn thought of the words of the priest-poet Kilian McDonnell, lines that always left him feeling slightly off balance.

No grand betrayals
we lacked the impudent will
we died of small treasons.

Please, God, Bryn prayed, *forgive me my small—and grand— treasons. Let your mercy rain down on us all. On me, your unworthy servant, on Charles Cullen and Pietro Montaldo, on your wounded, divided church, and especially on Laura Spivak, Frances Hellerman, Ann Marie Ellsmere, and all the victims of injustice and violence.* The freighter seemed to have moved an inch or so to Bryn's eye. Good enough. We are God's holy people, he reminded himself. All saints and sinners. So be it. Peter Bryn Martin, Bishop of Cleveland, turned from the pier's rail and headed back up Ninth Street. He had work to do.

ACKNOWLEDGMENTS

I am grateful to the following individuals for contextual and technical information relating to *Under Pain of Mortal Sin*: Stephen N. Fliegel, the Robert P. Bergman Curator of Medieval Art at the Cleveland Museum of Art, who arranged a private viewing of the extraordinary *Caporali Missal* that figures in the plot of *Under Pain of Mortal Sin*; William M. Denihan, former Safety Director of the city of Cleveland; Brian Dombek, former Secret Service Agent; Cecilia Liberatore, S.N.D. of Collinwood Neighborhood Catholic Ministries; Dale Hilton of the Cleveland Museum of Art; Professor Paul V. Murphy; Dagmar Celeste; Alan Klonowski; and Maryellen Dombek, retired Outdoor Education Specialist for Cleveland Metroparks.

Readers of early drafts include: Marie and Timothy Glasow, Cathleen Walsh, Karen Walsh, Margaret Cessna, H.M., Rose Marie Kramer, H.M., Mary Ellen and Robert Toth, Catherine Heimburger, Jane Cunin, Stephen Foley, Maryellen and Daniel Dombek, Carol and Richard Graff, Dr. Ronald Naumann, John Scarano, Gail Roussey, and Julie Myers. Their critical reading and feedback fueled the writing of later drafts.

Work on *Under Pain of Mortal Sin* began while I was writer in residence at John Carroll University. I remain grateful for the personal and institutional support I received from Dr. Jeanne Colleran, Interim President; Dr. Margaret Farrar, Dean of the College of Arts and Sciences; Dr. Sheila McGinn, Chair of the Theology Department; Kathryn Merhar, former administrative assistant in the Theology Department; and Suzanne Grazia, administrative assistant in the Department of Campus Ministry.

Finally, this story would not have seen the light of day without the expert guidance of Michael Coyne and Gregory Pierce, publishers of In Extenso Press and ACTA Publications, respectively.

To all of the above, my heartfelt thanks.

Donald Cozzens

Other Books from In Extenso Press

AVAILABLE FROM BOOKSELLERS
OR FROM 800-397-2282 • INEXTENSOPRESS.COM
DISTRIBUTED EXCLUSIVELY BY ACTA PUBLICATIONS